Tales of the U'tanse

Tales of the U'tanse

Henry Melton

Wire Rim Books
Hutto, Texas

WRB

Tales of the U'tanse © 2012 by Henry Melton
All Rights Reserved

Printing History
First Edition: December 2012
ISBN 978-1-935236-48-1

ePub ISBN 978-1-935236-49-8
Kindle ISBN 978-1-935236-50-4

Website of Henry Melton
www.HenryMelton.com

Character images © 2012 by Djamila Knopf
http://shilesque.deviantart.com/

Printed in the United States of America

Wire Rim Books
www.wirerimbooks.com

Acknowledgements

Jonathan Andrews, Jim Dunn, Linda Elliott, Mike Lynch, Alan McConnell, Jim Reader, and Tom Stock, the first explorers into this unknown territory. Their scouting reports were essential.

Table of Contents

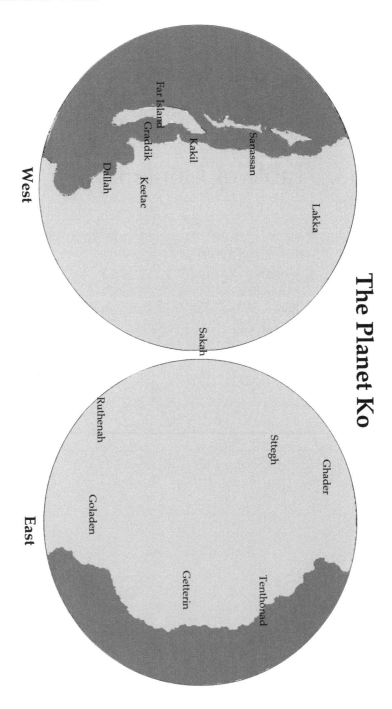

The Planet Ko

West

East

Far Island
Graddik
Kakil
Sanassan
Dallah
Keetac
Lakka
Sakah
Ruthenah
Sttegh
Ghader
Goladen
Getterin
Tenthonad

Before The Arrival

After thousands of years of being nothing more than the 'arm-pit' of the constellation Orion in the sky of the Human Home World, Betelgeuse had the last say. It was getting old, as stars go. For all of human history and more, it had been a red giant, bloated up and just hanging on.

Then the time came. The star collapsed and exploded into a supernova—not a tidy one. There were lobes and flares in this gigantic eruption. One of those flares just happened to be aimed at a much smaller star, Sol, the parent star of the planet called Earth.

Human technology was based on tiny structures called semiconductors, and they fried under the onslaught of powerful electromagnetic pulses. Then, high velocity particles blasted that atmosphere, bathing the planet in sickening radiation. Many died, but as the Star faded, people had learned to stay out of the star light and were posed for survival and recovery.

It could have been much worse. The Cerik are predators and it was as natural as breathing for them to wait in hiding until prey were weakened and distressed. If it had not been for our ancestors, the first of the U'tanse, all of Earth and all of the humans would have been prey for the chase.

Abe and Sharon, Father and Mother to us all, fought the Cerik for all of human kind, and they won, at the cost of their own freedom.

That is the great secret we share, behind our telepathic blocks and our acts of servitude to our Cerik masters. Two U'tanse defeated a Cerik clan, and we have inherited all of their power. Someday, when the time is right, the U'tanse will move, and we shall reclaim our freedom.

1

Genesis

"Honey, I'm home."

Abe Whiting, AKA, Aie, the U'tanse, closed the airtight door behind him and slipped through the first of the low-ceiling bubble-like chambers, making sure the lock was secure and the air was set to remove the poisonous nitrates from the air. When the dots on the wall changed color, he removed his leather breathing mask.

"Sharon?"

There was noise deeper in the warren of chambers that the extinct Delense race would have called luxurious. There were times when he really wished he were telepathic like his wife. He was sure it was Sharon, but sometimes she got a little... strange when they were apart too long.

But her protective suit, a head to toe leather outfit they both used when outside in the normal air, was hanging in the closet, so the noise was probably her. He began peeling off his outer wear. The less exposure they had to the toxins native to this planet, the less work she had to do to keep them both healthy. Three or four days of unprotected exposure without her psychically enhanced healing and no Earth-born life could survive.

Unfortunately, other than a few rags they'd salvaged from the trucks raided by the Cerik when they were planning to invade Earth, there were no other clothes. Their masters were hunters. They excelled at the chase and the kill, but they had no manufacturing, no cloth making, nor sewing. Even the leather suits were Sharon's handiwork.

He showered, his invention, and turned on the lights in the darkened living chamber.

"Aieeee!" She pounced on him, snarling, showing her teeth. Her fingernails, deliberately grown thick and sharp, scraped at his skin. His head hit hard on the floor.

"Sharon. Honey. I love you." His voice was low and gentle. He made no move to fight back.

She blinked. Her hissing stopped. She shook her head, as if fighting off a bad dream. "Abe. Sorry." She began to get up, but he held her down.

"Hey, I like it like this."

"Your head hurts. I'll fix it."

"Later. It's been two days. I like cuddling on the floor with my wife."

Slowly, she relaxed, and settled into his arms. "It's the Cerik thoughts. They're too much."

He kissed her. "I know. I'll make Tenthonad understand. We have to stay together, always." She needed constant human contact, and human thoughts, to keep her brain on track.

She smiled, a little sadly. "How did your work go?"

He knew she could read it all out of his mind, but it was nice when she just let him talk.

"I brought two more Delense factories back on line. As usual, there was no real damage. They just had to be tuned a little.

"One of the Cerik smashed the main contol center to bits when he got angry that the machine wouldn't make his processed animal feed. He just tried to claw it into submission. Luckily, there was a standby system I could make work."

She sighed. "Do the Cerik really understand what they've done to themselves by killing off their Delense?"

"You're the telepath. I'd say no. They didn't really appreciate what their slave race did for them."

"I hope they appreciate you."

"Tenthonad does. His clan is gaining ground like mad. He's charging big tracts of land for every factory I bring back."

"He's not so happy with me."

Abe stroked her head. He was grateful her long white hair was growing back, now that she spent most of her time in Earth-friendly air. She'd lost nearly all of it when she was first captured. He understood why she was reluctant to have children, in this hostile environment, to be raised as slaves—if they even developed their minds properly on this world of predators.

She was reading him—absorbing his idle thoughts and his deep desires. Abe wanted children, badly. If there were just a way it to make it happen... Until then, she would have to be vigilant. She shifted her legs around his and moved her hips. Abe's eyes closed as he breathed in her scent.

. . .

Asca the Telepath approached Egh the Scientist, rattling his claws to be acknowledged.

<Yes, what is it?>

<They are mating again.>

<Again? It seems like they do that every day. Is there any sign that she is bearing cubs?>

<No. And I don't think she will, until she decides to.>

He knew roughly what she was doing, killing off her mate's seed with her mind even as she requested more from him. It made no sense, but he wished he had her skill. Think of the power a warrior would have, if he could repair injuries in his body! But he knew of no Cerik with that skill.

<We need to make her breed! Without more U'tanse, Tenthonad's position in the Faces is in the wind.> And his own as well, but he didn't need to say that. They had returned to *Ko*, the Home World, without a treasure world claim. Their ship had been damaged so badly that the navigation log showing the position of the U'tanse planet was corrupted past recovery. Tenthonad had barely survived the challenge of his own clan.

But the male, Aie, had proved the value of the U'tanse by quickly restoring the ability of the clan to feed captive Runners. Every Large Moon, it seemed he found new ways to restore Delense machines that had been thought lost forever. Other clans were trading lands and runners for the services of the little alien.

Asca suspected the U'tanse female of being responsible for losing the path back to her world, that *Rakla-del*, but he couldn't prove it, and he dared not suggest it, for that would be to proclaim that he was too weak a telepath to tell whether she was lying or not. Admitting weakness was unthinkable.

. . .

Egh's Second waited patiently, just outside the chamber, listening to the two. He had long practiced the habit of listening without thinking. Asca might be a weak *name* with no Second of his own, but he was still a telepath, and one should be trained in *ineda* to deal with his kind. He would think later, when the telepath was busy with other concerns.

...

The Cerik Home Planet, called just *Ko*, "all lands", rumbled underfoot, but then, it always did. Its moon, nearly as large as Luna, was in a much more elliptical orbit, reaching close enough to trigger landquakes and volcano eruptions on almost every pass. Within the history of the Cerik, lands had sunk beneath the waves and new mountain ranges had risen. Within the *oral* history of the Cerik—there was no written history. Reading was elusive, one of those skills some of the slave races used. Part of the genius of the Delense, the extinct Builders, had been the ability to craft machines that could be run with the slash of a talon, and instruments that showed their results in cartoon-like images—all so that their masters could run some of the machines themselves.

Abe tried to ignore the quake. He had grown up in seismically quiet Texas, and quakes were those things that happened in far off California. Now they were common. He sighed. The Delense construction had lasted this long. It had to be safe. He would get used to them, eventually.

He put on his favorite, and only, robe. He loved it. Sharon had made it from a box of red automotive utility rags that they'd scavenged from the wreck of a truck that had crossed the star lanes with them. She'd made herself a housedress out of rolls of cheesecloth that she'd likewise salvaged from the grocery store supplies. He was so lucky to have married a woman who never worried about how much skin was showing.

He sat at a desk that was totally Delense in construction. It was good enough for him—flat and hard like a desk ought to be. The beaver-like creatures the size of a bear had been engineers after all. With a stool the right height, he had a workspace that felt right at home. He picked up the stack of school notebooks that had never made it to the school supply shelves and clicked a ball point pen. If he never made it back to Earth, and if they started a branch of the human race here on this planet, his children would need a history. Until he ran out of paper, he'd write down everything he knew, everything he remembered, everything about Earth, the human race, and where they came from.

A tiny scrap of loose paper like a bookmark fell out. In Sharon's crisp lettering, was a list of other slave species scavenged from planets nearly destroyed by the supernova. Abe knew some of the information already, but they never discussed their plans to escape. Not verbally. Not in a manner a passing telepath could discover. Anything that hinted at less than total loyalty to Tenthonad and his clan had to be passed in this fashion, and kept loosely in the mind, free of any overtones of excitement or fear. It was a difficult, long range plan, but being unarmed slaves on a planet with a poisonous atmosphere limited their options.

...

The next day, Abe and Sharon appeared in their leathers before the High Perch. They knelt, as befitted their status, to the left of Tenthonad. Egh and his Second approached and scraped the floor with their claws.

<Speak.>

Abe was learning quite a bit of the Cerik language, although he could barely form the words himself. Each time he went out on a project alone, he really missed Sharon's ability to translate.

Egh tapped his claws again. <Sanassan clan has been attempting to breed Geisel Runners from their Treasure Planet for a generation with no luck. When it became known that U'tanse Builders were living here with no signs of early death, the Sanassan Scientist requested my help.>

Tenthonad growled low. <I have tasted the blood of a Geisel, when twenty-seven were released at the beginning of the Face. Finding a way to breed them here is a worthy goal.> He turned to look at the female U'tanse. But then he spoke to Egh. <What have they offered?>

Egh gave a dissatisfied grumble. <They have offered eighteen Geisel.>

Tenthonad snarled. <They offer a minimal breeding set, which will be worthless if they die early, and which the Sanassan would make of no account if their own breeding program is successful. We get only enough for a single hunt and they get a valuable trade item. Tell them nothing until their offer includes lands or old Delense machines.>

Egh rattled his claws and backed away from the High Perch. His Second was slow to move, but followed Egh out.

Abe felt his eyebrow twitch, an indication that Sharon had read something of importance in someone's mind and triggered the nerves in his face. Who was it? Tenthonad, Egh, or his Second? Another twitch. So it was the Scientist's Second.

When they were alone, Tenthonad asked, <Aie, if you were asked, could you extend the life of these runners?>

<For the Name.> He'd gotten that phrase down pretty well. <I would suspect the food or air of *Ko* makes the Geisel die soon. What do you know of the Sanassan Treasure World? Does it rumble?>

Tenthonad made a dismissive gesture with his claw. <No matter. Egh would know.>

Abe grimaced. Tenthonad had wanted a 'yes' or 'no', not a discussion. <I would breed them in a burrow, with processed food and special air. They will not breed and run at the same time.> It was a guess, but his master was plainly more satisfied with that answer.

<So there will not be great herds of Geisel runners.>

<No. There will not be.>

Abe tried to have confidence. He had to make everything work, even here, practically naked, with no tools other than what he could cobble together from the race that had failed the Cerik before him.

I wish I had Hodgepodge. His thoughts flickered briefly to recall his right hand man, his little brother, his little robot friend that had never failed him.

Sharon took his hand and squeezed it.

. . .

The snap across space had severed all ties, even the psychic ones, with home and family. They had no idea where Earth was. Even if it had been only fifty light years, that still meant two thousand stars to check. The Cerik search for treasure planets had been crude random walk through the stars, utterly dependent on automated Delense tracking software to get them back home. The Cerik were not very interested in space. Having gone out at night a few times, Abe understood why. With the atmosphere constantly filled with volcanic dust, stars just weren't very visible. Their legends mentioned their moon many times, but Abe didn't couldn't tell if there were any other planets in this system.

What's more, the Cerik eyesight was best for looking across the plains hunting runners or looking down at prey beneath their perch—not up at the sky.

The Delense had obviously discovered space flight, but until he cracked the nature of their history, he was in the dark how it happened. Delense 'written' records were often cartoon like descriptions with a nearly human math script, based like the Cerik on a base-three counting system, even though the Delense had 'hands' with four digits. The Fables Tenthonad loved told of the symbiotic nature of their two races happening back before technology was developed, and from the math, he believed it.

I wonder what the Delense told themselves about their history. Did they think of themselves as slaves?

It was an important concern. He'd made a deal with Tenthonad to save their lives. He could live with the conditions, but assuming he had children, it would be binding on them as well. Unless he misunderstood human nature, that couldn't last forever.

. . .

Egh ordered his Second to relay Tenthonad's rejection to the Sanassan Clan.

Second snarled, <You are the Scientist. Why not play your part? Or have you forgotten your *name*?>

Egh quickly turned into a defensive crouch at the overt challenge. <A Second's words are all the Sanassan deserve. Perhaps you need to remember your position. You can be replaced.>

The Second Scientist wasted no more words. He lunged close and scraped the hide of his elder. His attack was well planned, with Egh caught in a narrow space between machines and a low ceiling to prevent a leap to avoid the attack. Egh's hide bubbled as his blood hardened instantly when exposed to the nitrates in the open air, sealing the wound. The sound of their screams quickly attracted others in the area. They kept their distance as the battle for succession proceeded. Everyone felt their own blood quickening as the scents of battle filled the chamber.

. . .

Sharon grabbed tightly at Abe's arm.

"What?" he whispered. They were still under Tenthonad's perch, having not been dismissed.

"Egh. He's…"

A growl came from above. <Little Telepath, speak aloud.>

She shifted to the Cerik language. <You have a new *named* Scientist. Egh's eyes have been taken.>

Tenthonad shifted slightly on his perch, unconcerned. <I smelled as much.>

Abe saw the shine in his wife's eyes. Once again, she was feeling the blood lust that was the everyday experience of their masters. He was perhaps the only one who was dismayed at the loss of the old Scientist.

Sharon shook her head. "No. I miss him too." But she was plainly divided between Human and Cerik sensibilities.

Tenthonad ordered, <Return to your burrow. I will call for you later.>

Abe and Sharon backed out of the *Name's* chamber.

"Come on! Hurry!" She tugged.

"Problem?" He ran beside her. Their breathing masks limited how fast they could breathe. Talking while running was difficult.

"Clat, the new Scientist—he hates us."

And a Cerik in a blood fever was likely to act first on his hate, even if his *Fa* would be angry. They were in immediate danger of his claws. Tenthonad knew his people. That's why he dismissed them. He wanted them barricaded away.

They reached their quarters and Abe applied a lock code so that a Cerik's talon wouldn't open the door from the outside. If he understood the way it worked, Tenthonad had an override code, but it wasn't the *Fa* of the clan he was worried about.

He began peeling off the leathers. "Sharon, tell me everything you know about Clat."

The remote look on her face told him she was off in the minds of the Cerik, learning all that she could.

"He has a half-formed *ineda*. He hasn't been trained for it, and that could get him in trouble."

"What?"

She looked his way, and then shook her head as she tried to focus on the here and now. "Clat was Egh's Second. He hates us because we're becoming more valued scientists than his *dance*. He thought Egh was too weak because he worked with us. Our death would be the best thing that could happen, as far as he's concerned."

Abe nodded. "The Scientist *dance* was created after the extermination of the Delense, to take up the slack when they realized they'd killed off their only technologists. And the Cerik aren't very good at it. Their minds don't work that way. But can you tell what Tenthonad is going to do?"

Sharon shook her head. "His *ineda* is tight. I can't read him. His new Second isn't quite as well trained, but he doesn't know what Tenthonad is going to do either."

"But he knows we're valuable, right?"

Sharon changed to her house dress and sat cross-legged before him. "If I read the politics right, it's still up in the air. The Face—that's like the planetary ruling council—is disturbed by our presence. There are some long memories. When the Builders revolted, they *flicked* the main city, complete with the *Names* of most of the clans—burned it like a nuclear explosion. The city was a... holy place? Think Jerusalem or Mecca. They intended to use the chaos to make a mass escape into space, with many thousands of Delense hijacking space ships and scattering to various planets. Instead they inspired the Cerik to track them all down and exterminate the whole race.

"The idea of a second race of Builders, us, is disturbing to many."

"We get the blame for what the Delense did."

"Something like that. Tenthonad will become legendary, either for making a dumb mistake to keep us, or for being wise enough to correct the mistake they made by eradicating the Delense. No one knows which, yet."

Sharon stared at the floor solemnly. "Our lack of cubs complicates the issue."

Abe nodded. He was aware of it. He, repairing damaged machines, was valuable to Tenthonad. The U'tanse as Builders could be valuable to the Cerik, as a race. But if they had no children, Sharon was a dangerous wild card.

She nodded. "Tenthonad has never forgotten my taste. I'm sure he has considered the option of taking my eyes and keeping you busy repairing machines until you die of atmosphere poisoning or old age."

"But that's not what he wants." Abe was sure of that. Tenthonad looked at him as the restoration of the old days, where Builders and the Cerik worked together to build a star-spanning empire, ever growing and ever more powerful. The loss of the directions back to Earth was a bitter blow.

Sharon spoke. "You can say it out loud. You can't help but think it."

He nodded. "Tenthonad would fight to the death to preserve the U'tanse as a race. He's done it before."

"And Clat is a direct challenge to that. He represents the current order, with the *dance* of Scientists trying to make the most of what the Delense left behind. The sooner we're gone, the better."

Abe sighed. "And his killing of Egh was the traditional way of succession. Tenthonad can't punish him for that."

. . .

Tenthonad could still smell the blood of Egh as Clat crouched before him, proclaiming the loyalty of all his *dance*.

"Bleed, all of you!"

The three remaining Scientists slashed their forearms and small splatters of blood made it to the ground before hardening.

He made no pretense that he was happy to lose Egh. The old one had never been less than loyal.

"Have the Sanassan been rejected?"

Clat rattled his claws. "My righteye notified them on the distant-speaker device."

The new *name* of the Scientists glanced at Asca, crouched at Tenthonad's right. The presence of a telepath at his first meeting was ominous. Clat struggled to keep his thoughts even and free of his long term plans.

Asca was too experienced to let any of this show in his eyes or his stance. Clat was a youngster at these games and if old Egh had just kept his wits about him, he'd have sent the assistant back to heal with the cubs.

Two things were interesting to him. One was the half-formed *ineda* that the Scientist had managed without any real training. When he told Tenthonad about it, it wouldn't be a good day for Clat. In general, only those who desired to take the High Perch, those who trained telepaths, and thieves used the *ineda*. Which was he?

The other point of interest was the distinctive sense of the female alien telepath, also smelling the thoughts of this one, so plainly an enemy of the U'tanse. It was as if he and she were watching from opposite sides of the room, aware of each other.

He wished he understood her better. But one didn't poke too deeply into the jaws of a demon who could not be killed.

...

Abe was asleep, his head across her leg as she sat with her back against the wall. They at least had a bed beneath them, a low pallet made with large plastic sacks stuffed loosely with native grasses. It was luxury compared to the ceramic floor where she'd slept during the first part of her imprisonment. Part of her mind was watching the politics of Tenthonad's perch, fingers crossed for a little more bloodshed. But in spite of the Cerik nature, their culture wasn't random slaughter. There were rules and traditions. She was tempted to breach the filtering tissue in Clat's lungs and trigger a few blood clots, but a slave actually killing one of the masters was too dangerous. Abe walked that line all the time. The idea that he could get rid of his keepers with a few button presses had crossed his mind. But that's the kind of thoughts that had triggered the extermination of the Delense.

She watched Abe's chest rising and falling, his dreams tangled with memories of sunlight and software. There was a scar on his arm that she needed to repair one of these days when their lives were less stressful. She was deep in his cells every day, repairing lung damage and occasionally tinkering with his hormone levels, but there was always more that could be done. *I'll need to tell him, someday.* She hadn't revealed everything she'd done to him. It was his nature to forgive, so sometimes she skipped the whole process of confessing her transgressions. But some day, she would have to tell him all. For now, he accepted his greater strength and stamina without question, or chalked it up to a different gravity. He didn't miss his depression at all. She knew she couldn't let him drift into hopelessness, or they would be lost. He was her anchor.

And then, a few hundred yards away, Clat felt the jaws of panic nipping at his thoughts and clamped down, hard, trying to put up a barricade against anything that could betray him.

Asca scented it. The clumsy *ineda* still leaked, but Clat's efforts showed plainly his technique. It was the method of a Cerik cub who had trained to become a Telepath and then failed in the process. This one had not started off to become a Scientist, but had become one by default. Asca reviewed the differences in techniques in his mind. There was no doubt.

Sharon observed it all, silently like a Cerik on a perch over his prey. Step by step, she absorbed everything that Asca had seen and had known about the *ineda*. It was just what she needed.

That was the moment. The need of her mate to have children, her own biological urges, her fears of raising brain-damaged telepaths, Tenthonad's dream of a new race of Builders and her own mother's vision of a grand destiny—in that instant they all merged into a clear dream of her own.

She reached into the cells of her husband and shifted a few hormones. He stirred in his sleep as dreams became darker and more basic, more urgent.

"Abe," she whispered. "Abe. Wake up. It's time."

His eyes opened and he turned to her.

...

Asca watched as Clat backed out of the chamber and patiently awaited his *Fa's* command.

<Telepath?>

<For your Name.>

<Do you have anything to report?>

<Much about your new Scientist. And another thing, perhaps even more important.>

<Oh? Tell me.>

<Your U'tanse are breeding.>

<Not just mating?>

<No. The female has made it known to me. There will be many more U'tanse Builders for the Name.>

...

After the sweat had cooled, and Abe had drifted off into as peaceful a sleep as she had seen, Sharon still monitored the new life that was happening within her. So much depended on choosing the right sperm. Her children had to be just right. She and Abe were Adam and Eve here. There could be no defective genes to show up in the next generation. They all had to have her psychic abilities to protect themselves from atmospheric damage, but more importantly so that the mothers of the next generation could guide the evolution of the U'tanse just as she was doing now, and as her mother had done to create her. As well as she could manage, they must inherit Abe's skills as well, to become so valuable to the Cerik that no one could imagine living without them. Each child must also be different, to preserve the limited diversity in their genetic heritage.

Abe, as the only non-telepath, would have to become the patriarch to the new race, to teach them all how to remain human. As Eve to a new people, she had to hone the skills her mother used to raise her to be a unique person. It was up to her to make her children individuals and not just nodes in a hive mind. With what she'd learned today about the *ineda*, that now seemed possible.

Of course, the Cerik would have to be taught their place as well. That would be trickiest job of all.

Someday, when her descendants re-discovered the Earth, maybe then they could do without the Cerik, but until then there was a role to play, and the right words to be said. All the while, behind the *ineda* of the U'tanse, their true spirit would remain.

Mercy Run

1

James bar Bill worked out the family tree on the chalkboard by himself. He didn't want to go to Father with this. The birth rules had changed just last year. Mother had announced that the ratio of girl babies to boy babies was to drop from four-to-one to three-to-one. He thought he had the whole tree worked out in his head, but now he felt he had to draw it out and see it.

It will be nice to have more boy cousins. Just to have someone more like himself to talk to.

Not that there was *really* anyone like him, other than Father of course, but guys were different. For one thing, they weren't as involved in babies as the girls were.

He was of age, as of last week. Any day now, one of the cousins would show up at his cell and he'd be expected to get her pregnant. He'd never done it before, and it worried him.

It isn't fair. They all know how it works. They're all telepaths.

He sighed. The Father of them all, without telepathy, had thrived here on the Cerik world, but he had been the only one. Everyone else was born a telepath, by design. The women who monitored the gene pool had wondered if anyone else *could* be born without the gift, so they tried. He was an experiment. James knew that.

But it left him alone. Mother had three sons and fourteen daughters and it was plain her goal in life had been to increase the number of U'tanse from the original two until they had a population that would survive on this hostile world.

That meant babies. Lots of babies. Every girl of age appeared visibly pregnant most of the time.

They all know how to have sex. There was no privacy in a world where all your relatives are mind readers. Somebody was likely reading him right now.

He'd be required to do his part to keep the gene pool well-mixed soon enough. He looked over his diagram. If he understood the current rules correctly, several times a year, any female who wasn't an ancestor could choose him. That included the six of his sisters on his father's side and three on his mother's that were of age, although with the population fast approaching a hundred and fifty, word was out that siblings would soon be off limits as well.

Cynthia bar Bill poked her head into his cell. His older sister smiled at the marks on the board. "What are you up to?"

He flushed. She had heard his thoughts. Every girl was a telepath, that was a given. There would be no female experiments like him. Every mother-to-be had to be fully capable of controlling the sperm cells within her body and to psychically choose one that was free of defective genes.

"I was just seeing who was on which side of the chart."

She came closer and put her hand on his shoulder. She had cared for him since he was a baby. "Don't worry about your sisters. Everybody understands the new incest rule. Father and Mother wouldn't have allowed it for the first couple of generations if it wasn't absolutely necessary. Lots of things had to be changed for the survival of the U'tanse."

"I know all that. It's just...."

"You think that if you can chart out all the cousins on your board, you'll be able to predict who will come for you. James, you think too much! When the time comes, it'll be perfectly natural. You were born with the right instincts. And you don't have to worry. You will enjoy it. All the guys do."

She took the other shoulder, too, and stared down into his chest. At least that's what it felt like.

"Are you feeling any effects from your last time outside?"

"No. I wasn't in the air very long, and I was wearing the breather."

"Good. Remember, if you have too much exposure, any of your cousins will help you heal the lung damage—not just your sisters."

He flushed. It wasn't fair. They had made him without any of the psychic skills. He couldn't read minds. He couldn't see into his body and heal the damage of the Cerik atmosphere like every one else could. He was the only helpless one.

She shook her head. "You're just like Father. He's not helpless. No one—no U'tanse, no Cerik would say that."

As she left, he practiced the mind blocking techniques. His *ineda* wasn't very good, according to his cousins, but he'd only been practicing for a few months. He was sure he was doing something wrong, but people were having trouble describing what it was. Since he couldn't read their minds, they had to explain verbally, and English just didn't have some of the right words.

They always try to make me feel better by comparing me with Father. It's all a scam. I'm nothing like him.

2

The ground rumbled, and by long habit, he rolled to the ground and waited out the shakes in the reinforced cavity in the side wall, shaped for the long dead Delense Builders that had created the complex in the first place. His cell, like all the rest, was part of a labyrinthian burrow built by that previous slave race.

While the Cerik overlords could navigate the maze of tunnels and chambers that made up Home, and occasionally did, to inspect the U'tanse, they were creatures of the open skies and the broad plains, and didn't care for being underground.

He put his hand on the cool, densely packed clay. His cousins could all tell the progress of the quake with their minds, but he had discovered as a child that he could detect when the quake was over, or whether it was just paused, by the vibrations in the wall.

He wasn't afraid of the quakes anymore, not like he had been. When he was little, a lot of things had frightened him. Not any more. Except the Cerik, of course. He couldn't help but shiver when they came around.

Something changed. He could hear the silence.

He'd wondered, in a population where all were all telepaths, why there was always a chatter of voices echoing through the corridors. People like to talk, he guessed. But right now, they all stopped. That meant there was some kind of call to action—a telepathic call to action. Everyone stopped what they were doing and listened.

He got to his feet and went out into the corridor. Carl bar Abe pointed at him. "Rockslide at the entrance. Get your breather and come help."

He ducked back into his cell and grabbed the face mask. All the men and boys were heading out, as well as some of the older women. Some of the little cuties were staring out of cells as they passed. He straightened a little as he walked, going with the adults to deal with the problem.

A strong man in his leather outdoor suit was directing the work. A few strands of thin gray hair sticking out from his cap marked him instantly, as did the faded letters "ABE" on his shoulder. Father was in charge, even at his age.

He pointed, "James. Grab a shovel and help Hank."

Several tons of rubble had collapsed to the left side of Home's main entrance and spilled out in a rough fan over the ground. Some of the original reinforcements left by the Delense Builders were exposed by this latest quake. He could hear some of the older ones discussing whether to rebuild the entrance, or to simply clean up the rocks and dirt.

Hank bar Abe pointed at the pile he was to work on. But then he said to James, "Father will have them rebuild." His voice was just a little muffled by his mask.

Obviously his thoughts were hanging out there for anyone to overhear.

Hank smiled as he shoveled dirt onto a sledge. James struggled to match him. "You're Bill's boy," Hank said.

He nodded. Hank was his maternal grandfather, but with a family tree like theirs, nobody paid any attention to such things. He wouldn't have thought about it himself if he hadn't just worked on the relationships.

Hank asked, like a test, "What would you do? If it was your decision."

James looked up at the bones of the old entranceway reinforcements. "I'd build a stone facade, like the building sketches in the Book. You know? I'd make Home look U'tanse, rather than Delense."

The older man chuckled. "Who knows? You're not the first to make that suggestion."

. . .

They were two hours into the task when a Cerik arrived. James paused and set down the rock he was carrying.

Father spat out a reply to the Cerik in his own language as if it were an insult, but James knew that was how it was supposed to sound.

<We can handle our own repairs. But we would be wasting less of the *Name's* time if we were allowed decent building materials. The Builders loved mud, but the U'tanse know stone and metal.>

The Cerik, three times the mass of a man, sat on his massively muscled rear legs and made a dismissing slash with his claws. <Mud or rocks makes no difference. The *Name* requires your list.>

Abe nodded, <He will have it today.>

<I will send the boat at sunset.>

Abe growled, extra loud, <For the *Name*.>

The Cerik bounded away, far faster than any man could run.

James startled as Hank gripped his shoulder. "Are you okay? Do you need a break?"

"I'm okay. What was that? Why are they sending a boat?"

"You don't know?"

James shook his head, his face flushed. "Not a telepath."

"Sorry. You should have been told. Twenty-seven of us are being sold to the Ghader Clan. An old Delense burrow is being set up for them. It's on the other side of the continent. They'll need a boat to fly them there. It's been set since the last Face. Our *Name's* clan is getting nearly three hundred miles of coastal plain in exchange."

James felt a knife twist in his chest. "Who is going?"

Hank shrugged. "Father hasn't announced the list. Don't worry. You'll probably stay here. The last time this happened, it was a mix of first and second generation adults—no cuties, no babies. Setting up a new colony is hard work and they won't have time for child care for a while. Plus I'm sure their new overlords will want to get some of their own factories repaired as soon as possible."

James swallowed at the implication that he was still a child. "Will we be able to say goodbye?"

Hank shook his head. "It doesn't sound like it. But the Festivals were part of Father's deal with the *Name*. Certain members of the colonies will get to meet up on a regular basis. We have to keep the gene pool mixed, even if we're physically separated. It's possible you'll get to see them again, although it may take awhile."

. . .

The sunset deadline changed everything. The cleanup was put on hold. People hurried down the corridors, anxious to check on their closest friends.

When the silence descended, James tossed his shovel to the side and began running. A broken-hearted wail echoed through the curved tunnel and other cries joined it.

Cynthia caught him up in a hug as soon as they saw each other. Her eyes were full of tears. "James, I'll have to leave my babies!"

He held her hand as they walked hurriedly to the nursery.

He could do nothing but stand beside her as she kissed and hugged her little ones. Her sisters made what promises they could. A large number of mothers were having to turn their children over to sisters that already had large families.

The nursery was deafening. Little ones, all telepathic, were caught up in despair that couldn't be contained behind *ineda*. They couldn't be comforted. He picked up a three year old cutie and an infant and attempted to coax the older one to help comfort the baby. The trick had worked for him in times past, but nothing he tried was working today. All he could do was hug and cuddle them.

Watching the others, he was a little grateful for his telepathic deafness. He could at least turn his eyes down to puffy eyes and runny noses and give some comfort. None of the others could look away from the exiles' torment.

3

One by one the twenty-seven gathered at the main exit. Mother and Father were there as well, giving some last minute words of comfort and advice. James had followed Cynthia, but he held back when his sister found and clung to Simon bar Tim.

He nodded, suddenly aware that Cynthia and Simon had been friends, close friends, for as long as he paid attention to such things. Maybe everyone else knew it already. It was good that she would have someone like that going with her.

There was a sinking feeling in his stomach when he heard that Hank, his grandfather, was to be the leader of the new colony. It made sense, but it was one more broken link in his family.

The boat floated down from the sky and a Cerik pilot opened the door and snarled at the group. Father barked back, and the new colony filed in through the door. Soon, the boat lifted away, and James went back inside. The normal chatter in the corridors was muted. He wanted to find some friendly face, someone he could ask to link to Cynthia and just check to see if she was holding up.

On cue, another sister, Eliza bar Tom came into the corridor. She had been crying, but she gave him a smile. "Cynthia asked me to check up on you. Have you had anyone look at your lungs? You were working outside, weren't you?"

He shook his head. "I'm okay. Can you talk to her? Is she okay?"

Eliza looked aside. "Not yet. Mother told us all to give them all a breather, so that they can bond together as a tighter family. We can talk in a few days, but not now."

He sagged. "Okay."

She took his hand. "Remember. I'm here for you, whenever you need help."

He sighed, "It's just not fair."

She chuckled. "You must have been reading the Book. Of course it's not fair, but that's the world we live in. We're all the possessions of the *Name*, to do with as he wills. We're just lucky he pays attention to Father. You were too young to remember when Oscar's colony left, but it was like this. Now they're thriving. Kakil's Clan is thriving too, thanks to their U'tanse Builders. As long as we do that—repair their abandoned factories, fix their machines, design new buildings and dams for them—then they'll value us. If we fail, they'll kill us all, just like they did the Delense."

She shook her head. "The *Name* won't feed us and let us grow numerous out of the kindness of his heart."

He didn't attempt to agree or disagree with her. It was hard to argue anything with a telepath unless your own opinions were rock solid. He wasn't there yet.

...

His other grandfather, Carl, had taken over the entrance construction. There had been a day of rest after they'd cleared away the rubble, but then a shipment of custom metal rods had arrived. James was fascinated by the process of building the new structural framework for the entrance.

The rods came in several standard sizes, some straight and some curved, manufactured at an automated factory—a facility Father had brought back to life a couple of decades earlier. The metal rods fitted together, and then a chemical was painted on one side of the joint. As it reacted to the surface of the metal, the contact points of the metal bonded with each other, making an unbreakable whole. Piece by piece they built the skeleton around the entrance. Pallets of carved stone from another factory arrived shortly thereafter. Hours later, after fitting the grooved stones to the metal framework, James was worn out.

Carl slapped him on the back on the second day of it. He looked up at the brown-tinged sky and the fat sun near the horizon. "Good work. Come on in. There's no need to work when the light goes dim. That's when the accidents happen."

Once they got inside and pulled their masks, Carl sniffed and curled his lip. "James, are you bathing regularly?"

"What?"

He patted him on the shoulder. "Come on with me."

They walked down the twisty pathway towards the bath. "James, your body is changing, as I'm sure you know. One of the effects of that change is that you'll need to bathe more frequently. After working all day, you stink. Just get in the habit. We've got a wonderful bath. Make use of it."

The two of them undressed. James was embarrassed to confirm that he really did stink terribly. He'd have to swap tunics and run his leathers under the UV lights. Why hadn't anyone told him this before? Did everyone else just wait until his back was turned to hold their noses?

The bath was about a hundred feet wide and twice that in length. The original Delense design had it connected to the river nearby via tunnel. They had been semi-aquatic swimmers that had built riverside burrows before they had become slaves to the Cerik, and this pool was built to their specifications.

Once the U'tanse moved in, some changes were made. The air vents were closed off so clean filtered air filled all of Home's chambers. And supposedly there was still an underwater passageway to the river, but it was screened off to keep the native wildlife out of their bathing waters.

There was also a wide bench built into the perimeter of the pool so people could sit and talk while up to their chest in the water. There was a cutie pool isolated from the main waters that he'd used many times growing up.

There were several groups already in the big pool. A dozen were out in the water swimming, but twice that many were sitting on the edge, talking. Not surprisingly, the largest group was exclusively girls, chatting and giggling.

Carl chose a spot off to the side. James stared at the waters. He'd been in the big pool several times, but he'd never made it across. It was deep and intimidating.

Carl frowned and checked his waistline. "You've got air-burns. When is the last time you had your outdoor suit re-fitted?"

"Um, about a year ago."

"It's time to get a new one. Boy, you're a man now. You can't count on your sisters to take care of you. Don't even show up for work tomorrow until you've got a suit that fits. Do you want me to heal this?"

He shook his head. "No, I'll find someone else."

A woman swam up, "Hey Carl. How goes the construction?"

His grandfather turned his full attention to the woman about his age. "Hope," he nodded. "We'll be done in a couple of days, one way or another. The *Name* has a job for me and I can't put it off much longer."

James turned his attention back to the far side of the pool as it was clear the two of them had other business. He slipped into the water and sculled with his hands to keep his head bobbing above the surface. He was still build-ing up the courage to attempt a swim across when a girl splashed up to him.

"Hi. I heard you need some skin healing? I can do that. Do you want me to?"

"Uh. Fine, yes." It was a good excuse to put off his swim for a little bit.

A glance at Carl showed that he and Hope were entwined and busy, he swam up to a vacant spot.

"I'm Pam, by the way."

He nodded. "Oscar's daughter. I was just going over the family tree the other day."

She sat on the seat beside him. She was small and the water was almost to her chin. She flushed. "Yes, I am still a cutie, for a couple of months yet. So don't get any ideas."

He hadn't been, but now he was blushing as well. He kept his eyes out on the waters while she ran her hands over his burned spots. For as long as he could remember, Cynthia had done all the healing he needed. And now she was gone.

She was reading his thoughts. "My father left before I was born. I've never seen him directly. But we talk, sometimes, in our heads."

"I won't even be able to do that."

"Sorry." She concentrated on her chore. After a couple of minutes, she said, "That'll do it. The dead cells will probably rub off in a day or so. I found a little melanoma. You should be careful. Especially…"

"Since I can't heal myself, or even sense the damage."

She smiled timidly. "Sorry. I guess it's a sensitive issue?"

He shook his head. "The world isn't fair, I've been told. It's okay as long as I have nice cousins ready to help."

She flushed again. "Thanks for letting me practice on you. It's the first time I've gotten to work on someone else's body."

4

When he woke the next morning, James dressed and carried his mask and leather outdoor suit over his arm. He remembered fragments of a dream that were rapidly fading. Pam had been in it. Maybe because she was a girl that wasn't a sister.

When he was younger, he'd believed that dreams were really a sign that his own telepathic sensitivity was just locked below the surface, and that someday, he'd be able to join the telepathic conversation like everyone else. But Cynthia sensed his wishes, and made him face the truth. Everyone could read him, but he would never be able to do it. His dreams were just tangled fragments of the day that everyone had, even Father.

In a large chamber off to the side of Home, a number of animals were confined in fenced pens. That's where he needed to go. He tapped the circular pad of dots that controlled the airlock and stepped through. The air inside the chamber smelled mild enough, so he didn't bother putting on his mask. He opened the other door and winced at the bright lights and the strong leathery stench of the livestock.

June bar Abe stood at the doorway of her warehouse, built into the side of the chamber wall. "James, I felt you coming. Come on in."

Just like the times before, he couldn't avoid looking at the lines on her face and her graying hair. She was one of the oldest of Mother and Father's children and after doing her duty bearing a dozen children, she took on the task of managing the animals. She was still strong and agile, but she no longer sculpted her body to stay looking young like some of her sisters did.

She took his leather suit and checked the seams. "When did you get this one?"

"Um. About a year ago."

"You're growing rapidly. Maybe you should plan to get a fitting a couple of times a year for a while." She checked the racks of outfits with a frown on her face. "I've been running low on men's suits, low on everything, really. I had to give spares to all of Hank's colony. It'll be a while before they set up their own corrals."

He frowned. "I'd think you'd run out of women's suits first. There's so many of you."

She chuckled. "Yes, but half of us never go outside. Cerik don't really understand that women can think. Their females don't. They're happy for us to stay inside and breed, but they aren't comfortable working with anyone but the men. No, my supply problems are just bad planning on my part. Everybody knew the twenty-seven were leaving. I just kept putting off making the replacements.

"Now strip. I need to measure you."

He sighed and slipped off his tunic and stood up on the platform with his arms held out. He'd been through this before.

She pulled out her knotted strings and began measuring. She didn't write anything down. As with better than two thirds of the population, her memory was flawless.

"I can put together a temporary top that could work with your existing pants to keep the air out, but it'll be tomorrow before I can get you a properly fitted suit. How urgent is this?"

He shook his head. "I don't know. Carl said not to come back…"

She held up her hand to stop him as she stared off into space for a few seconds.

"You're off the hook until tomorrow. I checked with Carl. No building crew duties until you get the new suit. So, you're all mine today." She rubbed her hands with a satisfied smile.

He nodded and pulled his tunic back on.

The pen, under bright lights hung from the ceiling, had several dozen Geisel runners milling nervously about. June handed him a pair of leather gloves. "Father calls them 'antelope'. Supposedly, they look like some animal from the human home world. Not all of these are ours. We get to harvest some for the leather, but if the *Name* wants to chase down some fresh meat, he always gets the best of the lot. They're off-world, like us. That's why we can raise them in filtered air, and I don't have to wear a mask all day."

She pointed to the bales of leafy feed. "While I work on your suit, take two of those bales to the far side of the pen and put one bale in each ring. When you're done, I'll have more chores for you."

"Okay." He put on the gloves. There was a wheeled trolley just big enough for a bale. He had to roll the bale up onto it, but with only a couple of spills, he got the food in place.

The runners knew what he was doing, and he was nearly knocked down by the crowd of beasts pushing their snouts in close to sneak a bite. They were quick. The instant he put his hand out to pet one, it scampered a dozen feet away. He nodded. The Cerik would love these—something tasty to chase.

June loved having a laborer at hand, so she kept giving him new chores. There were fences to repair and a water tank to mend. By the time she had completed the new suit for him, he was tired. The farm work used different muscles than the construction, and they let him know it.

He stopped at the pool, taking to heart Carl's advice, but no one bothered him. He swam a little and then dozed in the water.

. . .

Carl shook his shoulder, waking him.

"Hey, you'll get all wrinkled that way."

James nodded. "Sorry. I guess I'd better get back to my cell. I'll be back to the job tomorrow."

"Maybe. Get dried off and go visit Father. He needs to talk to you."

What did I do wrong? James raced back to his cell to drop off his new suit and mask and hurried over to the Library.

Several years back, when he was feeling particularly lonely, Cynthia suggested he learn to read. Father and Mother had forced all their children to learn the skill, but as the population boomed, and with efficient ways for people to get the information they needed quickly with just a thought, fewer people each generation took the time and effort to learn it.

There were only so many books to read, after all.

The two trucks hijacked by the Cerik scouts had supplied so much of what Father and Mother had needed to survive. There was food, until they had learned how to make do with local plants and animals, and to grow crops from the sampling of Earth seeds. But there were other goods as well. Intended for a grocery store, there were things like pots and pans, sewing materials, aspirin and cold medicine. There were also 112 books, mainly cookbooks, children's picture books, and a collection of novels.

In addition there was an expanding collection of hand-lettered note-books—the Book. Father had spent more than fifty years writing down everything he knew. There was the history of Father and Mother, and how the U'tanse came to be. There was his paraphrased version of the Bible, as well as he could remember it. Mother had, after much urging, written her volume as well, spelling out in detail every thing she knew about her powers and how they could be used to grow a population free of the incest-caused buildup of defective genes.

Of course much of this was common knowledge, learned by osmosis as everyone read the thoughts of their elders. Not even the Cerik used a written language. Everything was done in Delense-crafted pictographs or oral traditions. No one really *needed* to read anymore.

No one except James.

He had spent a lot of time in the Library growing up. He'd read the Book several times, noting how it kept growing with each pass. Father kept adding to it. Parts of it were incomprehensible, especially the parts dealing with human sciences that had no counterpart here on the Cerik world. But he loved the histories.

Father had spoken to him several times as he read, happy to see someone reading. But he hadn't been there in over a year. He'd read everything, and there were only so many times he could enjoy reading about how to cook things using foods and spices that were little more than fantasies on this world.

He walked into the Library, with the strawbag chairs against the wall and racks holding the bent and worn covers of old friends bringing a smile. A few of the titles caught his eye, but he kept on walking, stopping before the wide door at the other side of the chamber. None of the cells where he and his cousins lived had doors, but with Mother and Father, it didn't seem strange. Large letters proclaimed 'WHITING'. They had strange names—Abe Whiting and Sharon Dae. It was a puzzle he wanted to understand some time.

The door opened before he built up the courage to reach for it on his own.

Mother stared at him, assessing him. She always looked at people the same way. She was a strong, if older woman. If anything, she looked younger than her daughter June.

"When we began to write our children's names on the family tree," she said, obviously having read his thoughts, "we added a mark, a dash or a bar, following their name to mark who was the father. The tree was matrilineal, mothers and their children, so we had to track the father's name that way. So you are James bar Bill, to be distinct from James bar Abe. Our names worked nearly the same. Abe's father was probably named Whiting. My mother's name was Dae."

He nodded, still a little confused, but he wasn't about to question Mother.

She tilted her head slightly. "Block your thoughts for me."

He felt a moment of panic and then started practicing the *ineda* exercises—the rhythms and calming visuals. There were others, but he hadn't learned them yet.

Mother shook her head. "You need more practice. We'll see about getting you a trainer."

She waved him inside. "But Abe wants to talk with you. I won't keep you."

5

Father was writing when James walked in. He looked up, smiled and closed his book. "James, have a seat."

They stared at each other for a moment.

Abe's smile showed some wrinkles on his face. He asked, "How are you doing? And remember, I can't read your thoughts. I'd appreciate it if you kept that in mind."

James smiled. "You're the only one. Apparently my *ineda* doesn't work either."

Abe nodded. "I get that feeling from time to time. The whole place gets the news and nobody thinks to tell me about it."

"Yeah." James sighed. "I didn't know about this new colony until the day it happened."

"You lost someone?"

He nodded. "My sister Cynthia. The others will be able to talk with her eventually, but not me."

He frowned, and nodded. "A mother figure."

"What?" James didn't understand.

Abe stood up. "I'll explain later." He reached into an open box and pulled out a small sphere he could easily hold in one hand. "Come with me."

They went out another door into a large work chamber. There were several large Delense machines in various stages of disassembly. He was puzzled how they could have been brought into this place. Several were too large for the main entrance.

"Catch." He tossed the sphere in an easy arc towards James.

He reached, but it bounced off the tips of his fingers. He scrambled to catch it as it rolled across the floor.

"Sorry."

"No problem. Throw the ball back."

James picked it up. The sphere was firm, about the density of wood, and covered with a leather skin, obviously sewed on. He hefted it and tossed it back.

His great-grandfather snatched it easily out of the air and threw it back to him.

This time it bounced off the edge of his hand, but he caught it with the other before it got away from him.

"Back."

James threw it back. Father was good at it. He caught it and returned it, all in one relaxed sequence.

This time, he was quick enough to catch it. He threw it back.

"When I was a child, back on Earth," he said, as he kept the ball in play, "throwing a ball was one of the basic skills every boy learned. Some people were very good at elaborate games, built around balls."

"I haven't seen one before."

"There aren't many of them. I've had to make them all myself. I've tried to get all of my sons and many of my grandsons interested, but it never lasted."

"Only boys?" His hand stung as he caught the last one. Father was throwing them faster now.

"On Earth, it was mainly a boy's game, although many girls were good at it, too. In our place here, there are too few boys of the same age growing up together. But that is changing. I am trying to bring some of the old human traditions back to life."

James asked, "Because of the changes in boy-to-girl ratio?"

He nodded. "Yes. In your lifetime, the birth rate should even out. The heavy female population was only to increase our numbers as fast as possible."

"Because the Cerik wanted more of us."

"Right. And because we could have easily died out in the first few years. If one angry Cerik had killed me before I fathered a son, it would have been all over." He grinned. "Sharon has amazing skills, but she hasn't managed parthenogenesis yet."

"Partho-what?" He threw the ball faster, and it few in a flatter arc. Father snatched it automatically.

"Parthenogenesis. That's where a mother could give birth to a daughter without the father's sperm. The whole population would be female."

James chuckled. "It almost seems like it. I can go whole days without seeing another guy."

Father nodded. "And it's not a good situation. A lot of what we've had to do is horrible, long term."

"Do you mean like the incest thing?"

"Yes, that's one. But that should be fairly easy to phase out over time. It's not terribly hard to match up a pair that aren't siblings and that are true cousins, now that we have the numbers. Most of the animals from Earth naturally avoided mating with siblings without any rules or traditions. It's probably built in. We've forced the incest out of necessity, but I'm confident it will die out.

"There are other, worse situations that we'll need to fix—like the lack of parenting."

"I don't understand."

Father held the ball for a moment. "James, how close are you to your biological mother and father?"

"Umm. Well, not very, I guess. I know who they are, and where their cells are. I don't see them much."

He nodded. "It's what I see everywhere. Nearly every child is raised by older sisters. Your sister Cynthia raised you, correct?"

James sighed. "Yes. And I kinda feel lost without her."

"Our situation, the nearly perfect health gained by having healing abilities and the conscious decisions to have many children, has left us with more children than the biological parents can care for. Both Sharon and I did our best with the first generation, but even we had to rely on the older ones caring for the younger. There is no model of parental care any more. When our birth rate comes down, I fear no one will have any role models to fall back on."

James didn't understand the problem, but obviously if Father was concerned, it must be important.

"Sir, why was I... made the way I was?"

Father tossed the ball back to James, but he just held it for a moment. He was more interested in the answer to the most important question of his life.

"Why you're not telepathic?"

"Yes."

Father looked away. "I will tell you, but after your *ineda* training is complete." Then he turned and locked eyes with James. "I need you to put it out of your mind for now. You will get all your questions answered, then. Understand?"

James held his breath while his mind raced over the ramifications. There was a reason. It was important, and their Cerik masters could not know it.

So he couldn't be told until he could block his thoughts.
He nodded. "Okay."

6

It had been a pleasant visit, but it was getting late. Father was loved by all, and if he gave everyone the same personal attention, it was clear why. He certainly had to do some difficult things, such as choose which of his descendants would be ripped out of the community and sold off.

James walked the darkened passages, glancing into some of the cells as he passed. Most were dark, opaque caves where some cousin slept. One had a couple, still making noises. That was one of the things that bothered him. From all he knew, sex shouldn't take all that long, but he often saw or heard evidence that some people took a lot longer at it.

I'm just not ready yet.

He thought back to his visit with Father. *"You will get all your questions answered, then. Understand."*

He shouldn't think about that now. He visualized waves rippling across the bath and tried to follow them all the way across in his imagination.

There was a figure waiting in the darkness, just outside his cell.

Oh no, not tonight.

As he approached, he made out the face and hair.

"Hello, Alice."

She smiled. "It's been a while, James. Can I come in for a minute?"

He nodded. "Sure." He went in and tapped the light on.

In the glow of the light bar, he got a better look. His birth-mother looked like she'd just gotten out of bed. But she looked healthy and active—and not much older then Cynthia.

She chuckled. "Yes, Mother called after I'd gone to bed, but when she calls, you listen."

"Mother called? Why?"

Alice bar Hank shrugged. "She just said we should have a talk. She didn't say why."

He waved at the bed. "Sit there. It's a lot more comfortable than the stool."

She looked around his cell, and focussed on the partially erased family tree chart. "You erased the ones that left."

"Um. Yes, I was just trying to see if there was a pattern to who was chosen."

She nodded. "You got a chance to visit with Hank before he left."

"A little. We worked together."

"How did he look? I hadn't seen him in a while."

James thought back. "He smiled a lot. In good shape."

She nodded, probably looking at his memories. "He'll make a good leader."

They were silent for a moment.

"When you walked up, you were upset that I was standing outside your cell. Why was that?"

"Oh, that was before I knew who it was. I was relieved when I recognized you."

"You were expecting some girl?"

He nodded, looking over at the chalk marks. "Yes."

Alice probed gently. "Some girl that would want to spend the night?"

He took a big breath. "Yes. It's about that time. I'm of age. It's my duty."

"But you aren't ready yet."

He nodded, staring at the floor.

Alice waited. Then she said, "You know. A lot of people have the same problem."

He looked up at her.

She nodded. "Sex feels good, and we have instincts that drive us to it. Add to that the duty to the U'tanse to increase our numbers, and sex has become a duty that everyone accepts.

"But not every day, and not every time someone asks."

She leaned back against the wall. "Father and Mother, neither of them had sex until they were fully matured adults. Mother had this same talk with me. Their world was different. Men and women paired up, often for life, and they only had a few children. We're the strange ones, if we're still human."

"Still human?"

Alice looked at him and smiled. "They worry about that—Mother and Father do. How many generations of forced breeding does it take before genetic drift makes the U'tanse no longer human? That was a question when we designed you. Could we even have children that were not telepathic any more?"

"So… I wasn't a mistake?"

"No. You weren't a *random*." She shook her head and shuddered. "There's been only one *random* child. My birth mother Lillian and Oscar risked it. I was only about four at the time, but I still remember when she died, barely a week old. Death is rare among us. It was pretty traumatic for everyone."

Abe remembered the marker when he'd memorized all the names and dates from the official family tree in the Library. Siren had been her name.

Alice nodded as she confirmed his thoughts. "But we're still human, with human instincts, even if we've tinkered with some of the mental skills. And people mature at different rates. I wasn't quite ready either, when I came of age. Mother told me to set a broom by the entrance to my cell."

"A broom?"

"Yes. If we had doors, we could close them to signal our need to be alone. We don't, so it's a simple signal that everyone knows, when you desire to be alone, to ignore your thoughts and don't come in. Prop a broom in the doorway and no one will come to you for sex. In my case, I had that stupid broom propped up there for five months. Until I was ready."

James nodded. "Thanks. I didn't know."

"And that's our fault. It's hard for us to remember that you can't hear the constant chatter. In a way, you're lucky. It's endless. Even now, I can feel all the dreams around us. You, at least, can lay down, pull a pillow over your head and block us all out."

He smiled faintly. He wasn't quite ready to be grateful for being deaf.

He found the little broom and set it against the entrance.

She nodded. "So, I should leave." She stood.

"I didn't mean you."

Alice put her hand on his shoulder. "It's late, and you're tired. We can talk again sometime."

He watched as she walked down the darkened passageway, then adjusted the broom so he wouldn't trip over it, and yet where it would be visible. No telling how long he'd need to leave it there.

. . .

After the second corridor, James knew it was a dream. He looked at every cell he passed and there was a broom, just like his. Inside, his cousins were all frozen solid and motionless. He wanted to go shake them and wake them from their spell, but the broom barricaded the entrance.

But then, one of them fell over, and all the brooms vanished. People all came to the entrances and suddenly, he realized he was naked, without even a tunic. They stared.

He wanted to get back to his cell and dress, but someone important had told him to show up without delay. He had to keep going.

7

Luckily, it was considered impolite to make fun of someone else's dreams, although James thought he saw people looking at him as he walked to his appointment in the morning. But it could have just been his imagination.

Hanna bar Hank was his new tutor. She quizzed him about what *ineda* techniques he knew, and then described more. Some were obviously rooted in Cerik history, like which animals to eat immediately after slaughtering and which to let cool. Still, Hanna wanted him to at least be familiar with every known technique for blocking his thoughts. She quizzed him, but with his excellent memory, it wasn't as if he were going to forget.

"Then come with me. Let's walk. Every time I reach your thoughts, I'll let you know."

It was like that for days. Every morning he was quizzed and coached, and then they went for a walk. It took him nearly a week before he realized what she was doing, taking them to so many different workplaces. They toured the enclosed gardens where corn and beans and rice were grown—all plants from the human home world that had ridden as bags of seeds in the trucks. Some had survived the vacuum, but others hadn't.

They revisited June and her animals and she was happy to have him move more feed bags for her. Another day Hanna and he toured the air-moving machines that filtered the nitrates from the outside air and made it breathable in the Home.

But when she had to dig him out of the guts of a derelict Delense land transporter, she chuckled. "Well, it seems we've found your calling."

"What?" He set down the threaded power coupler, making sure it locked back into its proper place.

"It seems you have a talent for Delense machines."

"Oh. I was just trying to figure out how everything works."

She nodded. "I'll recommend you get a better tutor tomorrow. One that can do a better job at giving you the answers you need."

He frowned. "I thought you were my tutor."

"For the *ineda* exercises. With your memory, all that remains is continual practice."

He realized he'd let his chants lapse when she called him out of the machine. It had gotten so that he could keep his surface thoughts tied up in the exercises for hours on end, without much effort. "Sorry."

"You're doing well. Just keep them up, or I'll have to track you down and give you a refresher."

. . .

As James walked to the bath, he pondered what would have happened if he'd paid too much attention to one of the Geisel runners or spent too much time helping with the rice harvest. No one told him that he'd have this kind of test to check his interests. Or was that one of those things that everybody knew—except him?

The idea of having someone explain how the Delense science worked was exciting. U'tanse science was mostly obvious things. A fan with tilted blades pushed the air. A faucet opened and closed a hole for the water. It was all obvious.

Supposedly, back on the human home world, there were exciting and mysterious things like "computers" and "radios", but when he read Father's descriptions of those sciences, it was obscure. He didn't know what the words meant.

It was the same with the Delense devices, but at least with those, you could take one apart and see what the pieces looked like.

He shed his tunic and dove into the water. The splash of cool shook his *ineda* patterns and he used the swimming strokes to rebuild them.

He would have to work hard with his new tutor, whoever it was. He didn't want to be like Susan bar Tim, who lived three cells down from him. She changed regular jobs every few months. Five years ago, she probably went through this kind of examination. If she hadn't found her place, then there was no guarantee he could follow his interests either. She hadn't even lasted in the nursery, and they were always in need of help.

Pam bar Oscar was frowning at him from the side bench. He turned toward her and floated into the seat beside her.

"Your *ineda* is a lot better," she said.

"That's all I've practiced for a while."

She nodded. "I've heard. A number of people, who shall go nameless, have attempted to pick your brain after you put up the broom."

"Oh? I thought the whole broom thing was to keep people from intruding."

"That's why they're nameless." She grinned and splashed a handful of water at him. "Do you need any healing?"

He shrugged. "I haven't been in the outside air in a long time, but you can check, if you want the practice."

She nodded, and reached for his wrist. He relaxed, keeping his thoughts clear. The *ineda* was no obstacle to healing. Sensing his cells was something they could do whether he was blocked or not. The legend of the Arrival told of Mother probing the insides of the Cerik's ship and controlling the atmosphere settings with her mind. His inability to see the insides of the machines had made him think that he would never have what it took to be a master mechanic.

But Father, with the same limitations, had become the greatest of them all, and it looked like they were going to give him the chance to follow in those big footsteps.

Pam released his arm. "Your lungs were fine. That melanoma I found last time is gone. I did fix a small infection on your hand, though."

He glanced at the wrinkled fingers and remembered a scrape he'd gotten while climbing through the machines.

"Thanks." He smiled.

She flushed and crossed her arms across her chest. "I need the practice."

"Yes. You're getting close to coming of age, aren't you. Have you decided who to breed with?"

She looked off across the water and shook her head. "I'm not quite ready yet. I've got a tutor, a couple of them, helping me through the training. I even got to observe."

"You mean you watched when a couple…"

"No! I mean after he left." She was flushing bright red. "I was invited into her mind as she did the sorting and culling, making sure that all the right genes for the psychic talents are expressed, and checking for dangerous combinations."

He asked, "Like what?" He knew he'd never understand what they did, but it was fascinating to hear about it.

She tried to explain, but she kept running into concepts that had no words. He visualized thousands of little swimmers glowing unimaginable colors that she could separate and kill, until there was just one left to fertilize the egg.

"It's a hard job, and the original humans didn't have to do it. They just let the fastest swimmer win, and it was all *random*."

She said the word like it was a curse.

He nodded. For the U'tanse, it was. The chance of a fatal gene combination was much too high to leave it up to chance. Every recessive in Father and Mother's original genes would have too great a chance of meeting its match and being expressed. No one knew how long it would take before all the bad ones were weeded out of the mix. He was fourth generation, and from what he'd heard, it was no better now than before. Everybody was a descendant of that first pair, no matter whether they were siblings or cousins.

She sighed. "At least I've got some choice. It's not like the first couple of generations when there were only a handful of boys and you had a fixed rotation."

"Oh? You get free choice?"

"Not quite. My tutors have already done the consanguinity calculations for me. It'll be up to me to recheck it before each pregnancy, but at least I've got a list of names that I don't have to worry about. You guys have got it lucky. You don't even have to worry whether it'll be a boy or a girl. Stick it in and you're done."

It was his turn to blush. His *ineda* patterns circulated in his head and he dared not let them slip. He'd done his own calculations and sooner or later, he and Pam would have to pair up for the night. He had to be gone before she could read his thoughts in his body.

"I've got to go. I want to swim another few minutes. Thanks for the healing."

"Yes." She looked puzzled.

"See you again soon." He said and eased off into the water.

That was a stupid thing to say. He liked talking to her, but the topic of conversation was too dangerous.

He visualized his broom. It was there for a reason.

8

Bonnie bar Abe led him to her work room.

"You have a good memory?"

"Yes."

He stared at a large painting on the wall. "Is that a Delense?"

She nodded. "It's full size. I find it helps, when I get stumped, to take another look at the designer who built the machine I'm trying to fix."

James looked closely at the figure. It had to be fifty percent more massive than an adult U'tanse and walked comfortably on four limbs. Covered with a water-repellant pelt, it had a large vertical tail fin.

"Father calls it a beaver, but his sketches of that Earth animal look much more crude. Take a look at the Delense forearms. When they sat back on their rear legs, those fingers were every bit as flexible as ours, and each could oppose the others. But see how the plate on the side of the hand could be used to dig. Although they were machine users, most of Home was built by 'hand'."

"Did you paint this?"

"No. Not completely. Belle, my birth-mother, started the sketch from some history videos produced by the Delense. They had made the videos for the *Name*, and we only had access to them for a short time. I helped with the coloring and shading when I was old enough, but…" She pulled a book from the table. "These are mine."

James carefully turned the pages. Each was a sketch of a piece of Delense technology showing how a Delense hand would operate it.

"Oh."

"You see something?"

James nodded, tapping at the image of one of the machines. "I was trying to work with this thing in the big workshop, but I was holding it wrong."

"Maybe. These are just my best guesses."

. . .

Each day he showed up and Bonnie handed him a Delense gadget. "Fix it."

It was a test. The first was a fluid pump, and he could see that the sealing clamp was snapped off. He dug through the big shelf of parts bins and found the replacement. There was even a little finger-sized pry bar perfectly designed to replace that kind of clamp. He fitted it on a test fixture and it pumped water fine, with no leaks. He handed it to Bonnie and she told him where to put it—in the parts bins to fix something even bigger.

Other days were different. After three days of puzzling and testing, an L-shaped device as big as his arm defeated him. It had no external seams or ports other than a seemingly useless screw ring. Bonnie made an empty shelf. "Put your failures here."

He hated that shelf—all his failures. But he couldn't help thinking about them. Each morning as he walked in, he looked them over, occasionally picking up one for another look.

Bonnie said nothing. She worked at her own repair jobs, usually ones much larger than the gadgets she handed to him.

He wondered when he'd advance to the bigger devices, the ones that they had to bring in through the big overhead hatch. He'd seen only one delivery, and they made him leave until they could purge the outside air. He was happy to be gone. The small boat that settled down between the rows of equipment was being piloted by a Cerik, and those claws made him nervous. The way the pilot slashed at everything made him afraid someone could be carved open by accident.

He told himself that it was safe. He just didn't believe it in his gut. Everyone knew about Sue bar Carl, the eight-year-old girl who snuck outside and was eaten. It had happened fifteen years before he was born, but every child in the nursery knew the story—and it wasn't a fable. It was even marked on the official family tree.

But he guessed he would have to prove himself on the little repair jobs before he could graduate to bigger ones, and when he was older, go off on those expeditions to repair the Delense factories like Father still did.

9

Two months went by, long enough so that he could almost tell what was likely broken before he picked up his next device. The Delense had some gadgets that were marvels of elegance and rarely broke except by physical trauma, but there were others that always had the same broken latch or burned-out heater element. James was sure he could make an improved in-line heater if he could just make a new element with a thicker end.

Unfortunately, the U'tanse didn't have access to the factory that made those elements. A different Cerik clan owned it, and they were happy to trade replacements to the other clans. They snarled at the suggestion that any U'tanse could re-program their factory.

James walked to the bath toying with the idea of raiding their parts bins and making a little depositor to rebuild those heating elements with thicker metal. Unfortunately, that wasn't his job, and nobody was likely to take the suggestion of someone as young as he was.

He felt his *ineda* slip a little. *I can't have that.*

He'd been told that some people kept their *ineda* up constantly, but most didn't. However, once he started keeping his mind blocked all the time, he found that more people talked to him. It was a revelation. Some people did want to know what he thought, and if they had to talk to find out, they did.

He took the opportunity to calm and compose his mind and lock it down tight as he undressed. Uncertainty was like an itch. Hanna hadn't come to give him an update on his *ineda* progress. He was mostly confident that he was doing it right, but he couldn't be sure.

Walking out into the bath chamber, he saw a half-dozen girls stretched out next to the water, chatting among themselves. So much bare skin after a long day working on machines inspired him. A plan came over him. He looked around. No one had raised their head to look his way. He smiled.

Easing into a run, he turned at the last second and jumped high, making the biggest splash he could right next to them.

When he came back up to the surface, the naked girls were all on their feet, squealing and yelling at him. He smiled and ducked down below the surface, heading out into the middle.

It worked. No one could read me. It was a complete surprise to them.

He savored the memory as he swam all the way across the bath and sat on the other side. Maybe it wouldn't be wise to swim back just yet.

...

His birth-mother Alice was waiting outside his cell when he returned. *Uh, oh. I'm in trouble.*

"Come on in," he invited, before she could say anything.

She looked at the broom still propped up at the entrance. They sat.

She chuckled, "You made a splash today. I wondered if you'd taken down the broom."

He frowned, "No. Why?"

She laughed and shook her head gently. "James, that stunt was the perfect way to turn every girl's attention on you. It wasn't just those who got splashed. They were so surprised that every U'tanse caught the ripples. Cynthia asked me if you were okay. She felt it and couldn't get through your *ineda* to check on you. You had always been so shy."

James asked, "Is she doing okay?"

Alice smiled. "Yes. They're working hard on the new colony. There's so much work to do, both to build their new Home and to satisfy their new *Name*. But she's been watching you. She's proud of your *ineda*, but she checks in through your neighbors and your tutors."

Conflicting emotions churned in his head. He was happy Cynthia was looking in on him, but the thought that his *ineda* was causing her worry bothered him.

"Please tell her I'm doing fine, and I'm enjoying my technical training."

"She'll be happy to hear it. But how are you doing on that other issue?"

He looked over at the broom. "I'm still... a little reluctant."

Alice shrugged. "It's up to you, but you should know that practically every girl that has you on her consanguinity list has just given you a second consideration. You're now a man of mystery, and quite a few of them would love to knock over your broom."

...

Bonnie looked a little excited when James showed up for work. "Hold off for a little bit. Father is coming in from a trip with some new things."

"I didn't even know he was gone."

Mother walked into the room. "Secret trip. The *Name* has been negotiating with one of the rival clans for some time, and part of the deal was for Abe to get one of their factories running. It's the Getterin, and they've been rejecting everything U'tanse since the Arrival. They're part of the Cerik block that wants us all eliminated. This is a big deal for us."

Almost immediately, the overhead hatch opened with a whoosh of air. The Home always kept the clean air at a slightly higher pressure than the outside air to keep the poisons from leaking in.

James held his breath, and contemplated retreating behind the air-sealed door to the interior. But he didn't want to miss this.

He exhaled, and tasted the outside air. It wouldn't kill him. Not quickly.

The boat settled down into the work area, where there was always a space kept clear for deliveries. Father stepped out of the hatch, pushing a wheeled cart.

The roars and snarls that the pilot and Father exchanged were harsh to the ear, but anyone who ever planned to be working with the Cerik was trained in the language. James didn't trust his pronunciation, but he could understand the gist of what was being said. Father complimented the Cerik on his piloting skills. The pilot ordered him to unload quickly because the stench of the U'tanse and their machines made him queasy.

Mother tapped James on the shoulder. "Go help him unload."

He hurried over and Father nodded, handing him the wheeled trolley. "Get another cart."

James pushed the first one hurriedly to the wall. With barely a glance at the cargo, he grabbed an empty cart and ran it back to the boat.

It was the first time that James had seen one of the flying craft up close. He followed Father back inside, glancing at the Cerik lounging by the wide display panel that controlled everything. There was a three-dimensional view of the landscape showing.

The Cerik snarled at him. <Hurry up, cub.>

James entered the cargo area and helped Father move the pile he'd just freed of its straps into the cart's large tub. It took a couple of trips, and they were barely clear of the hatch when it closed. The propulsion beams nearly knocked him down, buzzing loudly as they grabbed the air above and shoved it down for lift. The boat cleared the overhead hatch and was soon out of sight.

He moved the cart to where they had unloaded the others and the vents high in the wall began blowing like a windstorm, pushing clean air inside even before the hatch had finished closing.

Father and Mother were talking quietly, holding hands. He couldn't hear what they were saying, but he was quickly distracted by the new devices.

Bonnie was already hovering over the carts, sorting the items into stacks by type.

"What are these?"

"I have no idea. Father must know, but he hasn't told me yet."

James took one of the gadgets in his hands. It looked like some kind of instrument. One whole side was the reflective white enamel that made up many of the Delense control pads.

On the back was familiar-looking screw ring. He brought it over to his failure shelf and picked up one with a matching ring. They connected easily. The control pad lit up with a control pad and something that was obviously text began moving and changing on the flat side.

"What do you have there?" Father said, looking over his shoulder.

"I don't know. Is that Delense text?"

"Yes." He watched the markings move. "What is that thing you plugged the diagnostic panel into?"

"I don't know. I'd never figured it out." He watched the lettering pause, and then change again. "I didn't know the Delense had a written script."

Father nodded. "I've seen hints of it over the years, but nothing like this. The Cerik can't read. I don't think they have the brain centers necessary to process symbolic script. That's why the Delense displayed everything in 3D modeling and vocal output for our masters."

James handed it to him, and Father ran his fingers over the text to see if it showed any interactivity. "Still, I've often thought that the Delense had to have some kind of text of their own, if only to express and preserve technical details. This is a helpful discovery. Thank you, James."

Tapping the control ring, he turned it off. "Bonnie, could you take this to my office. I'll need to spend some time at it."

"Yes, Father."

He turned back to James. "The air will take a while to clear out. The two of us need to be elsewhere. Come with me."

James had to agree. He could feel a slight tickle in his throat. Maybe he could meet up with Pam at the bath later to get it healed.

10

They walked the halls, heading so far into the mountain that it was all new. James had never realized the tunnels continued this far.

"Your tutors all report that your *ineda* has gotten solid. That's good."

"I'm glad. I've never been… confident that I was doing it right."

His great-grandfather chuckled. "Don't I know it! Everyone else can at least see a reflection of themselves in other's thoughts. We don't have that option."

He paused when the corridor ahead didn't light up as usual. "Here, take this." He pulled a hand-sized device from a recessed shelf in the wall. He twisted the small pipe-shaped thing and one end lit up and projected a strong beam of light.

James took it and probed the darkness ahead. There was more corridor, but it looked different.

"U'tanse construction," he guessed.

"Right. Come on."

They stepped into the new section.

"What's this thing made of? It feels strange."

"It's plastic. Human made. When the light dims, shake it and it'll get stronger."

"What's plastic?" James shook it and something metal moved inside. The light increased slightly.

"It's a biological material. Certain substances like oil can be triggered to shift from a liquid to a solid state. I'm vastly simplifying the chemistry, but since we don't have the source materials, it's not a technology we're likely to develop."

"I don't remember that in the Book."

"Oh? I guess it's time for an update then." He chuckled again. "There's always something I've forgotten."

They walked on a little more into the long featureless tunnel. "Father, you said that when my *ineda* was better that you would tell me why I was made without telepathy."

He sighed. "Yes, I did."

The silence continued for another minute as they walked.

"James, there were several factors that urged us—the U'tanse concerned with our genetic future—to see if we could make a true human, like me.

"Now, I'm not saying your cousins aren't human. We all are very close to the original human stock. Any of your brothers or sisters could walk the streets of Austin back on Earth without attracting any undue attention.

"But the psychic gifts that they all have were very rare back there—so rare that many people believed they were little more than fantasies. And we have bred all of your cousins to excel at that. It was necessary."

"Because of the defective genes."

"Right. Every mother had to be able to pick and choose the genes of her children-to-be. The men were made psychic too, because it gives obvious advantages in working with the Cerik."

"Then why was I... left out?"

The tall dark figure walking beside him, wrapped in the shadows, was quiet for a moment. James was tempted to shine the light into his face to see his expression, but refrained.

"James, it's time for the secrets. Secrets that must forever remain behind *ineda*. Can you do that?"

"Yes."

"Be very sure. At any time, Cerik telepaths could reach for your mind—in the Home, as you work, in these corridors, as you sleep, as you laugh and as you cry. You must never think of these things without a strong *ineda* sheltering them."

James swallowed, imagining the beast masters reaching for him in the dark. "Yes. I can do that. I will keep secrets secure."

"Good."

Father put his hand on his shoulder.

"Someday, we're going home, back to Earth. When that day comes, the U'tanse must not be a separate species. On that day, we must still be human."

. . .

James stared across the waters, sitting alone, far from the others at the bath. He had much to think about.

We don't belong to the Cerik. It was contrary to everything he'd been told. Since the days when his sisters cuddled him and told him the stories of the monsters outside who must be obeyed and who controlled everyone's lifes, he'd just accepted it. The Cerik were the masters, and the U'tanse lived to serve.

It had been obvious. Maybe the U'tanse were smarter and had fingers and could make the machines, but the Cerik were bigger, stronger, and faster. Any Cerik could snap up any U'tanse like little Sue. They were only safe because they were useful to the masters of this world.

A world where we couldn't survive on our own. The air was poison. The only food they could eat had to be grown under the same isolated conditions. Without the *Name's* assistance, they would die out quickly.

Any resistance was unthinkable. The Delense, also native to this world, had been the first slave race, the creators of all the technology the Cerik claimed as their own. They had rebelled one time, and the entire race was wiped out.

It was stupid of the Cerik. Since the rebellion, their technology had been slowly collapsing on them, with no tool-makers, no builders to help them—up until the raid on Earth that captured Mother and Father. And that had been just good luck on the Clan's part. They had been after prey and hunting grounds. Father had made a deal with the *Name* of that expedition after it was clear that they could never return home to Earth. He had promised to serve the *Name's* clan, and in turn Father and Mother would be protected from the rest of the Cerik, who saw them as nothing more than prey to be chased and eaten.

That much was common knowledge. At least among those cousins who had bothered to learn U'tanse history.

But James had learned more today. Father and Mother had promised to serve, but they had not pledged their descendants. From the Arrival, they had kept a secret resistance. The location of the human homeworld was deliberately destroyed so that there would be no more raids for slaves. Shared with only a few of their children, grandchildren, and, with him, great-grandchildren, was a plan to gain control of the space flight technology, to re-discover Earth, and to return the U'tanse to their true home.

Father knew he would never leave. Trapped as they were in protective enclaves on a poisonous world, it was taking a very long time. But when the pieces came together, Father had explained, the U'tanse needed to be human, and to have the will to regain control of their own destiny.

But with savage genocidal masters, resistance had to be careful, cautious, and kept totally secret.

He had learned the real story of Sue's death. Yes, she had been a willful, curious girl who had chafed at living forever underground. Yes, her carelessness had gotten her killed and eaten.

But the most powerful of the U'tanse had worked undetectably and cautiously, to identify and track the Cerik who had been the first to kill one of them.

Skills that could routinely heal were used to alter the killer's chemistry.

It was well known that the U'tanse tasted good. Mother had been attacked and her blood sampled by the expedition's *Name*. There was nothing they could do about that.

But shortly, the Cerik killer developed painful internal cramps, followed by cancerous tumors cropping up all through his body. He died in agony within the month, and none of his fellows dared to give him the traditional killing slash through the eye sockets that a dying Cerik would normally expect.

The word spread far and wide. U'tanse might taste good, but they were deadly poisonous.

All of this happened under tight *ineda* by the select few, as the U'tanse family mourned. It was a secret that could never be revealed.

Interestingly, the Cerik never told Father what had happened to the killer. They were keeping secrets too.

And so every little cutie was told the frightening story of what would happen if the Cerik got a hold of them, and presumably a different tale of horror was told to Cerik cubs.

11

Deep in thought, he didn't see Pam approaching until she splashed up on the bench beside him.

"Hi."

"Hi, there." He smiled, but he was tense. Pam had been affecting him—showing up in his dreams. Now was not the time to let his *ineda* slip. His brain was too full of important secrets to let his hormones sabotage them.

"I almost missed you. What are you doing down here? Hiding from me?"

"No. No. I was hoping you would show up."

She smiled. "Oh, do you need anything healed?"

"Um. Maybe. I was exposed to the air without a mask today."

"Let me check." She took his hand.

He watched her closed eyes, and found himself dwelling on her nose. Better that than let himself pay too much attention to other parts of her body.

"All done." She opened her eyes. "It wasn't much."

He stared back at her. After a moment, they both realized they were still holding hands, and dropped them.

"Um. How are things going with you?" he asked.

She leaned back against the stone wall. "Oh, still training for my first pregnancy. I'm not a cutie anymore, so it's coming up."

"That's right. When was your birthday?"

"Three days ago. But I won't really be fertile for a few days yet."

He nodded. It was impossible to be brought up surrounded by pregnant and soon-to-be pregnant sisters without knowing a few things about womens' reproductive cycles.

"Are you all excited about it?"

She looked down, and nodded. "Yes. Sort of. There's the sex, and the sorting. I'm afraid I'll mess that up, but my tutors tell me I'll be fine. And then there's all that waiting and monitoring so the baby comes out healthy."

"And you've got your sisters to help."

Pam chuckled. "Yes. Seven of them older than me. And every one is full of advice. They've got about a dozen different opinions about who…"

"Who… is to be the sperm donor?"

She winced a little and nodded, looking away.

He took a breath and quickly blurted out, "Well, if I'm anywhere on the list, you'll have to defer me until the next pregnancy." His heart beat pounded rapidly.

"Oh?" She looked sad.

He nodded, trying to make light of it. "I have a work trip coming up, maybe tomorrow. I'll be away from home for quite a while."

"Oh."

"Sorry. This just came up, but they tell me it's important."

She sighed. He took her hand. She looked at him, trying to read through his *ineda*.

He wasn't going to relax the telepathic block, but he could talk.

"You know, up until this came up, I was having some second thoughts about the whole broom thing. But now… I'll just have to wait until I get back."

She said quietly, "You were on the list."

They sat in silence for a moment. He gave her hand a squeeze. "You know, I've been around Mother and Father a bit lately."

"Oh?"

"Yes. It made it pretty clear that they're really from a different world."

She asked, "What do you mean?"

"Well, there are a bunch of things. They actually live with each other. I don't think they have separate cells. When they greet each other, they hold hands, like this."

She looked at hers and he gently released his grip.

He gestured, trying to put into words what he was trying to express. "I mean, they have *always* lived together, since the Arrival fifty-some years ago. Even, as he said, when he was doing 'Lot's duty' with his first few daughters, he still lived with Mother and refused to continue once his first son was old enough to impregnate that generation.

"It's like he's bound to her alone. And she's the same. When I made a copy of the Family Tree, I didn't see anything but 'bar Abe' on any of her children.

"And the way they talk—once the U'tanse population is large enough, I think they'd be happiest if there were as many men as women, and they paired up for life like they did."

Pam said, "Wow. That sounds so strange."

James nodded, "Not likely to happen in our lifetime, unless we live a long time. You'll work down your consanguinity list, having a child with each man in turn. I'll have sex with each cousin who comes and taps me on the shoulder. That's the way it works.

"Still—I think it's nice, what Father and Mother have."

Pam thought a moment. "My sister Chrissy spends a lot of time with Dale bar Oscar, even though their daughter is over four years old by now."

James nodded. "People pair up. I hadn't paid much attention to that until my sister Cynthia left. She had a favorite man, too. I guess Father and Mother are just an extreme example."

Pam looked out over the water. "I was hoping you and I…"

"We will, eventually. But it's not our time. And you can't wait for me. I really don't know how long I'll be gone."

"I'll miss you."

"And I'll miss you, too."

12

Mother was sitting across from the table. James couldn't help but feel that she was scanning every cell of his body, looking for a way past his *ineda*. Her skills were legendary. Even though almost everyone had inherited her psychic abilities, none of them had been tested in battle, as she had been, against the Cerik. Two decades of experience on the human world in Earth years, hiding her existence from the non-telepathic, and six decades of Cerik years here, shaping the life and culture of a rapidly growing population that were all as gifted as she was—more than the Cerik, more than Father, she was the one people feared the most.

She smiled, and it wasn't her most natural expression. "I can't read your thoughts, but your face is an open book. I'm not that much of a monster."

Father chuckled. "Hey, you scare me most of the time. Give the kid a break."

She leaned forward. "Did you have sex with Pam last night at the bath?"

"Sharon!"

James clutched fiercely to *ineda* patterns. He swallowed and tried to calm himself. "No. We didn't."

Father was frowning, tapping the table with his fingernails. Mother was ignoring him.

"Why not? You're both of age. She's all primed and ready. She's studied it. She's even sampled the passion as she prepares for her first pregnancy.

"And you're a normal young boy, dreaming of her. You get an erection every time she comes to visit you at the bath."

James was reeling with conflicting emotions. He knew she was testing him, but the things she was saying…

"I decided that it wouldn't be fair to her. I was going to be leaving and…"

"That's a lie! You had that broom up in your cell long before this mission came up."

She paused and lowered her voice. "Isn't it true you're just afraid? You know you're the most inexperienced boy in generations. You can't observe how it's done like all the others. You know you'll embarrass yourself the first time you try to hold her—the first time you'll try to stick your penis in."

Father got to his feet. She didn't stop.

"Isn't it true that you know all your sisters gossip about how the boys perform their duties? Aren't you just scared witless that you'll be just like Chad and your sister Pearl when he took three days before he got her pregnant? First he ejaculated early, and then he couldn't get an erection.

"Aren't you just frightened that the same could happen to you?"

"Sharon. Are you done?"

James was shivering. He couldn't say anything.

Mother nodded, leaning back. "Yes. You did well, James. Your *ineda* held."

She turned to Father. "He can do it."

"I think that…"

"You're right. I was out of line. I pushed too hard. But lives are at stake. All of us. And Abe, if he hates me for it, he won't be the first one."

She walked out. Father sighed and sat back down.

"Are you okay, James?"

He nodded. He took a deep breath. "How did she know all that stuff? If my *ineda* is good, then how?"

Father spread his hands. "She's good at what she does. She's been spying on our masters since we've been here—all from inside these chambers. She's been watching all of us. Even before you were *ineda*-trained, we knew you were special. And even with your block, she can still follow you through other eyes. She was probably watching you through Pam, or even just monitoring your body remotely. It doesn't take telepathy for that—not for my Sharon."

James sighed. "I don't feel special."

"Still worried about the sex thing? She was just hunting for anything to push you out of your comfort zone. She wanted to see if your block would stand up to emotional shocks. She said it did. You have the skills we need."

But he was still in turmoil. Maybe the test was over, but his heart was still pumping. His arms were shaking. Had he really been just as frightened of being inadequate as she'd said? He worried, but…

He looked up. Father was watching him with concern.

James mumbled, "Sorry."

"Take your time. Emotions dump chemicals into your blood. You can't turn that off instantly."

James tried to get his mind back under control, but Mother had spilled his composure like a tub of corn. It would take a while to collect all the pieces.

"Can we talk about what I'm supposed to do? I'd like to get my mind off of the sex stuff."

Father nodded. "Yes, but it's a complicated situation. If there's something you don't understand, stop me."

"Okay."

...

"James, do you think you could handle a solo mission, dealing with a Cerik, that might last many days?"

He shivered. "I don't know. I'm scared of them."

"Do you know the language?"

"A little. I can understand what's said. I don't know about my pronunciation."

Father chuckled. "Don't let that stop you. No human can pronounce Cerik and the Cerik don't even try to speak our language. Our mouths are shaped differently. The biggest key is to keep your mouth open. Never use your lips."

James had heard that before, when he'd been tutored in the language.

He sighed. "That's just an excuse, I guess. It's the claws, and the way they move."

"They do it on purpose, you know."

"What?"

"Slash at you. They like to see the U'tanse jump. It reinforces their self-image as masters of all. They'll never injure you by accident. They have excellent control. If you bleed, they did it on purpose."

"But... I don't know if I can do this."

"What if a life depends on it?"

"What? Explain."

"Rita bar Oscar is about your age. Martha bar Carl was her birth-mother and went to the new colony just a couple of months ago. It was too much for young Rita."

James tried to visualize her. There were so many young girls his age that he couldn't quite place her. Ftom her name, she was one of Pam's sisters by different mother.

"What happened?"

Father stared at his fingers on the table. "She was a timid girl. Always a little unsure of herself. More than most, she clung to her birth-mother."

"Attachment," he guessed.

Father nodded. "A particularly bad case of it."

One of the articles written by Mother in the Book was a detailed description of the affliction she'd named 'Attachment'. It was the biggest fear of the telepaths.

James knew where his every thought came from—from inside his own head. No matter how confused he might be, those thoughts were his. It had to be the same with Father.

The rest of them had a harder time of it. When a thought could just as easily originate in some other skull, it required more effort to know your own mind.

Father rubbed his forehead. "When we arrived here, it took some time before Sharon would agree to having children. Her own mother had gone to extraordinary lengths to insure that Sharon would grow up as separate person, and not just as an appendage, with no personality, no will of her own.

"Sharon suffered from it, too. There were times when she'd get deeply into my mind, or even into the Cerik." He sighed. "I've got the bite marks to prove it."

He straightened up in his chair. "But with the *ineda*, which we learned from the Cerik, she was able to raise her children. I almost messed that up."

"What? How?"

Father shook his head, "I taught my daughters a song."

"Song? What's that?"

He sighed deeply. "One of those things the U'tanse has lost. It is words chanted with a set rhythm and tone."

James couldn't quite imagine it. "What did that do?"

"You see, when a group of people sing a song, they act together. They say the same words so their voices overlap. They think the same thoughts, all at the same time. I think that's the purpose of songs. It's great, for the non-telepathic. It brings people together.

"But with my little girls, once they learned it together, and sang, it began to stick. They walked together, with the same steps. When I asked a question, they all answered as one person. It took several days, and some rather traumatic efforts, to separate them."

"Traumatic?"

He sighed. "Pain. If one of my daughters was in pain, the others disconnected. I never want to have to go through that again."

He shook his head. "No more songs. Not for the U'tanse. It's a great loss, but it is necessary. I want you to forget about it. Don't try it. Don't even experiment when you're alone."

James nodded, although he doubted he could forget. But he could refrain from thinking about it.

13

No one had noticed Rita's affliction the first few days after her birth-mother left. Everyone was depressed, and it was normal for Rita to seclude herself in her cell. Added to the stress of her looming coming of age, no one had been too surprised when she missed her training.

Mother came back into the room. She waited quietly as Father talked. James nodded to her. He was beginning to understand.

She joined in the narrative. "The telepathic can see an echo of themselves in others. It's normal and we expect it. But when Rita's sister noticed that she was eating her meal in time with her, she was shocked to see more than an echo. Rita's mind was a mirror, echoing her every act and thought. She knew the signs. She wrapped her thoughts in *ineda*, and after a moment of confusion, Rita latched onto the mind of another cousin.

"I was notified, and we moved her here, into the depths. We've tried everything, but if Rita is still there in that body, we can't find her anymore."

. . .

Rita was being fed in a special, locked cell. Mother explained, "She's underweight. We tried an isolation trial, where no one was in the cell with her and she would have to read changing instructions to find the food and feed herself. It wouldn't help to link to the mind of another, since no one except her keepers could read the instructions, and we all had our minds blocked.

"But it didn't work. She locked onto one of the infants. She just cried helplessly. And that's dangerous for the real infant as well. We had to give it up. She was starving to death."

James nodded, understanding on an intellectual level. He watched from the doorway. The girl looked dazed, sucking at a bottle. It was a thin version of Pam, and she didn't appear well.

"How can I help?" But no sooner had he said the words than he felt so helpless to do anything. How could a person deaf to the telepathic world be of any help?

Mother looked at Father. He pointed down the corridor and said, "Follow me."

. . .

"There are at least four independent groups of Cerik telepaths that monitor us." Father gestured to a shelf of written reports in a smaller room much like the Library. James opened one of the bound volumes on yellowed earth-paper with thin blue lines. It contained page after page of reports where Mother or one of the older generation had detected the echo of the U'tanse in a Cerik mind. The newer ones were scrolls of *shash* paper.

"The *Name* has his spies, but there are others. None of them trust us. They lost a city to their previous slaves. They don't intend to make the same mistake twice."

James nodded. "You explained. We have to keep our *ineda* up."

"Yes, but this isn't a problem we can hide. Rita is keeping no block. She's wide open. I don't know which group put the pieces together, but the *Name* now knows that one of ours has a strong case of attachment. Some Cerik are telepathic—more than traditional humans, but much less than the U'tanse. It is extremely rare, but attachment has happened to them as well. When a Cerik cub becomes attached, it is killed immediately.

"The *Name* demands that we get rid of Rita."

James took in a deep breath, trying to get an idea of what Father meant. "How?"

He shrugged. "The *Name* would be happy to have us kill her, or failing that, turn her outside where one of them, or the air itself, would kill her."

"We can't do that!"

"I agree, and I've been working for weeks to find an alternate solution that the *Name* would approve."

"What's wrong with just keeping her here, and hoping that she'll get better?"

Father pulled out a wide scroll and spread it on the table.

"This is a chart of the stars, as seen from this planet."

James looked at the dark dots on the whitish surface. There were thirty or forty of them, much more than he'd ever glimpsed in the sky on those rare occasions when he'd been out late.

"Did the Cerik make this?"

"No. These are my own observations. Many of these stars can only be seen on the darkest of nights, when the volcanos have been quiet and the moon is on the other side of the globe."

"I've never seen so many."

Father chuckled. "From Earth, you could see thousands. But the air there was clear."

He stabbed a finger at one of the smaller dots. "The Cerik don't care much about other worlds, but when their Delense Builders discovered how to fly in space, they went here first. In spite of its faintness, it's one of the closest stars.

"What they discovered there frightened them badly."

James thought he mis-heard. How could the Cerik be frightened of anything?

Father continued, "On a planet around this star is a world much like the Earth, from the Cerik legends I've heard. It is blue with oceans. And it is populated by beings more like humans than Cerik or the Delense.

"Their first ship sent a scout boat down to the surface to see if the animals could be eaten. The boat landed, but the Cerik never reported in. A second boat was sent, ready to attack any danger, but it vanished silently as well.

"Now, the Cerik are not inclined to back off from any threat. A third boat was sent to get close enough to observe where the first boats landed, and then destroy them with a bomb that would burn the whole area."

"Burn their own people?"

"Yes. They decided to destroy the boats to prevent giving enemies access to them."

James remembered a tale—the story of how Mother and Father were captured from the human home world. There were similarities.

"The third boat was in constant communication with the big ship. As they got close to the ground, the pilot became... something else. For an instant, there was battle on the boat as the pilot's mind was taken over by the creatures on the surface. But soon all the Cerik changed, and the third boat was lost. Fragments of the communications told a tale of minds being 'eaten'.

"The Cerik call them the Ferreer. Long distance pictures showed them as green, standing upright on two legs and having two arms. The Cerik left that world alone. In their later explorations, they discovered other worlds, also populated by the Ferreer. In each case the story was the same. Any pilot that got too close lost his mind and became one of them, landing the boat safely and walking peacefully among the green ones.

"The Ferreer are the nightmare goblins of Cerik folklore, but all too real. If the *Names* could destroy those worlds, they would. As it is, since they've seen the Ferreer on multiple worlds, the green ones must have access to space travel. If they were inclined to come after the Cerik, they just might."

James shivered. "They frighten me too."

Father gestured at the map. "One theory is that the Ferreer are a race of attached telepaths. They have a hive mind, but one so strong that they could overwhelm a partially telepathic race and take those minds over."

James absorbed the idea. "Do the Cerik think this?"

Father nodded. "And from our experiences, I believe it too. Rita is dangerous to us, as well. We've spend a great deal of effort attempting to break her attachment, but we can't afford to let her stay here. We could feed her and take care of her physical needs, but she is a seed of a much more dangerous problem. How many attached telepaths does it take to form an unstoppable hive mind? The U'tanse are close to a merged consciousness already. Too close. The Ferreer can take over even untrained, partially telepathic Cerik minds. What would happen to one of the U'tanse?"

He shook his head. "The Cerik are natural killers. Their solution for the attached is probably reasonable for them."

James didn't like it, but Father's assessment made sense. "But we can't kill Rita." He knew in his heart that they could... but it would be traumatic to the person who did it. It would be traumatic to everyone. There had to be another solution.

Father was silent for a moment, then he asked, "What if we could take her to the Ferreer planet?"

James considered it. "She would attach to them. If she could eat the food and breathe the air... I guess she wouldn't be lonely. She's already given up what made her Rita. And it's not likely she would ever... un-hook from the hive mind."

Father nodded. "That's what we thought. But there is a problem."

James saw it. "We don't have space ships."

Father shrugged. "The *Name* does. He has more than he's using. The Cerik have been retreating from space since they lost the Delense. If we had a year to design a way to send a ship without a pilot, there would be no problem."

"The pilot."

"Right."

James thought about it. "No Cerik is going to deliver Rita there for us."

"No. Not a one of them."

"And none of us can pilot."

"The *Name* would never allow it. I've been here fifty years and they have never allowed me to fly anywhere myself. Not even in a little boat."

"So, is there any solution?"

Father gestured as he explained. "Theoretically, a Cerik pilot and a non-telepath could take Rita to the Ferreer system. The Cerik could keep a safe distance in the main ship and the non-telepath could attempt to land a boat, unload Rita, and escape before his brain was taken over.

"I've offered to do this. But the *Name* wouldn't allow it—he wouldn't allow *me* to do it."

"And I'm the only other non-telepath."

No sooner had he said it, when the next question came. "What if the Ferreer can take over a non-telepath?"

Father sighed, "It's a risk. We're dealing with Cerik story-telling here. We don't know the hard facts. Sharon doesn't think they could. She could cause muscles to clench in another body. She's even communicated with me via facial twitches, but landing a space ship? Not likely.

"Still, you would be risking everything. If the Ferreer can take over your mind, Rita would be saved, but you'd be lost. You'll have to make that decision yourself."

"Why would the Cerik let me at the controls of a boat?"

Father tried to be honest. "The *Name* expects you to fail. But he considers the loss of an untried cub less than that of the boat he's already gambling."

James frowned. "He's risking a ship, too. And the pilot. What does he get out of it?"

Abe shrugged, "Good relations with his valuable slaves, and he could possibly gain some strategic information about the Cerik's most dangerous enemies. If the *Name* could brag to the others at the Face that he had gotten a boat to the surface of the Ferreer world and retrieved it, he could gain prestige."

James tasted the idea. "I'd be proving that U'tanse could be tactically valuable—weapons, not just repairmen."

"Yes. What do you think about that?"

14

He had little more than a day to get ready. Once the *Name* was informed that the plan was coming together, he was impatient for them to be gone.

James had two training sessions with Mother. One was to refresh everything he knew about *ineda* and the other was a session where he suffered her attempts to take over his body. It was disconcerting to feel his arms twitch, and his eyelids to flicker, but he was always able to keep control.

In the parts bins were pieces of a boat's controls. They were inactive, but Father wanted him to be familiar with their position and feel. The plan was for the Cerik pilot to give him simple training on how to get the boat down to the surface and back up again, but the Cerik were always impatient, and poor trainers. Father had seen many a pilot in his years of service and knew roughly how to fly a boat even though he'd never been allowed to touch the controls. James listened carefully.

He wished he could sleep in his own cell, on his own bed, but the hike back to the main living area was considered a waste of time and a distraction.

I wish I could say goodbye to Cynthia and Eliza and Pam. But Father is right. Don't start thinking of failure.

He woke with a slight headache. Someone had retrieved his leathers and his gas mask. At least part of the trip would be in Cerik normal air and there would be no one to heal his lungs until he returned. He checked to make sure that the filtering chemicals were fresh, even though he expected someone else had already taken care of that. Best to be sure.

Grace bar Hank brought him a large sack. "This is food and water for you and Rita."

He looked into the bag. Biscuits. Nothing tasty, just edible.

"Thanks."

Father hurried in. "The boat is arriving early. Come on."

James took the offered hand and they hurried down the tunnel.

"Where is Rita?"

"They're already ahead of us. Sharon has tinkered with her sleep center and she'll be out of it for a day or so."

...

There was only one boat landing site inside the Home. Since he'd been working there for weeks, it felt very comfortable when he walked in. Abe signaled him to put on his mask. The boat was already down. A Cerik was watching the people gather.

Rita was bundled into a blanket and carried on a push cart.

Mother came up to him. "The boat pilot is telepathic. Don't let your *ineda* slip. Once you're on the main ship, I'll check out the its pilot. If he's telepathic too, I'll twitch your eyelid three times. If he's not, only once. Got it?"

He nodded. Supposedly the pilot that was going to take him to the other planet was non-telepathic, for his own safety, but the Cerik were tricky. If the U'tanse had a double-cross planned, they'd want to know about it. James was already aware of a dozen ways this could go wrong.

Rita was sleeping deeply, with slow, steady breaths. She was wearing a gas mask as well. Although she had been trained to heal herself before she attached, it wasn't likely she would be that self-aware.

"Take good care of her." Mother patted him on the shoulder.

"I will."

<Don't waste my time! Get inside.> The pilot growled and headed for his control screen.

There was no ramp for the cart. With the supplies slung across his back, he lifted Rita and stepped up into the hatchway. The floor shifted and the hatchway began closing behind him, blocking the buzz of the engines.

He's lifting already! To keep from stumbling, he set her down where he stood. With one hand on her head to keep her secure and another on his food bag to keep it from spilling, he struggled to keep everything still. *We're in the air, Rita. We're flying!*

He kept his *ineda* secure, but he couldn't hide his excitement at being in a boat, actually flying.

As the boat cleared the overhead hatch and moved out into open air, the deck stopped shaking. Since he hadn't had time to move to the interior hold, he was right behind the piloting station. The Cerik waved his claws through light beams and moved a targeting icon high on the screen.

I'm going to have to learn how to do that. I need to watch.

Carefully, he positioned the bag where it would remain upright and shifted to where he could get a better view.

The Cerik appeared to be ignoring him, but if they had gone to the trouble to send him up with a pilot who was also a trained telepath—which were two very different Cerik *dances*—then he was sure that his *ineda* was being constantly tested.

He wished he could ask questions as the Cerik adjusted the flight path, moving them farther and farther around the curve of the planet, but he was too timid to form the Cerik words.

A ship icon appeared on the screen, and claws adjusted the path again, aiming them at the interstellar vessel.

With Father's coaching still fresh, he saw the slash that activated the automatic docking. The pilot eased back on his rear legs, watching the screen shift to a visual image of the rapidly-growing ship ahead of them in orbit.

Nearly everything in the Delense-designed ships was automated for the Cerik's convenience. The docking bay on the larger ship opened up. Their boat eased in and settled down on the dock.

James moved back to Rita's side. As he expected, the pilot yelled at him to unload. Not waiting, the pilot bounded out of the boat and through a hatchway into the main ship's interior.

The air was still swirling, not yet equalized, but he knew they wouldn't wait for him. He hurriedly carried the food bag into the interior passageway and then went back for Rita.

She was still thin and didn't weigh much, but she was limp and difficult to carry. There were no carts in sight, so he knew he'd have to take care of her himself. Cerik never helped the U'tanse.

Father's words echoed in memory. *"Don't wait for orders. It just makes them irritated. If you look like you know what you're doing, most of the time they'll leave you alone."*

There was no time to scout out the ship. He needed to be ready when they were.

It's cold. And the air was stale, from what he could smell through the gas filters in his mask. *Has this ship been empty and idle up here in space?*

He'd need a warm, safe, and poison-free compartment to keep Rita.

15

He examined and rejected the first five places. Some had doors that wouldn't seal. One was full to the brim with dried and brittle vegetation the previous crew never bothered to remove.

Others had equipment of various kinds. He wished he had time to look at them, but getting Rita safe was the first order of business.

Echoing down the passageway, the snarls of the two Cerik yelling at each other gave him a sense of their direction. He could hear the boat pilot refusing to help the ship pilot. The ship pilot claimed that it was an impossible task to bring the ship back to life single-handedly.

Good enough. He found a chamber that was relatively small, with a door that sealed and environmental controls that worked. Following Father's instructions, he adjusted the air so that it contained no nitrates. There was a hiss and the air circulated to match the settings. The temperature was already set correctly, even though the walls had not warmed up. *Just how cold had this place gotten?*

It would have been difficult to reactivate a ship this size if it were frozen solid with unbreathable air. How had the Cerik pilot managed it?

...

He put Rita against the wall and moved a big storage bin close, so that she couldn't roll around if the ship shifted while moving. He checked the air again and then went outside.

It's the fourth doorway from the intersection. His memory was excellent, but he worried that somehow he would forget where he'd left her.

Perhaps it would be safest if he just stayed out of sight—but no, the Cerik would come looking for him.

He followed the growls and snarls. James walked slowly, checking other doors. This was a huge craft, compared to the boat. Dozens of people, maybe hundreds, could ride inside.

Right before the intersection, he stopped in his tracks. There was a window to the outside. He hurried up close.

The sight of the red-brown planet *Ko* below was majestic enough. There was a large continent, with a long island following the coastline. The land moved below.

No, we're moving, flying at great speed. The daylight faded as they moved into night. He looked for the stars, but the glare from the sun and the still-lit parts of the planet made them hard to see.

Down the corridor he heard, <Where is that U'tanse cub? If he dies on me, They will give me a whole new set of scars.>

James tore himself away from the window and ran down the corridor.

...

For all the echoes of his snarls in the corridors, the ship pilot was smaller than the boat pilot who had brought him up here. He was still large enough to tear any U'tanse to pieces.

James took a deep breath and yelled, <For the *Name*. The female is secured.>

The Cerik turned and laughed at each other, probably at his accent. James was just glad they weren't angry.

The ship pilot pointed to the control panel, <Builder, fix the air so it doesn't stink so bad!>

James moved. The Delense controls were standard, but he had no idea what kind of a stink they were talking about, since the air always stank to the U'tanse.

He had been coached on what it took to keep the Cerik happy and healthy long before this mission came up. It was part of U'tanse standard education. He checked the gasses, but they were in the proper ratios already.

Human fingers, and the Delense fingers before them, could work buttons that Cerik claws couldn't. He went into the menus.

At first, it seemed that everything was okay. Gas ratios and temperature were set at standard. Then he dug into the current status reports. Like everything Delense, these were graphic charts rather than numbers, but it was designed to be easy to read. The standard gasses were in the correct portions, but there was a tiny dot, blinking to show it existed, of other things. And it was increasing in size.

Is something leaking? Did a pipe break?

He needed to identify the problem quickly. If there was a frozen pipe, then it might rupture now that things were warming up.

The Delense menu system was very deep. He started digging.

<What's taking so long! It's getting worse!>

James pulled up a chart of the ship, and overlaid the trace gasses as a color.

The concentration was strongest in one area. He traced the corridors with his finger. There was where the the boats were docked. There was where they entered. *Here is where Rita is. There is…*

He yelled at the pilots, <There are old rotted things in storage. I'll need to seal them.>

He raced down the corridor, pausing just an instant to check on Rita. She was still breathing gently.

Starting with the dried vegetation he'd found, he turned off air circulation in that room and sealed its door. He then worked down the corridor. Three others had old vegetation. Two had piles of rotting animals. They weren't too visibly decayed, probably because they were still frozen, but they would get much worse. For now, he sealed off the rooms.

<There were rotting animals in the hold. I sealed them off.>

Both Cerik snarled. The boat pilot said, <They didn't empty their prey last time. That's your problem, not mine. I'm going.>

<Fine, you're useless anyhow. Better a U'tanse cub.>

They roared at each other with some final insults and the boat pilot stalked off. James stepped to the side to be well clear of him as he left.

The ship's pilot stared at James, swishing his claws through the air. Off in the distance, there was the metallic clang of a massive door shutting. The boat was gone.

16

<I'd take your eyes if the *Name* wouldn't take mine when I return.>

James had been taught to keep his eyes down on the deck. If he had claws, he should have been tapping them on the floor. Be submissive.

The pilot growled, <A trip to the Ferreer planet is death. I know why I was chosen. Why were you?>

James cleared his throat. All the running had already given him a little hoarseness. Yelling only made it worse. <I am the weakest of the U'tanse.>

The pilot turned his back. <Of course you are. Go check the power of the engines, but don't turn them on.>

James backed out of the control room.

I wasn't told I'd have to help with the ship engines! What do I do now?

There was, of course, a Delense map of the ship and a little searching of the menus showed him where the main engine controls were.

Not good. He looked at the chart of the engine power, showing iconic bubbles of different units of energy. There was certainly enough to heat the ship and circulate the air, but if he understood the icons that compared energy supply and engine demand, there wasn't enough.

He walked back to the main control room, carrying a multi-wrench in his hand. *Has the Name sabotaged the mission from the beginning, or is he just ignorant of the ship?*

At the entrance, he raised the wrench, and rattled the tool against the wall. Cerik underlings rattled their claws to request entrance. Best if he tried to follow the protocols.

<You have news?>

James stepped into view. <Energy is very low. There is enough to push, but not to leap.>

<It is as I expected. Go activate the pushing engines.>

He backed out.

I can't run back and forth like this. I don't have the energy, and I don't dare exhaust the chemicals in my gas mask. He toyed with the thought of exchanging Rita's gas mask for his. *Maybe later, if I have to. She won't be roaming the ship.*

...

James was making the trek back to the control room when his right eyelid flickered on its own.

He paused and waited. Was that Mother, signaling him that the pilot was not telepathic, as she promised, or was he just getting tired? After a few seconds, with nothing else happening, he resumed his pace.

I can't drop my ineda. Not yet. If Mother can reach me from the planet below, the Cerik telepaths can too.

With the pushing engines activated, the pilot snarled at him. <It will be a day until we reach the charging point. I will be in *dan* shortly. If you wake me, I will get hungry and there were no other prey loaded for me.>

The threat was plain enough. The Cerik often fasted in a *dan*, sleeping, until the next hunt. If no food was provided for the pilot, then the mission had to be completed before hunger made him forget that the U'tanse were poisonous.

James backed out and worked his way back to Rita's chamber. He paused at the window.

Things had changed. The planet, with its thin brown halo of atmosphere was noticeably smaller. The ship had shifted its angle. There were stars. He watched for several minutes, trying to fit them to the dots to the map that Father had drawn. There was some overlap, but even with the glare of the planet, there were many more stars in sight than had been on the map. It was spectacular. No one on the ground could imagine what the sky was really like.

17

His hand paused on the door. *Get in quickly, before much of the nitrated air gets inside.* In one fluid twist, he opened it, entered, and closed it behind him. The lights brightened automatically, and only then did he notice that Rita wasn't where he'd left her.

He barely saw her out of the corner of his eye before she slammed him to his knees. There was a slash of her fingernails across his chest and then she caught his wrist in her teeth.

The finger-slash was inconsequential, but the bite hurt. He tugged his wrist free and rolled. Maybe in her mind, she was a Cerik, but her body was still that of a lightweight and undernourished girl. He pulled her arms down to her side with little effort and held her tight.

Her eyes were wide and she tried to bite at him again, but he kept out of her range of motion.

It's time. I need to open up.

There were many stages of *ineda*, from a tight, featureless block of all thoughts, to repetitive patterns of thoughts that would distract a telepath from deeper thoughts. And *assertive* thoughts.

While it was impossible to keep yourself from thinking certain thoughts, another technique was almost as good. Force your thoughts onto certain channels. Keep yourself filled with thoughts that weren't dangerous to reveal.

Rita needs to lock onto me, not the pilot.

He stared into her wild eyes. "Rita! I'm James."

She was panting, still struggling, but her eyes blinked and some of the predatory glare faded. He had her pinned down with his weight, and he worried a bit that he was hurting her. Her attack had knocked him down, but there really wasn't anything she could do to him.

He eased his grip, concentrating on looking at her. *You look a lot like Pam. Do you know her? We're all three the same age.*

Her stomach rumbled, and he chuckled. She chuckled too, echoing him.

"Come on. Let's get you some food."

He rolled off of her, and she rolled in the opposite direction. They both got to their feet together. He kept his eyes on her, and she kept staring at him.

The biscuits were funny, at first. She was clearly more hungry than he was, but she couldn't eat unless he was eating. The first two went down as a synchronized duet. She bit and chewed exactly as he did. Then they drank water together.

Will this work?

He reached into the sack, as did she. He gripped a biscuit and brought it to his mouth. He mimed eating, and she mimed eating as well.

"Later." They both said the word and put the biscuit back into the sack.

It was interesting what things happened exactly alike, and which were close. Her steps were shorter than his, so as they walked back to her blanket, she had to make an extra step.

"I need to rest." They lay back down, staring at each other. He bunched the blanket at one end to make a pillow. Her hands started to follow his actions, but he was done before she could match him.

Thinking for a moment of Pam, he put his arms around her. He let his *ineda* firm back up, and for a moment, she struggled, not against him, but within herself.

"Rita? Can you hear me?" Her eyes didn't connect with his. A second later, she went limp.

"Rita?"

Where was she? Was she unconscious, in sync with the pilot's *dan*, or what?

He opened his mind, and she looked into his eyes, her arms tightening around him.

"Rita, what will I do with you?"

She echoed, "Do with you?"

Her eyes began welling up with tears.

No, those are my tears. Poor, poor Rita. How did you ever lose yourself?

. . .

He had thought that holding a girl, and sleeping with her, would be a wonderful experience. Maybe if he had stayed home with Pam, it would have been. But the long night was a struggle. If he opened up, she was just a puppet, mirroring as well as she could his thoughts and actions. If he sought the security of *ineda*, where he could think his own thoughts, she became a slave of the sleeping killer, luckily in a motionless trance. He forced himself to keep her there, holding her close, more for his comfort than hers.

Father's comment doesn't apply.

As he had been coached about this mission, Father had commented that it would be very easy to have sex with Rita, since she didn't have a will of her own. But that would be a bad thing. If she became pregnant, it would be a *random*, since she would not make the necessary sperm selections. Even if the baby came to term and was viable, it would be immediately absorbed into the Ferreer hive mind, with no choice, and no chance at all of having an independent will.

He'd explained how even though it was the exact opposite of what his normal U'tanse duty called for, even if she seemed to express sexual desire, he should refrain from following his instincts.

No chance I'd do that. If she touched me, it would just be me touching myself.

This was not the time for that.

. . .

Something brought him awake. James opened his eyes and barely remembered where he was when Rita's eyes opened too.

Only, she wasn't mirroring him. He could see the killer in her eyes.

He rolled free of her, and snatched up his gas mask. The pilot was waking out of his *dan*, and he'd brought Rita awake with him.

She wasn't really mirroring him, but her mind was reacting to her environment as if she were Cerik.

I need to be out of here.

He glanced at the controls near the door. Had Rita ever been trained in Delense menu pads? If so, could she use that training, the way her mind was now?

James tapped the menu a few times, and slipped outside. There was a thump against the door. She had tried to attack again.

He rested his head against the door and eased his *ineda*.

Rita, calm down. Bundle yourself up in the blanket and go back to sleep.

He couldn't hold her long, but if he could just calm her down, when she slipped back into Cerik mode, maybe she would go into a *dan* herself.

It was all just guesswork. He'd put a slight overpressure in the room to keep the door pressed tightly shut. Maybe it would be enough to keep her from opening the door and getting herself in trouble. He wished he could put her back asleep like Mother did, but he never had that kind of skill. He couldn't even make himself go to sleep when he needed to.

The window showed nothing but stars. The planet had to be elsewhere. The star field, with no glare to wash it out, was like nothing he'd ever seen. He soaked it up, especially around the edges, hoping to match up some patterns with ones he'd seen before. Unfortunately, with so many stars visible, it was hard.

A growl echoed through the ship, coming from all directions. The pilot must have turned on a sound system. Why hadn't he done that before? It would have saved him many trips running down the corridors.

<U'tanse! Come here!> Cerik always sounded angry, but this time, James couldn't help but shiver. Something was up.

18

He ran to the control room, and barely started to pull out his noise-making wrench when the pilot yelled, <Get in here. You're not a Cerik.>

James stood in the doorway. <I am here.>

<Get to the engines. Use the shouter and tell me the energy levels.>

He ran. Back in the caverns of Home, his job fixing Delense machines had put him on the track to work with the most powerful and incomprehensible of technologies. He remembered something Bonnie had said.

"All machines have to have a source of power to run them. Many of the devices we repair have simply run out of the power stored in them. Often we can 'repair' something by connecting it to the charger and moving power from one device to another."

"What happens when we run out of powered devices?"

"I tell Father and he arranges to get something brought in that contains power. And before you ask, yes, there's a limited number of to devices we can use for power. Father is still working on the puzzle of where the power comes from in the first place. The Cerik say it comes from the stars, but they won't, or can't tell him how."

James had wondered what the pilot meant when he'd said that they were moving to the 'charging' point, but he'd been too distracted to think much about it then.

A whine was coming from the engine room. The power chart was blinking on the display. *Where did all this power come from?*

He'd imagined there might be some factory in space that made the power, but he could see nothing nearby. The pusher engines were running hot. One was aimed at *Ko's* large moon. Another was aimed out into the stars.

Not a star. Something big and massive out there. Another planet?

He watched the power grow for a few seconds, filling shaped bubbles on the screen. *What happens when the energy storage gets full?*

He tapped on the menu system, discovering the shouter. <The power is coming fast. It will be full in minutes.> The whining noise had gotten louder.

He remembered disconnecting a power connection the second day he'd been working to repair devices at Home. There had been a flash of light, and there had been black deposits all over the connector. Bonnie had rushed over at the noise and scolded him for severing a connection while power was flowing.

What kind of flash would be created with this much power?

The pilot shouted, <Is there enough power for a leap?>

<Enough for six leaps. There is a whine. I don't like it.>

<Kill the pushers! We can't over-charge!>

There were several other words interspersed in the pilot's shouts, but James had never heard them before. And he was too busy to worry about them. He shut off the pusher engines, but the whine just increased.

<Leap engine!>

James fumbled through the menu, then gave up and slashed at the light beams as if he were a Cerik. The screen flashed momentarily, and he felt like something snapped inside his head.

The whine faded. James checked the power. <Power is stable. One leap quantity was consumed.>

<U'tanse, you're the maintenance guild. Check the ship for damage.>

James sighed. Another task he wasn't trained for. He reached for the menu pad.

· · ·

He paused at Rita's door. The overview of the ship from the menu screens was superficially good, with nothing drastic failing. Maybe the pilot would be content with that, but James wasn't happy. A number of systems had triggered on their own when the ship's leap engines threw them across space. He needed to check what he could in person. He'd already had to reset the master lighting controls.

I just hope we went to the right place. The engine screens gave him interior information, but the pilot's screens were the only ones that showed where they were.

He put his hand on the door, and it opened effortlessly.

That's not good. He'd pressurized this cell.

The lights came up as he entered, his muscles tensed to be attacked from any angle.

Nothing. And Rita wasn't there.

She's out. He had to get her back before she accidentally encountered the pilot. He snatched up her gas mask from the floor and reset the air before he left. She was breathing bad air.

"Rita!" he shouted down the corridor. On impulse, he ran toward the window. The instant he was sure that the star patterns were different, he dropped his *ineda*.

Rita! If you can hear me, you need to get back into the safe air. Please listen to me.

If the only minds around were the three of them, or the two and a half of them, then a yell in his head would be better than a shout any day. Rita was the only telepath to *hear*.

There's no yelling from the control room, so she's not there. No telling what the Cerik is up to.

Rita walked up, silently, and startled him.

"Rita! You're safe."

Her face was remote. <U'tanse. The guild tried to kill me. Can't go there.> Her mumbling in the Cerik language was erratic. Was she linked to the pilot again? She stared off past his shoulder.

He turned. *The stars?*

She pointed. "They're that way. I can hear them."

James looked harder. *Is one of those...?*

She completed his thought. "...the Ferreer planet?"

So, she's linked to me, but she's telepathic. She could also read the pilot.

She mumbled in the Cerik language, <I'm not going any closer. I'm not going to have my mind eaten. Kill the U'tanse? Can't make up a story. The guild would read my mind.>

And then she coughed.

"Rita, we have to get you back into clean air." He slipped her gas mask over her face. She was passive and unresponsive.

"Come on, walk with me."

As he turned, she did too. They walked in step.

James wondered at her condition. She wasn't a mirror of him, but there didn't seem to be any personality in her. If she could just absorb enough of him to realize that she needed to stay safe in the clean air room, without trying to walk where he walked, then maybe he could complete his tasks.

And what did the pilot intend to do with them?

<Get them off the ship. Send them away, and the guild will read that I did my job. But how can I jump the ship back without the U'tanse to help? They're trying to kill me.>

James felt jealous. Telepathy was so easy with everyone else. He'd spent half his life puzzling over things that were obvious to...

"...everyone else."

He put his hand on her shoulder. "No need to gripe at you. You have your own problems."

He sat her down in the room and wrapped the blanket around her. "Stay here. Be safe. Get some rest. There are still biscuits and water in the sack."

He had no idea if she had enough free will to do what he said. But she had wandered off on her own. Maybe there was hope.

He re-pressurized the room and left. *I still have to make sure the ship is safe.*

19

Hours had passed before he approached the control room and rattled the wrench on the wall.

<Enter!>

He stepped in and tried to make sense of the navigation screen visible behind the pilot.

<Report.>

<The ship is now safe. Do you want to know what was damaged?>

<No. That's your job.>

James nodded. <What happened to us?> It wasn't really the place of a slave to ask, but he was too tired to care.

The pilot growled. For a moment it didn't appear he would answer, then he raised himself from his crouch. <Enemies gave me the wrong information. I'm a pilot, not one of the Rear Talon guild. The ship charged much faster than I was told. If I had waited another minute, the ship would have exploded. It was already too late to shut down the charging beams properly, so I commanded the ship to leap.>

He snarled and twitched with satisfaction. <I will have some eyes when we get back. And they think I'm dead. They'll never see me coming.>

James had no idea whether the Cerik was truthful or delusional. It wasn't his concern whether one Cerik killed another right now. They did that all the time.

He waited a moment, and then asked, <How long to get to the planet?>

The pilot growled low. <I'm not moving. We're close enough. Take the boat and get rid of your female. Remember, I am getting hungry.>

<I was told you would train me on how to fly the boat.>

<That was never my job. The one who brought you should have done that. Be gone and remember to use the distance shouter, so I'll know when you mind has been eaten and I can leave.>

The Cerik settled down into a *dan*.

James hesitated for just a moment and then backed out of the room.

. . .

I was never trained on this. I don't even know where the planet is. Does the pilot?

He reached the room and tapped the controls to equalize the pressure. She was waiting patiently with the blanket draped over her shoulders.

"Rita, we…"

"… need to leave." She stood up.

"Rita, is the pilot really going to let us fly off without any training?"

She just stood there, eyes unfocussed.

I guess he really is in dan.

"Come on then."

He picked up their sack of food and walked them toward the hangar where the other boat waited.

If the Cerik can fly these things, then how hard could it be?

The hangar room was large enough for several of the boats, but there was only one of them.

If I don't return, how will the pilot get back to the surface? Can he even activate the leap engine by himself?

He looked at Rita, so passive, so detached. *Are you listening to me?*

This was all to save her life—or at least to save the U'tanse from having to kill her.

Quit this defeatism. We have to get clear of the ship before the pilot does something stupid.

He made sure Rita was seated against a wall, in case they bumped against something, and then hesitantly activated the controls.

The menus showed several screens. There was a navigation screen that only signaled that they were inside the hangar deck. There were controls for the air, for weapons, and for the engines. He quickly set the air to U'tanse standard.

Power was low. *They'd given Father the dregs of their vehicles, hadn't they? Had the* Name *written me off from the very beginning? Was it just a gesture—pretending to Father that the* Name *considered the U'tanse important?*

He glanced back to where Rita sat waiting for him to take care of her. *That's it, isn't it? She was tired of taking care of herself and just gave up. But that doesn't let me off the hook.*

He looked through the controls. Somehow the boat had to be able to get more power. Maybe the ship could power up in the middle of space with the pusher engines, but he doubted the boat could do the same. *Little devices get power from the bigger ones.* That was the rule at Home.

After digging through the Delense menu pad without finding something obvious, he tried the light beams. Cerik had to be able to power their boats and that's all they used. James slashed with his hands, trying to mimic the talon gestures.

Ah! There it is. In the navigation screen, there were bubbles like on the main ship's power settings. He directed one of the bubbles to the image of the boat. There was a hum and shortly, the boat had increased its power levels. James kept at it, adding iconic bubbles until the boat said it was close to full.

The external hull doors were illustrated on the navigation display. A gesture caused a warning signal, and after a moment they began to open. Using the gesture controls was simple. Everything was automated. Presumably, the hangar air was pumped out, or else there would have been a gale on the deck when those outside doors came open.

Just go with the flow. The Cerik don't worry about all this stuff.

From Father's coaching and from what he'd seen on the boat ride up from the surface, he soon directed the boat outside.

The navigation screen changed once he cleared the bulk of the big ship.

There were stars, faintly decorating the background. But there were other things as well. There was the ship, and there were a dozen balls.

Which is the Ferreer planet?

Rita stepped up beside him. "I hear them."

"Is it the Ferreer you hear?"

She pointed at one of the balls on the screen. "They call me."

He hesitated. She was almost acting like a person. Had the people back Home made a mistake? They said they couldn't find Rita's mind anymore. Had it come back?

She stared intently at the display.

"Rita, I have to know. Are you back? Do you want to go to the Ferreer? I won't take you there unless you want to go."

It was a silly thing to say. They were committed. What was his alternative? Hijack the big ship, kill the Cerik and learn to fly it by himself?

But he couldn't turn her over to a hive mind if she were struggling to regain her identity. He just couldn't.

Rita turned to him. "We need to go there."

"Rita, do you know what will happen there? You'll get absorbed into an alien mind. They won't even be people like us. There will be no way back."

"We need to go there. We will have a place."

He sighed. "You will have a place. I can't stay there."

She looked back at the display. Maybe there was a hint of a smile on her face, but he couldn't be sure.

There is no help for it.

He slashed his hand through the web of light beams and a pointer extended from the image of the boat to the planet. The big ship began moving off. They were on their way.

James frowned at the display. "How can I make us go faster? It'll take days at this rate."

...

It was his fluttering eyelids that called him to a stop. He'd found the way to speed up the boat, and had dug into the Delense menu pad options. He could force it to go even faster, at the expense of all the automated safety features.

But that flutter wasn't Ferreer attacking his mind, it was just exhaustion.

He left the boat on automatic and settled down beside Rita.

"It'll take most of the day to get us there. I need to rest. Is that okay with you?"

She was expressionless. Her eyes were open, watching the navigation screen, but she might well be asleep or in a trance.

He looked into the sack. She hadn't been eating. He pulled out a bottle and coaxed her into sipping until her body's need for water took over and she gulped down the whole thing. He put a biscuit to her lips and she nibbled about half of it. He almost dozed off, holding her. *Enough for now.*

He stretched out on the floor, his arm around her, and closed his eyes.

. . .

She was warm beside him. "I'm glad you removed the broom."

He was content to hold her and not think about it. Warm, smooth, and curved, there was little to think about.

"We could stay together."

He grunted. "You know that won't work."

"They would let us." She held him tighter. "Everything would be different. You wouldn't be an outsider anymore."

He shook his head, "My duty…"

20

<U'tanse! Has your mind been eaten yet?>

James shook awake, wrapped in Rita's blanket and her arms.

"What?" He pulled free and got to his feet. <What did you say?>

<Have the Ferreer eaten you yet?> The angry voice came from the ceiling overhead.

Oh, the shouter. I forgot.

<No. My mind is still my own. I was sleeping.> He checked the navigation screen. <We are half way there.>

<Has the female's mind been eaten?>

James looked at Rita, watching him. <I don't know.>

There was a grumble of disgust, and the sound shut off.

James took a moment to compose himself. He had been asleep, but he wasn't sure she had been. He glanced back at Rita. She was half undressed.

His body was feeling guilty. He had a memory of holding her. *Surely we didn't have sex while I was asleep. I'm still dressed. I'd know, wouldn't I?*

He closed his eyes and took a deep breath. He'd dressed the little ones all his life. She was the same. Just more developed.

James made her get up on her feet and he tugged her tunic back into place. She was a little girl, in his care. He wouldn't take advantage of that. He combed her hair back with his fingers.

"Rita, are you in contact with the Ferreer?"

"They know she is coming."

What mind said those words?

"Tell them… Tell them to leave my mind alone!"

"You and Rita would be happy together. It would be no different than Mother and Father, a couple starting out on a new planet. Only this time, the Ferreer would be there to help, every step of the way."

James tried to ignore what she said. The closer they got to the planet, the more animated Rita's body became. She wandered about the cabin, looking at the blue planet growing visibly larger and more detailed on the screen and watching him.

He locked his mind down with his best *ineda*. It made no difference to her.

She said, "You don't need to do that. Those surface thought tricks work fine against point telepaths, but not against an endless array."

"I'll make my own choices. I'll do anything to keep my own mind."

He slashed his finger through the air, refining the target landing zone. The original one had been in the ocean.

"Don't do that."

"What?"

"Don't go straight in. It will overheat your craft. Remember how the boat pilot chose a gentle curve when taking you out of the Cerik world atmosphere? Use that technique to gently curve down to the surface."

"How?"

He had barely formed the thought when Rita walked a few steps closer and said, "We can read surface thoughts, and memories, and dreams that you can't even recall. We also remember the thoughts of Cerik who came before, flying boats like yours. We have their training. You would be wise to take this advice."

He didn't want to listen, but what they said made sense.

Rita approached the display and touched a point on the planet's image. "This would be a good landing place. It is flat, with clear weather, and we can get a reception party to take care of Rita very quickly."

It occurred to him that the Ferreer had total control over Rita. With their experience, they could probably land the craft with her.

"Yes," she said. "But wouldn't you enjoy doing it yourself?"

He looked at her face. The eyes were like Pam's, the hair and skin like Pam's, but the smile was old and wise. The effect was a unsettling.

"Tell me when I'm doing it wrong." The Ferreer wanted them to land safely. He could trust them to give him good landing advice.

He activated the distance shouter. <This is the U'tanse again. I am approaching the atmosphere.>

There was silence for a moment. <Has your mind been eaten?>

<I am still myself, but my passenger speaks with the words of the Ferreer.>

There was no reply.

Rita said, "He is frightened."

"The Ferreer are the monsters Cerik frighten their cubs with."

"The Cerik who lived here were content."

"None remain?"

"Their bodies gave out from old age. They were all male, so no new ones were born."

"Would you have allowed that?" The Cerik were *his* childhood monsters.

Rita tilted her head. "There are currently seven species, from various worlds, that live together as the Ferreer. Rita will be the first of number eight. And it would be wonderful if you stayed with her and became the father of more."

The display shifted into a map of the terrain below. Rita whispered in his ear, "See where the river curves. Aim for that."

James was having trouble making sense of the image. The only maps he'd ever seen were internal corridor maps of Home and fanciful drawings of the human home world. This was closer to Father's sketchings of Europe than anything else.

"The fat line is a river?"

"Yes. See where it bends. Try to land in the center of the curve."

James tried to put everything out of his head but the task of making the boat follow two gentle curves—the altitude and the direction.

New details of the land appeared as he approached. There were brown, cubical structures. Many small buildings were distributed evenly through tall dark green and black vegetation. Broad tan fields were circled by uneven rows of green.

Rita pointed. "That field is where you should land."

He slashed the air and placed the targeting icon right in the middle. The shifting view of the ground began slowing dramatically.

A moment later, they were down. James left the engines idle but in standby.

Rita smiled and took his hand, "Please come out and meet the People."

21

"The air is clean."

He nodded. Standing in the door, he was struck by the color. In Father's writings, he'd used the term 'sky blue', which never made sense to him, since the Cerik sky was a reddish brown.

But this sky was blue. It shaded from darker hues directly overhead to a pale color on the horizon.

"The Greeters of the People will be coming from that direction."

James fought the urge to run—to seal the door and climb back into the sky. "Greeters" could not dispel fears of "Eaters of Minds".

"Don't take my mind over."

Rita patted his hand. "I want you to stay with me, but I won't force your will."

"But you can do that, right?"

Rita's smile didn't waver. "You only know us through the stories of the Cerik. Yes, we had to stop them from scattering destruction across the world, but forcing a merger is not our preference."

"A merger? Only some of the Cerik were telepathic. Did you control their muscles?"

Rita watched the cloud of dust on the horizon. "No. It was a telepathic merger. In species like the Cerik, and the U'tanse, where there are some minds that cannot sense other thoughts, there is often a way to activate that ability."

"You could make someone like me telepathic?" His mind raced. *If that were possible...*

"Does that appeal to you? We could make it happen."

James considered it. How could he not? There wasn't a day in his life when he didn't stumble over some fact that everyone else knew, because they were telepaths. All his life, he was the one left out. And now, it was offered to him.

"How? How would you change me?"

"The U'tanse are new to us." Rita smiled, "This one is the first to have embraced the People, so we are still learning how your mind works. When the Cerik telepaths encountered the People, their motive was to learn our weaknesses, and so discover how to attack us. But as they linked in, their motives changed, and soon they became part of us.

"You are already aware that your sisters and brothers can control the cells of their bodies. They can also control your cells. We did the same for the others, who did not think of themselves as telepaths. The patterns of cells and their interconnections—developed over the life of the telepaths, were duplicated in the brains of the non-telepaths, opening up their new comprehension of the world."

James tried to imagine it. "You took brain cells and clusters in the non-telepathic Cerik and changed them to match the telepaths?"

"Essentially correct." The Rita-shaped person talking to him had become different, like a tutor, lecturing him.

"And you propose to do the same with me? To copy part of Rita's brain and overlay part of mine?"

"The part that opens up telepathy, yes."

James asked, "And what would I lose? What part of me would be lost when that part of the brain is changed?"

She shook her head. "Unknown. We have not known Rita and you long enough to completely understand those details."

He saw that the dust cloud was getting larger. A group of vehicles were approaching. James had a gut feeling that once the 'People' were represented by more than Rita, things would be different.

And would he even know it, if his mind began to change?

"No. I don't want my brain altered in any way. I've lived without te-lepathy. I don't need it. And I want to get back off the planet just as soon as I can. The pilot might abandon me."

Rita sighed. "I understand, but he's in *dan* right now. Don't you want to see the People? Surely Father will want to know everything you can tell him about us."

He wanted to be gone. He glanced back inside. "Will you have food here? Should I leave you the sack?"

"The People have an excellent understanding of biology. Compatible food will be found or made. The U'tanse will probably be easier to sustain than the Cerik. Merging minds did not change their need for freshly killed meat."

He looked her in the eyes. "Can I talk to Rita alone? Is that possible?"

She hesitated, and then over the course of ten seconds, she sagged.

Rita blinked, her eyes watered, and she moved in little abrupt shifts.

He took her hand. "Rita? Are you okay?"

Her voice wavered. "No. They left me."

"They'll come back." He squeezed her hand. "Do you know what's going on? Do you understand?"

She wouldn't look up his eyes. She nodded. "I want them back. I want the People."

He sighed. "I just needed to know."

She lunged forward and wrapped her arms around him, her face buried against his chest. "You were nice. I'll miss you."

He had no response, other than to hold her. He whispered, "I just had to be sure."

She sniffed, and then pulled back. He let her go. In a moment she straightened up, she smiled, taller and happy.

"Please don't leave yet. We have a present for you." The three vehicles were just pulling up next to the boat.

22

The Cerik ship hadn't left. James slashed, placing the target mark on the loading hatch and activating the automated docking sequence.

The pilot only growled at him over the distance shouter as he reported that he was returning from the Ferreer planet. One of the theories he'd heard growing up was that the Cerik's hunting growl set up a resonance in the bodies of prey, startling them into running, even when they were safely hidden. He had no idea if it were correct or not, but his instincts were crying out that he should flee; not go into the predator's den.

But he was at least happy to see the ship. The distances were so great that the landing boat's navigation display had lost track of the main vehicle.

Once he had lifted away from the planet with his cargo, he was horrified that he had no idea where the ship had gone. Only when he had made 'contact' with the pilot via the distance shouter did he notice that a marker appeared on the display while the pilot was growling at him.

The trip back to the ship took him only ten hours. Not only was he eager to be gone from the Ferreer planet, but also, the cargo was driving him crazy.

When the boat settled to the deck and the hangar refilled with air, he sighed and walked back to the cargo chamber, where he'd secured them behind a restraining gate. The big eyes all stared at him.

He chose one. "Sorry, girl." He snagged the rope collar around her long neck and pulled her with him out of the boat and up to the hangar hatchway. He shoved her through and slapped her haunch. She scampered away, her hooves clattering on the corridor floor.

He hurried back into the boat and activated the shouter.

<I have returned. My mind is intact. I have also brought some runners from the grasslands below. I have released one into the corridors.>

There was a great shout that echoed throughout the boat. The runners in the cargo area stirred uncertainly. James reduced the sound level. He repositioned himself so that he could watch the animals.

Outside, one of their own was being hunted. He didn't think it would take long. At least he couldn't hear it.

About ten minutes later, the shouter spoke, in a faint voice. <Release another.>

James tried to make his voice properly obedient. <Another will be released. It will take a moment. Please note that there are only five remaining.>

<Release another.>

Even quietly, there was no give in that voice.

James chose the next one. "Let's hope you're the last one. Come with me."

The grazer was compliant, and he had no trouble leading it to the door, until it opened.

Long-slitted nostrils opened wide and the animal bucked and tore loose from his grip, dashing at top speed, skidding on the metal floor. Quickly, it was gone.

James hurried back inside the boat.

It was longer this time. Again, James had been watching the animals in the boat. There wasn't a hint that these creatures had any telepathic connection to the ones that had gone outside to their death. That second one had sniffed something in the air, perhaps the blood of the first one, but that was all. As near as he could tell, the good-will offering by the Ferreer had no hidden telepathic nature.

They might not even last long enough to return to Ko, at the rate the pilot is gorging himself.

But James had been happy to accept them. The pilot had gotten very hungry while waiting. *Better them than me.*

The shouter spoke, <U'tanse. Get to the engine room. We will be preparing to leap.>

James nodded to himself. The pilot was sounding normal again.

<I am going there.>

. . .

The leap across the stars did not take long, but the pilot took care to position the ship into a stable orbit around the planet.

James only had a few minutes before he was called back to the boat. He found one of the kills. There was little but bloody bones left in the corridor, and some of those bones were gnawed into pieces.

Who cleans this up? He was the first U'tanse on a space mission. Did Cerik cubs get the cleanup jobs?

But it looked like this time, as before, the ship was going to be left as is, bloody and all. Would it power itself down? James didn't know. He spent the waiting time refreshing his *ineda* exercises as the Cerik piloted the boat down. He was again back in the world of his masters.

It had been nice, for a bit, to just let my mind relax. I won't get a chance to do that again any time soon.

He had been ordered to stay back with the runners.

<These will likely be sensitive to Cerik air, like the Geisel runners. I have set...>

<Stay put. I will give you orders with the shouter.>

James moved back a step. Just for a moment, as the pilot left the boat, he glimpsed the buildings outside.

This isn't Home. Where am I?

23

It had to be some large Cerik city. There were many buildings and courtyards wide open under the brown sky.

He tapped away at the menu pad until he discovered how to show a simple visual display of the surroundings. The map gave him the details in a small, oddly-accented voice. This was the Perch of Hagnel—the *Name* of the Tenthonad clan that owned him.

It made sense. The pilot had come to the *Name* to report on his mission. *I just hope that I survive it.* He wished Father knew he was back. He had great faith in Father. Father had defended the U'tanse since the beginning. But now wasn't the time to relax his *ineda*.

He watched the view outside. As near as he could tell, the boat had landed in a large courtyard. There were a number of Cerik around, and more were arriving. They all seemed to keep their distance from the boat.

Afraid of Ferreer contamination, probably. And that was one point in favor of his early death. Somebody out there was arguing for his quick slaughter, just to be on the safe side. Even the pilot was at risk for the same reasons.

James remembered the thoughts Rita had pulled from the pilot. Something about a guild that had sabotaged the mission. The pilot wanted them dead.

Could he have gone on a revenge hunt? And if so, what would happen to him?

I have to get back to Home.

The training he'd gotten all his life was simple. The U'tanse would survive if they were no threat and they were useful.

I need to be useful. He couldn't argue that he wasn't a threat. A super intelligent hive mind might have planted some hidden trigger in his brain—one that he wouldn't be aware of.

I have to be ready to report everything I've learned about the Ferreer. They might even demand I drop my ineda.

That's why assertive thoughts were needed. He needed to be ready to think only about his experiences on the planet and his strong opinions. *And nothing else.*

The runners began some kind of squabble among themselves. It was quickly over. *You obviously have no idea you're surrounded by hundreds of bloodthirsty predators.*

James looked them over again. Four was a dangerously low breeding pool, but if they could be cultivated as yet another rare food item for the Cerik, they could be very valuable. The Ferreer, those little green people with tails, had told him that the Cerik who had been absorbed had all liked the taste of this variety. They were a peace offering to a species who didn't understand what peace was.

From all he knew, he suspected they would be poisoned by the Cerik air, but the *Name* knew about that issue already with the Geisel runners and the U'tanse. The pilot wasn't concerned, but he'd need to make that clear if questioned. It would be sad to bring them here, just to have them curl up and die from the air.

On the display, there was a group of Cerik approaching from one avenue. The crowd began to appear more agitated.

<U'tanse! Release the runners.>

It was the pilot, speaking into some gadget, a shouter, strapped to his chest.

All of them? Surely not.

But that larger Cerik beside him just might be the *Name* himself. *Be subservient.*

<For the *Name*.> He managed to shout, without too much of a stutter.

He opened the gates and pushed them all out. He didn't attempt to follow.

The rule of survival here was to follow orders. No more. No less.

He hurried back to the display.

Poor things. The runners dashed back and forth, penned into the center of the courtyard by the very dangerous beasts all around them.

There was a shout. It didn't come over the boat's shouter, but it was loud enough to be heard through the hull. The *Name* was saying something very formal, some kind of chant. James puzzled out part of it.

He could only shake his head as the *Name*, the pilot, and one other large Cerik moved in on the runners. It looked more like a dance than a hunt, but a hunt it was.

The grazers were trapped, and from three sides, the giant beasts with formidable jaws and sharp claws closed in, until in an explosion of blood, all four were torn apart and eaten.

The surrounding crowd cheered, only wishing that they could have participated.

So much for a valuable crop. As near as he could understand from the stilted chant, the *Name* prized the publicly slaughter of beasts from the Ferreer planet far more than any economic considerations.

James shook his head. Maybe they were right. No other *Name* on the planet could claim to have taken blood from the Ferreer planet. That was a very Cerik kind of brag, and just might be worth it.

And if the pilot had been sent on the mission as punishment, he must have gained status to have been permitted to participate in the kill.

24

A couple of hours later, a different pilot came to the boat. He didn't attempt to speak to James, and James kept silent. They lifted, and after a brief flight across the landscape, the boat settled near the main entrance of Home.

<Leave.>

James did.

People began pouring out of the entrance.

"James! You're back. We thought you were dead!"

Only half of the people were wearing their masks, and they quickly moved inside. Father raised his hands. "We will celebrate his return this evening. But I need to talk with him first."

It was a long walk back to Father's office, with the corridors packed with smiling faces. After so long with the Cerik, and the Ferreer and even the runners, he was quietly surprised just how much their faces looked alike—just family. He tried to say thanks to everyone, but as he stumbled, he realized just how tired he had become.

Father led him into the office. Mother was already there. She looked him over carefully.

"He's okay," she said to Father after a moment. "And I don't detect any distortion."

He nodded. "That's good. James, it's wonderful to have you back. I suspect you have a story to tell?"

...

Some hours after he had lifted off on the journey with Rita, a line of fire had flashed in the sky. When Father had asked about it, he was told that the space ship had been destroyed in a charging accident. It had happened before. Mother had been monitoring his body at the time and she thought it was possible that he might have made the leap to another star, but she couldn't be certain.

All they could do was to wait and see.

James gave his version, stumbling a little as he forgot things and had to back up.

Father shook his head. "I wasn't aware that you were going on one of the large ships. I'm surprised the pilot was able to fly it by himself."

"I helped."

Father nodded. "I'll want a book written, detailing everything you learned about the ship. We'll need it eventually."

When he related the visit with the Ferreer, Mother looked very worried. "They consider themselves the next step in evolution."

"Right. They don't think of attachment as a problem. They had trouble understanding why I didn't want my brain rewired so I could participate."

Father scratched his chin. "It may seem like arrogance on their part, but it worked out in our favor this time. I had hoped you could get down, drop her off and leave before they could stop you, but they didn't take hostile action. The hive mind lasts longer than any individual. Maybe it's easy for them to wait until we 'evolve' and join them voluntarily."

Mother nodded. "And until then, they can study Rita."

No one smiled.

...

A feast was planned, but James demanded a bath and clean clothes. He was turned loose. There would be other interviews. He would be working for a long time, documenting what he had seen.

And the star maps will be the hardest.

From the beginning, Abe had hoped he could view and memorize the star patterns from both the Cerik space and Ferreer space. Combined with Abe's map from his memories of Earth's night sky, it might be possible to build a three dimensional map of the stars, with some hint as to where the human homeworld might be.

It was going to be a long chore, but some day, they might discover lost Earth.

25

James slipped into the water with a profound sense of relief. Did the Cerik bathe? He certainly hadn't seen any hint of a bath on their ship.

A familiar splash caught his attention. Pam swam up.

He smiled. "I've been looking for you."

She timidly approached. "I couldn't get close. There were too many people."

"Are you pregnant yet?"

She shook her head. "I was too upset when they said you might have died. Why didn't you let me know you were going on a space flight?"

He shrugged. "It was a big secret."

She settled up on the bench beside him. "I cried."

He put his arm around her. "I'm sorry. I *almost* died, if it's any comfort."

She poked him. "No, it's not."

"And I'm taking down the broom after the feast tonight."

She leaned against him. "Can I get my place in line?"

"You're the first one I've told."

"Good."

He sighed. He still had no idea how this whole sex thing would play out. He still might become a joke among the cousins, but it didn't seem that important any more. He had work to do, documenting his trip, and writing a book on how to fly a boat. And after that, he had to get back into the repair shop. The hands-on experience he'd gained using the devices gave him some ideas about some of his old failures.

"You know, I was given the chance to be a telepath."

"Oh? By the Ferreer?"

"Yes. And I was tempted. Tempted to be the new Father, starting another U'tanse family on their planet with Rita as the Mother."

He chuckled. "When I told that to Father and Mother, they both shuddered."

"They did?"

"Yes, they said that as proud as they were of how their family had turned out, they wouldn't wish that role on anyone."

Pam was quiet for a moment. "Did you think Rita was pretty?"

"Um. I guess. She reminded me of you. Sort of a Pam without a personality. That was the scary part. It is so wonderful being home, with real people.

"And I'm really glad you found me." He pulled her tighter.

After a moment, he said, "But I'd better get dry, and get dressed. I'm looking forward to better food than biscuits."

"And lots of girls trying to get your attention, I bet."

"They can just wait their turn."

Bones

1

The claws moved too fast for Karl bar Ezra to see, but suddenly there was a streak of bubbling blood across the torso of the pilot. The deck tilted as the boat lost control. Karl grabbed for anything to keep from falling. A large bale of three-inch diameter pipes strained against the straps and he pulled himself into a corner next to the hull. The boat's automatics attempted to stabilize the craft on their own, because the pilot was too busy fighting.

The pilot and the picker from the Getterin clan had been on the verge of battle most of the flight. The picker was furious that a U'tanse was on board and earlier in the day, he'd slashed at Karl. If Karl hadn't jumped out of the way, and if the pilot hadn't intervened with a few slashes of his own, the scratch on his leathers would have been the least of his problems.

Not that the pilot cared much about U'tanse either, but he could work with them.

Tom! Alert! Karl had barely sent the telepathic squawk when a bound bale of pipes shoved against him. One or the other of the Cerik had been slammed against the cargo. Howls of anger and pain thundered in the small, room-sized cargo hold. Karl ducked lower and wedged himself even tighter into the corner, as far out of the battle zone as he could manage. This was no quick slash-and-snarl, no simple jostling for status among workers. Someone would be dead soon.

. . .

The planet *Ko* had only one ocean, and one massive land mass. A third of the way west across the continent on the coast, Tom bar Abe heard the call, deep within the cavernous chambers of the U'tanse's Graddik Home. He paused in his discussion with Abbie bar Carl and Samuel bar James about the children's training schedules. He eased his *ineda* and reached out.

Yes, Karl. What's going on?

The pilot and the picker are fighting. Both are bloody and the boat is wailing.

He could sense the confusion from his cousin. Karl had been on a number of expeditions, making sure that the cargo they loaded matched the goods that had been specified in the negotiations. In this case, pipes from a Getterin factory. The picker was on board for a similar job, to select the right *ooro* for the payment. The Cerik made a big deal of getting the best of the lizards, ones fast enough to chase and fat enough to taste good. Once the U'tanse had started cultivating the *ooro* in tanks, instead of chasing them down on the rocks in the traditional manner, the Graddik clan had made a trading crop out of them.

But Karl had never been present at a Cerik fight before. Tom had. **Karl! Stay clear of the Cerik. Either of them could take you out by accident.**

I am! Uh, oh!

Karl?

The picker slammed the pilot up against the control display. It may have cracked. Uh! Uh!

Tom could feel Karl's queasiness. Was the boat spinning out of control? Karl picked up the question. **Yes! We're...**

Karl? What's going on?

Strong, gut fear came from the man. **The picker...** *ssitt.* **The pilot is dead.**

Tom could even hear echoes of the howl of victory through Karl's mind. The *ssitt* was a killing stroke, where one Cerik ripped out the eyes of another.

Karl, can you stabilize the boat?

Tom could feel other minds listening in. All across the world, the distress rippled through the minds of Karl's telepathic relatives. Even the Cerik telepaths who monitored them had picked up the scent of the battle. Some were listening to Karl directly, some were listening through Tom's mind.

Denton! Notify the *Name*. He had to get word to their master immediately.

He felt assent from the man who was in place at the *Name's* Perch, several miles up the coast. He had been one of the ones listening in.

Karl was motionless. It was all he could do, no matter if the boat were going to crash or not. It would be immediate suicide for a U'tanse to approach a hostile Cerik in the midst of *'eeh*.

The boat is wailing, and I think the picker is starting to notice. From where I can see, the display is cracked, but it's still showing some terrain around us. My gut tells me we're spinning, and I suspect we're going down.

Tom knew more about a boat's control than U'tanse slaves were supposed to, but decades of habit kept that knowledge buried. Even if he had information that could save his cousin, there were too many minds listening in right now.

He turned to a man in the room with him, "Samuel, see if you can find a way for Karl to gain control of a boat. His pilot is dead."

Samuel was a tenner, those one-in-ten of all males who weren't telepathic. His eyes widened. He had suspected something bad was happening, but deaf to the events, he had waited patiently for someone to tell him what was up. He reached for the stack of rolled papers in a bin nearby.

It was a show for those Cerik telepaths who were 'watching'. Anyone in this room of the Home, telepath or not, had extensive training in how to hide their thoughts from the Cerik, whether by traditional *ineda*, or by misdirection. Samuel quickly pulled one of the rolls and spread it out in front of Tom.

The text did talk about boats but there was nothing useful. Cerik wouldn't know that even if they could see the lettering through his eyes. Their brains didn't process symbols like that.

Karl. There's an override. Slash down along the left side of the control display and the boat should make the attempt to land on automatics.

· · ·

Karl understood, but he wasn't about to move anywhere right then. Between him and the controls, the victorious picker was drinking the blood of the pilot and bellowing his victory, unaware of the boat's distress. Nothing was more important than battle and victory.

He'll think of me any second now. If anything had pushed the picker over the edge into a murderous rage, it was having to ride in a boat with a U'tanse. He'd take care of that problem next.

Karl looked at the bundle of pipes strapped together next to him. It would hurt if they fell on him. He lay face down on the deck as close as he could manage to the pallet, and then flipped the latch that secured the strap. The pipes tumbled from the stack, burying him with a clatter that momentarily eclipsed the howls of the picker.

But it also turned his attention instantly to the hated U'tanse. He bellowed a hunting cry.

With his hands over his head, attempting to lessen the impacts, Karl struggled against the weight above him. He yelled in the Cerik language, <The pilot has trapped you! He has you in his *dul*! His boat will smash you!>

There was an instant of silence as the picker reacted to the insult. Karl could read his thoughts. For the first time, the picker noticed the smashed control display and the wailing of the boat. A trickle of fear crept into the Cerik's chest. He roared, <U'tanse! Fix this!>

Karl struggled against the weight above him. <I am unable!> He shouted the directions Tom had given him.

The picker, unfamiliar with the pilot's controls, attempted to make the emergency landing slash. The ship just wailed even louder. Either he'd done it wrong, or it was too late to do anything about the crash.

The Cerik jumped to the cargo hold and slashed at the disorganized pile of pipes that protected Karl, but his claws were not meant for dealing with the shifting, hard objects. He roared in frustration and jumped back to the command station.

Karl watched through the picker's eyes as he tried the control panel slash again, and then gestured at the main hatch. The doorway to the outside opened to a howl of wind. The ground below was rotating and growing larger. The idea to leap clear at the last minute grew in the picker's thoughts.

For a Cerik, it was a natural thought—they had massive hind legs for leaping, and were used to landing hard.

Karl knew better, but he was more concerned with trying to judge how soon they would hit. As fast as they were coming down, neither U'tanse nor Cerik bodies could absorb the impact.

The picker jumped clear, and Karl broke away from following his thoughts and concentrated on the small control pad on the wall of the cargo hold. Telepathy couldn't help now, but psychokinesis might. Using the same skills he used to repair damage to his body, he reached into the control circuits. Just as if he were tapping the control panel with his fingers, he worked the menu. There was a setting he frantically tried to reach. It was supposed to be used to stabilize shifting cargo. The same forces that pushed and pulled the boat through the sky were also used to provide a false gravity underfoot when a boat was in space. Special settings could be used to adjust the pull on the cargo, to either lock it down tightly, or to let the crates float while moving them into place.

The pressure of the pipes above him eased as he reversed the false gravity. He shoved himself free of the pipes and jumped deeper into the hold, where tanks that were to be used to transport the *ooro* lizards, showed water, now suddenly lighter, trying to slosh free. He pulled the cover free of the closest and ducked under the water's surface.

How soon... The thought barely formed when the boat struck the ground.

2

Tom looked up from his papers. He'd ridden Karl's thoughts all the way to the impact.

"He's down."

Samuel asked, "Did the boat land?"

"No. It was a hard impact."

"So..."

"I don't know. He's either unconscious or dead."

A telepathic wail echoed through the U'tanse. Beside him, Abbie held her hand to her head as the headache, caused by the emotions of thousands across the planet, was nearly overwhelming.

Samuel was unaffected. He asked, "What now? Do we send a rescue boat?"

Tom shook his head. "That's up to the *Name*. Can you get a location?"

He nodded. The tenners were deaf to the telepathic world, but they were unmatched at making sense of figures and charts. Quickly, he had a map sketched from the master chart, showing the path the boat would have traveled from the Getterin city to their location on the coast, with a mark where the boat would have been when it was interrupted by the fight. "It probably went down within this circle."

Tom nodded, and stared at the chart.

. . .

At the *Name's* Perch, Denton bar Simon memorized the chart from Tom's mind and rattled the taps on his shoes against the floor.

<Enter.> The *Name* was flanked by Tetedo, his prime Cerik telepath, a lesser *name.*

Denton approached to the proper distance and yelled, <Your boat has crashed, returning from Getterin.>

<I have been informed.>

The presence of Tetedo had made that obvious. Denton had expected it. He was waiting for an opening, any way to request a rescue mission. He couldn't demand it, nor even suggest it. An injured U'tanse, possibly in immediate need of medical aid, and certainly in need of a source of clean air—that was irrelevant. The loss was the *Name's.* He had lost the boat. He had lost the pilot. And of course, his U'tanse. He would demand action or not, and as expected, both Cerik had firm *ineda* to prevent him from reading them.

<Who crashed my boat?>

<The Getterin picker drew first blood. In the battle, the boat controls were damaged when the pilot was kicked against the device. Your U'tanse informed the picker how to save the boat, but he failed.>

The battle to the death was a minor thing. The *Name* would hardly make an issue with the Getterin's *Name* over the death of his pilot. It was the pilot's own fault that he lost the fight. Nor was the cause of the dispute of any importance.

The *Name* thought a moment. <What would it take to salvage the cargo?>

Denton spoke carefully. He had to be accurate, or it would come back on him if an effort was started, and then failed. <The boat went down within a nine-run of a point in the third mountain range. A second boat could circle the area to locate the place where it came down.>

The *Name* growled. <Is the cargo intact?>

<Unknown.>

<What does my U'tanse say?>

<There have been no thoughts since the crash.>

He slashed dismissively. <Days to find it. The U'tanse would be dead, if not already. And I would be stuck with damaged cargo. I'll tell the Getterin I owe them nothing. If they want more *ooro*, then they'll have to negotiate again.> He was clearly done.

Denton hesitated only a second, before shouting, <For the *Name*.> and backing out of the room.

3

Abbie sat with Linda bar Franklin, holding her hand. "The *Name* has decided not to send a rescue boat."

"I know. I was listening." Linda's voice was rough. She had taken it hard. Karl had been her favorite. They had been talking about moving to one of the couples cells. "It kills me that I can't find him. I keep thinking he's still there, but I can't…"

"You need to get some sleep. We have a team searching for the scent of his thoughts. He might just be unconscious. If he wakes, we'll know."

"But if he's still alive, his breather only has a few hours of chemical left."

Abbie nodded. It was hard, but Karl was gone. Maybe he still breathed, maybe his heart still pumped, but without a breather or without a functioning boat, the atmosphere would kill him soon enough. She watched as Linda fondled the necklace that Karl had made for her from a yellow-colored metal that he'd picked up on one of his previous expeditions. It would be hardest for her. Luckily, their daughter was too young to have formed much of an bond with her father.

...

Tom bar Abe was the oldest of the first-born generation still alive. He had two sisters left, Hope and Kayla, but they were all showing signs of advanced aging that not even aggressive tinkering with the cells of their bodies could stop. He hadn't been out of this Home for three years, and his assistant was taking over more and more of his chores. Karl's loss was just another sign that it was time he gave it up and notified the *Name* that he was done.

He chuckled, and shook his head. No, better not. The *Name* would likely come rip out his eyes as a kindness. Better keep breathing and pretending for as long as he could. At least he could still plan, and plot.

He fingered the tiny vial dangling from a strap around his neck and closed his eyes, reaching out for some sign of his lost cousin.

4

Water trickled out of the open hatch, spilling on the rubble below and instantly sinking into the soil. Nothing had happened for hours, and the creature whose nest had been overturned by the avalanche of rubble as the craft had skidded down the slope had finally gained enough courage to approach. The *lulur's* forelegs, just the first of a dozen pair spaced evenly along the long, tube-like body, sampled the damp soil and then stretched upward, as it reached for the dark opening, half a body length above it.

When the forelegs reached the opening and scraped the edge, trying for a grip, there came a moaning noise from inside. The creature dropped and scurried away.

Karl's pain almost pushed him back into unconsciousness, but two questions kept him awake. What was that clattery noise? And did he imagine that scent?

It came again, the extremely rare scent of cinnamon. And it wasn't his imagination. It was a command.

In spite of the pain, and his urgent need for help, he clamped a strong *ineda* on his thoughts. A wave of despair swept over him. There were a half-dozen secret orders he'd memorized in his training. This one was very clear. A telepathic scent of cinnamon, an Earth spice unfamiliar to the Cerik, meant only one thing.

You have been given up as lost. You will not be rescued. Stay under ineda. *Your order is to stay alive, by any means.*

He'd felt the personality behind that message. It was Tom, one of his favorite elders. There'd been a confidence under the scent—almost a second message. *I know it will be hard, but I know you can do it.*

Karl had no such hope. He breathed filtered air, knowing it wouldn't last. A scan of his body showed two broken ribs and a fractured upper right arm. There were bruises, all on that same side. The impact had been buffered by the water and the false gravity beams, but it hadn't been enough. The tank where he lay was mangled by the crash, and one of the bonded seams had ruptured, letting the water pour out.

Probably a good thing, or I would have drowned.

He struggled to get to his feet. It left him panting. The floor was tilted at a steep angle. With only one arm, he wondered if he could even get out.

His *ineda* didn't keep him from feeling the thoughts of others. Linda was in pain, cuddling little Debbie. He could feel the ache of her sinuses, and the tightness in her chest. It would be so easy to send a whisper of thought to her.

But what would that do? He was still going to die. And any public thought was just that, public. He understood the logic. A third of the Cerik clans wanted all U'tanse eliminated. Tracking down and killing him, now that he was alone and his protector, the pilot, was dead—that would be an a challenge to the Graddik *Name's* reputation. It might be worth it for his enemies to hunt for him, if there were evidence he was still alive.

Maybe that's just paranoia, but don't make it easy for them. All his life he'd been taught to act in the *Name's* best interest, and he'd seen what happened when a U'tanse, either by accident or on purpose, embarrassed his *Name*. U'tanse were still valuable enough that a *Name* wouldn't kill them casually, but people like him could be sent on hazardous tasks, without backup. Food quotas could be cut. The *Name* of the Ghader clan had three U'tanse children's right hands cut off when they had allowed a herd of grazers to escape their pens.

He had to stay invisible. He had to be dead to any seeking telepath.

That might be easy enough. His injuries might take care of the issue. The pain was sharp in his ribs as he climbed over the side of the tank and landed unsteadily on the sloping floor. He scooted on the floor toward the exit, rather than trying to walk.

It was bright outside. The red sun on the horizon was coming up. *I was unconscious all night.* The landscape was disconcerting. There was no flat terrain anywhere. The boat was tilted because the ground was just a sloping pile of rocks. The door was torn loose, killing the minor hope of sealing the boat and bringing its atmosphere controls back on-line.

Everything loose in the boat at the time of the crash had spilled toward the smashed control screen at the front of the craft, burying the dead pilot under a tangle of pipes and storage crates. Karl rummaged through the pile one-handed and recovered several water bottles and his uneaten snacks. The trip was only supposed to last a few hours. He sat in the doorway and ate everything. He would need energy. Healing took resources.

While his air lasted, he began the process of knitting the bones. There were several small diameter pipes in handy lengths and he made an splint for his broken arm to keep the bone from shifting. He found a comfortable place to watch the scenery while the most critical stages of the healing could be hurried along.

5

Tom put the tiny vial of cinnamon powder back into its case, alongside several other Earth spices. He could imagine the thoughts of other Heads of Homes, although all had minds that were tightly sealed. Over the past few decades, there had been a number of deaths as more and more U'tanse moved out of the Homes and spent their working days in factories and handling various tasks.

U'tanse were good for more than just technical jobs these days. While they weren't the only slave race, the only others that had made it back to the Cerik home world were the Dadada's, which were only used for transporting heavy goods, and the Uuaa for tree-climbing. The U'tanse had a more generally useful intelligence and body shape, and the Cerik were slowly discovering that.

The more we do, the more dangers we encounter. But staying safe meant staying slaves to the Cerik. Father spent all his life fruitlessly looking for a way out. Now, as his grandchildren were taking over leadership roles, something had to change, even if it meant more risk.

Only people like Karl will have the opportunity to try new things. If he can survive.

...

The Large Moon had passed, and when Karl drifted on the edge of sleep, tasting the first failures of his breathing filter in the tang of the air, the moon was noticeably smaller than it had been the night before. He had moved against the far wall to avoid being covered by the morning dew. It also gave him a bit more warmth. His efforts to bring some of the systems back to life in the cracked boat had not been very successful. The main controls were all inactive. Even the minor controls in the cargo bin were erratic. It almost acted as if the main power cell had been drained, although he couldn't believe that.

Karl hadn't been given the technical education so many of the U'tanse needed. He could run the machines, but he'd never had the knack of seeing how they worked and what would be needed to fix them. Still, even he knew that the energy of a cell had to go somewhere, and most likely would produce a lot of heat if it drained off in an uncontrolled fashion. Everything had gotten cold. He would have welcomed a leaky power cell right now.

Luckily, sleep was easier when exhausted. All his food was gone, and he'd used so much of his reserves healing the worst of his injuries. Psychic control of his body's metabolism brought a number of disturbing options. He'd been using up his body fat, but soon that would be as low as he dared go. Could he risk metabolizing muscle? Did he have any choice?

He forced his thoughts away from his immediate dangers and reached across the continent to sense Linda, having her own sleepless night. It was really too painful to bear, so he sought out little Debbie. At least she was deeply asleep, with no worries in the world.

Shortly, he drifted off himself.

6

The *lulur* could scent the decomposing body up in the dark opening. There had been noises inside for two days, but all was now quiet. It stretched its segmented body up until it could snag the edge with its forelegs. This time, its scratching noises hadn't triggered any response. Maybe everything was now dead. Time to feast!

The body under the rubble was decaying nicely. The *lulur* bit off some of the soft parts and ate rapidly before risking any more exploration in the dark. There was another body, but it was still warm and smelled funny. Hesitantly, it took a bite at the sharp-tasting, old leather.

. . .

Karl woke out of a deep sleep, to see a long creature, nearly as fat as his arm and longer than he was tall, chewing at his boot. With no plan and no thought other than panic, he swung at it in the reflected moonlight with a short segment of pipe at hand.

The beast made no noise other than the angry clatter of too many legs against the hard deck as it curled instantly around the pipe, making a writhing ball. Karl dropped it and grabbed another pipe, smashing it repeatedly until it stopped moving.

Coughing hoarsely, his heart beating far too rapidly, he panted, his back pressed up against the wall. *Is it dead?*

He was woozy. The attack had brought him awake, but he wasn't fully alert.

Nightmare. But the curled animal with too many legs, with blood still bubbling out of it, didn't vanish as his brain came back to full speed.

He poked at it with the end of a small diameter pipe. It was dead. He pushed at it, moving parts of it toward the opened doorway.

Wait. Do I want another dead animal out there? It'd just attract more scavengers.

He edged it over into the full light of the moon. Timidly, he poked at the broken segments. Disturbingly, his stomach growled.

He shuddered. This was hardly what he would call food, and very likely it was poisonous. Not many of the plants and animals on this world were edible. The chemistry was close to Earth life, but this atmosphere had taken biology off in different directions.

Father said in his Book that he'd made himself sick too many times before they got the Earth seeds growing. Trying native meat was trial and error, and only with Mother's help had he survived it.

His stomach growled again.

Do I have a choice?

He tugged at the broken outer shell of the animal and impatiently pulled off his gloves. The warm, moist flesh of the monster's muscle tissue called to him. He tore a piece free, lifted his mask and stuck it in his mouth. He chewed, and the salty meat, with a slightly bitter tang, went down quickly. He breathed, waiting for something to happen.

It didn't kill him instantly. He tore out some more, and ate that.

I need a knife. But he didn't have one. He hadn't needed any tools for this trip, so he hadn't brought his kit.

He smashed at another segment of the beast. He got it open, but this time, something from the organs had been beaten into the meat, and he had to spit it out. The taste was horrid. He spat until there was no saliva left.

There was still water in the boat, luckily. He washed out his mouth, several times.

I really need a knife.

He looked around.

Down in the rubble, the Cerik pilot's body was still mostly buried. One of his claws was visible.

Karl thought a moment, and then picked up a medium diameter segment of pipe.

7

The first time lightning struck the crashed boat, it was deafening. He screamed and clapped his hands over his ears. He had been feeling pretty good about his situation until then. Over the past three days, he'd moved the dead Cerik and parts of the scavengers down the mountain far enough so they wouldn't stink up the place.

His new knife made a significant improvement in his mood. He'd built a usable handle from a short pipe fitting and straps of the Cerik's skin wrapped tightly around the bone. He had no idea how long a Cerik claw would retain its sharpness, but for now, having a weapon to defend himself and a tool precise enough to let him carve the good bits out of those scavengers that were converging on the dead body—it let him think about survival.

But even if he could heal his burning lungs fast enough to stay alive, it wouldn't help to be deaf to the dangers around him. His ears were still ringing from the first lightning strike when another followed.

I've got to get out of here. The boat had crashed near the top of a ridge-line, and then slid down a bit on the rocky slope, but it was still near the peaks, and something about its construction was attracting the lightning.

He felt like a bug waiting to be swatted as he nerved himself to move. The rain was pouring down and the rocks would be slippery. He put his mask back on, even though the breathing filters were useless now. At least the goggles would keep the rain out of his eyes.

Karl coughed and then took a deep breath before jumping out into the downpour. Keeping his balance while following a widening run-off stream downhill, he searched for any shelter to wait out the rain.

The sky lit up with another strike on the boat behind him. The adrenaline surge kept him going.

There! He slid into a rock overhang. The surface was pale tan, much different from the brownish rubble all around. It was a fresh break, probably from the quake the day before. This mountainside was a dangerous place. If the air didn't kill him, or the beasts, then lightning or quakes might do the job.

A sheet of water formed a ragged curtain between the small dry patch where he sat and the glistening landscape below. *I should keep going. Forget the boat. If it can't be a shelter, then it's no good to me.* But he wasn't going to do anything until this rain stopped. He'd healed enough broken bones for now.

When he leaned back against the rock face, he could feel warmth seeping through his leathers. In spite of the limited room to move, this unexpected shelter was a welcome change from his unrelenting bad luck.

Should I bring anything with me?

There were pipes, and they made good pry-bars. He could maybe use one or two as clubs to hit things with, but he'd hate to carry the weight, if he had to travel far.

That was the question. Where was he going?

Anywhere is better than on the side of a mountain where the landscape shifts with every quake and the temperature gets so cold every night. And besides, he had emptied out the nest of those things he was eating. He'd need to move, if just to find a better hunting ground.

I wish I weren't so useless. If Father had found himself in this situation, he'd have repaired the boat and flown back to the human world in it. *Any* of his ancestors would have done something great. They could have at least repaired the boat's air systems and made it a safe home against the planet and its beasts.

He gripped his makeshift knife. It was at least something.

The real question hovered just at the edge of his thoughts. He wouldn't look at it. Pretend it wasn't there. How long could he live?

He rested his head against the rock and closed his eyes. His people were all there, chatting away, living their lives. There were too many to count, and the Homes had popped up all over the planet. Everyone had a place to sleep, family to share their lives with.

Everyone had a job to do. A clan to support. A duty. A *Name...*

He opened his eyes. *I no longer have a* Name. *I have been discarded. I owe allegiance to no Cerik master.*

He searched back in his memory. It was in the Book; he was sure of it. He'd read it when he had been in training—back when he was trying to improve his technical abilities. Training had included reading as an essential skill.

Their Home's copy of the Book had been a 'Utility' copy—just the words. Back when Father died, several copies were made that did their best to copy the messy lettering of his first years, the crisp lettering of his middle years, and the shaky text of his advanced old age—all in an effort to preserve as much of what Father had left them as possible.

But the words were interesting enough. It had been in the Bible volume, in the carefully worded 'commentary' section. Father talked about the Egyptian years. *"Moses couldn't just arise from within the Hebrew population to lead his people. He had to leave and return, as a free man. None of them had any personal memory of being free."*

Karl felt his stomach rumble, and put out his hand to cup the running water to drink. *Is that what I am? A free man? It's not very comfortable.*

8

The rain died down, but Karl didn't see any need to move just yet. The rocks were still wet and he had no urgent need to get back to the boat. Maybe this new perch would show more of the local animals. If one kind was edible, maybe he could find more to expand his diet. Everything depended on keeping himself fueled.

The buzz echoing from the rock face confused him. It seemed to come from all directions.

"A boat?" He got to his feet, sudden hope surging in him. He reached out with his mind.

The pilot above was excited, too. *<That's a boat! Broken and on its side—just like a Graddik. They never had good pilots.>*

Karl froze in place. It was another clan. The Graddik *Name* had not sent someone to rescue him. Why was this one here?

The buzz changed, pitching higher. The boat was coming in for a landing. He still couldn't locate where the noise was coming from, but likely it was near his crash site.

Should I run? The hand-made knife, formed from the claw of a dead Cerik, probably wouldn't look good. He untied it and the strap that held it, and stuffed them out of sight behind a rock.

The buzz of the engines stopped. Karl felt his heartbeat race.

The pilot was scanning the scene crouched in the doorway of his own boat, with not a hint of *ineda* to obscure his thoughts. He saw the bones and plates of the dead pilot on the ground nearby, but gave it no thought other than to wonder if it had been thrown free on impact, or if the U'tanse had moved it.

<If the prey is still alive, then I can take its head back.> It was a pleasant thought. First a hunt, and then a trophy of the expedition.

Karl stopped breathing for a moment. Nothing could be worse than a Cerik on his trail. There was no chance he could stay hidden. The Cerik were supreme hunters. That's what the word 'Cerik' meant. He was no more than a few hundred yards downhill from where the boat had landed. There was no chance of running—no chance of hiding. They always complained about the stink of U'tanse, even those who worked with him. A whiff of scent on the wind, and the chase would be on in seconds.

The hunter was still observing the scene. *<Ah,* lulur *carcass.>* There was the distaste of the true hunter for the carrion eater in his thoughts.

Lulur, *so that's what they are.* Karl had never heard of them before his first-hand experience.

But in the hunter's mind, it was becoming clear that the U'tanse had survived the impact. Almost without anticipation, he leapt across to the ruined boat and entered the darkness. Even from the distance, Karl could hear the clatter of pipes as the Cerik ransacked the interior, smelling him, but not finding his prey.

Frustrated, he left the dead boat and roared a full-throated challenge to the air.

Karl shivered. That was meant for him, and it meant his death.

Suddenly, not a hundred feet away, downhill from his position, came an even louder roar.

What is that? He crouched lower.

In his mind, he heard the startled Cerik ask, *<What is that?>*

9

It had been woken by the Cerik's challenge, startled into an angry reply.

It was close, very close. Karl could only lay flat on the ground and watch as it appeared around a corner. *Huge.*

The Cerik were three times the size of a U'tanse, muscular and wielding natural claws and sharp jaws strong enough to bite through anything. They were the top of the food chain wherever they went.

The challenger was twice that size, with a head so large even its short massive forelegs seemed incapable of supporting the cluster of horns and tusks. Everything, the head, the tusks, the body and the long spiked tail, were the same color as the surrounding rocks. Not content with defense, it was gifted with camouflage.

It didn't even notice the little U'tanse as it passed. The instant it moved on, heading toward the challenge, Karl ducked around the corner, out of sight.

The breeze coming down from the ridge had protected him from the new beast's stench. It's nest had been in a protected overhang much like the one he had sheltered in. Only this one was well-used and the ground was covered in decaying vegetation.

Karl had been a cargo specialist for a few years, and the debris and droppings told him much. Spike-head was a vegetarian. It probably used those horns to shred trees and the like before eating them.

Surprise radiated from the Cerik uphill. <*A* klakr! *A live* klakr!> A wave of battle-lust swept over him. In the distance, Karl could hear roars and challenges. In his head, the Cerik was in pure bliss. Almost like a chant, the ancient tale of *Uriko and the Klakr* played in his memory.

The beast's thoughts were more rudimentary. A *klakr* seemed to know *my territory* and *pain* and *rend*.

Karl wanted to run, to be far from the battle when it was over, but the Cerik's battle-lust was intoxicating. Barely thinking about it, he ducked back to where he'd hidden his knife and recovered it.

Up. He found a crease in the rock, barely large enough for his feet to find traction, and climbed to the top of the ridge. Crawling, he moved close enough to the battle to see, peering over the edge.

It was fast. The field of battle was blocked on three sides by rock cliffs, and the *klakr* had the pilot penned in. But a Cerik's jumping legs made him seem almost free of gravity. Barely had the *klakr* swung its spiked tail to take him out, when the pilot leapt over it like a jumping rope.

The chant in his head was still going strong, skipping around in the narrative to match the real battle. The pilot was living Uriko's tale, almost predicting the *klakr's* every move.

Karl was enthralled, caught up in the battle. *I would get a pipe and jam it into the beast's throat.*

But the Cerik didn't use tools. Not like that.

Time and again, the pilot danced in between the horns and left his marks on the *klakr's* hide. They were painful, and the beast was enraged—prodded to lash out even more.

It was stamina against agility—horns against claws. Twice, the Cerik took bloody hits from the spiked tail, but he recovered. Claw-tips sought out particularly vulnerable patches in the *klakr's* hide.

It was not over quickly, but when the heavy beast began to stumble, and the Cerik had time to plan his next attack, Karl moved back down the slope, out of sight. He could still feel the *klakr's* puzzlement and the Cerik's victory, but he needed to be out of sight, out of scent, and out of mind.

As the Cerik gave the final killing stroke, and began debating with himself how to cut the klakr's head off and get it inside his boat, Karl had found refuge. He was wedged inside a narrow rock shaft too small for a Cerik, even if he were located.

Through the pilot's eyes, he could see the bloody prize as he shifted it into the boat, careful to keep the horns and tusks from any additional scrapes. All those marks were from *his* battle, and he was bursting with pride over every one of them.

The whole idea of hunting down a U'tanse was erased from his thoughts. This was a prize worthy of a story, and down the line, possibly a *Name*. Who could compete with something like this?

When the buzz of the boat's lifters echoed off the rocks, Karl quickly wiggled out of his hiding place.

He flies home and makes his big splash. Buddies say, "If there was one klakr, *maybe there are others." I've got to be far away before they come.*

He didn't think of going back for a pipe or anything else. He had to be off the mountain as soon as he could.

. . .

A planet with telepaths made for lightning-fast gossip. A bloody *klakr* head in the courtyard of Ruthenah was too good a story for the local Cerik telepath to keep to himself, and once he lowered his *ineda* to chat with his peers in other clans, U'tanse observers picked it up.

At his desk, deep in Home, Tom nodded to himself as the information was relayed his way. He wrote down the details.

Don't spread this around. This is not news of Karl's survival, only that his body wasn't found. We have the location of the crash, but no motive for our *Name* to go retrieve it. If anything, the Ruthenah pilot's battle with the *klakr* will just give him more reason to ignore it as beneath his interest.

The other telepaths agreed. Nothing could keep the story from circulating, but it would be best if it had nothing to do with Karl bar Ezra.

10

When healing trances sometimes stretched into hours, and every day was a new landscape, he lost track of the days. Nothing was the same, but there were moments he treasured.

They ought to teach this to everyone. Karl was immensely proud of his new trick. He took fibers that grew from the bark of aging *kel* trees and packed them loosely in a cage of twigs. He concentrated on a small tuft of the fibers and using the same skills he used to heal his air-damaged lungs, or to press the control pad in the boat, he heated them until they began to pop into flame.

Carefully feeding the tiny ember, he started a larger fire—heat enough to cook the three small fish he caught.

The fish were a variety that Father had tested long ago. They were edible if cooked to denature some of the poisons in their tissue. And the taste of a familiar food was a comfort in this strange land.

He had found more *lulur* nests and had perfected his hunting technique, but they weren't common enough to sustain him.

His memory was good, but not perfect like some of his cousins. He needed a refresher. He had taken to listening in on children's lessons back at Home. He couldn't ask questions, without betraying his existence, but when a useful topic occurred, he listened. He paid a lot more attention than he had when he was a child.

He needed to know every edible food. He needed to learn how to make or re-charge the chemicals in his breather mask. Maybe someday he would go back up into the mountains and see if he could repair some of the boat.

But first, he needed to find a safe place to shelter. He moved from night to night, and now that he had discovered how to make a fire, it would be nice to have a place to keep one burning.

A small cave where he could barricade the entrance against predators would be ideal. He visualized it. A place where he could make a soft bed. A place he could keep warm, and keep the hungry things out. A place where he could spend the hours he needed to keep himself healthy, and to learn how to survive.

A comfortable, if lonely, place to live.

The ground shook beneath him. *Quake.* He glanced up at the sky, but the moon was small. It shook again.

Something was wrong. Quakes happened at Large Moons.

He was on open ground. There was nothing to fall on him. He didn't need to seek shelter.

Burn. Move. It was a strong thought, and very close.

He looked at his little cooking fire. That was the only one around. On impulse, he picked up the remnants of his meal and kicked dirt on the ashes. The shakes beneath his feet rumbled in a rhythm.

And then everything moved.

He dropped to his knees, holding his twig with some uneaten fish safe. The ground, a circular patch twenty feet in diameter with him in the middle, shook and then began walking towards the nearby stream.

His food held high, he scooted free of the mobile patch of ground and watched as it walked to the water and large flipper-like feet, dozens of them, attempted to splash water up on its back.

He set the fishes on a rock and ran to help.

He'd built his cooking fire on the back of some kind of animal, hidden as a low mound in the dirt. He crawled back up on its back and kicked the remaining ashes into the water, keeping at it until he was sure that they were gone.

Strangely, once he had started, the animal had stopped its own efforts and waited patiently for him to put the fire out. Then, once it was out, the animal walked back to its original location and with its flippers vibrating in the soil, it settled back down. Again it was almost impossible to see, except for a circular disturbance in the dirt.

"What kind of a thing are you?"

Like a tiny dust devil, there was a puff and a hole appeared near the middle of the circle.

<I don't understand what you said.>

Karl sat down on a rock, a little shaken. <You speak Cerik?>

<Was that a question? If so, yes I do.>

<I'm sorry about the cooking fire. I didn't know you were there.>

<You weren't supposed to. If it weren't for the fire, you never would have known of my existence. What are you?>

Karl didn't know what kind of protocol there was for this kind of introduction. <I am Karl bin Ezra, a U'tanse, formerly of the Graddik clan.>

There were still some flipper activity, because even as they spoke, Karl could see ripples around the circle become more and more indistinct.

The creature's voice was very low-pitched, almost a rumble. <A U'tanse? I am unaware of your kind. Are you one of the captives or a native of this world?>

<The U'tanse were taken from another planet.>

<A captive then.>

<Yes. What are you?>

The creature was silent for a moment, and for a few seconds, even its mouth hole vanished under the dirt. Then there was another puff. <I do not wish to be known.>

Karl was a little offended. <I told you who I was. I, too, do not wish the Cerik to discover me. I would like to know who you are.>

It was silent for another few seconds. Then it rumbled, <You ask for *soso.*>

Karl nodded. A completed trade was the closest the Cerik language came to the word fairness. <Yes. That is what I seek.>

<Survival often abandons *soso.* But tell me your story, and then I will tell you mine.>

...

Karl was so hungry for someone to talk to that he was happy to take the limited offer. He gnawed the fish's plates and bones as he talked, giving the hole in the ground the story of the U'tanse, from Arrival to his unfortunate crash.

<So the Delense have been killed?>

<Yes, long before I was born. You didn't know this?>

<I have suspected something. The Cerik do not like being betrayed, although they will readily betray others. I suppose it is in their character to have eliminated them all.>

<Yes, there was an attack. The City of Faces was destroyed.>

The character of his rumble changed. <That explains it. Without the City, the Cerik would not be the same.>

Karl wondered what that meant, but he was more interested in his dinner companion. <I have told you my story. It's now your turn.>

116

There was a long rumble. Then he began.

<The Bababa live on another world. The Cerik call us Dadada because they can't pronounce our name. It was a perfect place with Ba on Ba on Ba.>

Karl already had questions, but he decided to wait.

<I was five, resting on my Ba when the world shook and the Cerik appeared. It was a time of confusion and pain. I was thrown out of the world and into a little one with many other threes and fours and fives. After a time, I appeared on this world. It was a long, and confusing time, before I learned to speak the Cerik words.>

Karl asked, <How long did that take?>

<Long? I don't know. I had five legs when I was taken, as I said, and eight when I began to speak.>

<Wait a minute! You mean you grew more legs?>

There was a rumble. <You are a flicker like the Cerik, with two legs and two manipulator limbs. The Ba are different.>

<Okay. Go on.> He wasn't going to understand more until he heard more.

<I was a toy—a pet for Cerik cubs. They learned to pounce on me. That's what we all were, at first, a moving target. We were chosen because we were rugged, and lasted longer than most pets. Most of the other Ba are gone, worn out as the cubs got larger, and more aggressive. Those of us who learned the language were sent to carry loads.>

<Like carts?>

<When I started, I could carry as much as three carts worth, and I could be given directions and deliver my load without a caretaker. Over time, I grew and carried much. I have moved buildings.>

11

The High Perch of Graddik wasn't very high. All that counted was that the *Name's* rear talons were firmly seated on the highest bar in the chamber. There was nothing higher than his head, not his visitors, nor the trophy heads mounted on the walls. The ruler of Graddik had chosen Kallu as his name when he had killed his predecessor, and it irritated him that hardly anyone knew it. Three hundred years ago Graddik had killed most of the beasts around him and his Builders had treated the heads to prevent crawlers and hung them on the walls to yellow and grow dusty. The clan would be called Graddik until he had made some mark that eclipsed that legendary hunter.

There was a clatter of claws on the floor.

<Enter!>

Tetedo, his chief telepath entered, and crouched submissively. Kallu made him wait for a couple of minutes. They had worked together, culling out dangers to the clan for years now. Experienced survivors of the climb to power, they said much by their silence.

<Speak.>

The telepath maintained his posture. <Eager cubs from Sanassan went hunting for a *klakr*, but came back empty.>

Kallu waited a moment, but his telepath was going to make him work for it. <Was there any information of interest?>

<This time, the picker was found. A quarter run to the east, shattered bones and plates were discovered on the rocks. No sign of battle. He had jumped from the boat and smashed himself. *Lulur* had taken care of the rest.>

Kallu growled low. <Any sign of the U'tanse?>

<None.>

They sat in silence. It was a known fact that a U'tanse could not live without a protected burrow for their special air. Since they were brought here by Tenthonad, none had escaped. Other than a cub or two, none had even tried to escape.

Tetedo was thinking the same thing. <The U'tanse all believe he is dead. His mate hoped the longest, but she has given up.>

Kallu knew that. <The Face is in two moons.>

That was the deadline. Kallu, as *Name* of his clan, was free to do whatever he wanted. However, at the Face, where the *Names* of all the clans gathered in the new City of the Face, questions would be asked, and anything could happen. His Second might suddenly need to *Name* himself. The clan might lose hunting lands. In times past, entire clans were slaughtered or absorbed for an offense against the Face.

It would be much safer if he had the bones of the missing U'tanse. Even bones in the hands of an enemy would be safer than a mysterious missing U'tanse. The new Builders were valuable, but only as long as they could be completely controlled. There could be no repeat of the revolt of the Delense.

Kallu had just a moment of regret for not sending a rescue boat at the time, but it faded. The past was swallowed and gone.

12

The Ba rumbled, <I saw the crash, and then later the battle up in the mountains. I've been watching you the whole time.>

Karl coughed and then frowned. <How could you possibly see that? I've been walking for days. The mountain pass is not visible from here. How fast can you move?>

<No. I haven't moved. I said it wrong. It has been many years since I spoke to anyone. When I say that I saw you, it is hearing. The crash, the battle, and your footsteps echo through the rocks. That is seeing.>

Karl looked around the blowhole. The Ba's vibrations had flattened out any irregularities. There was no other sign at all that he was down below the ground.

<So you don't have any eyes? You don't see light?>

<I've been asked before. I don't know eyes. What happens above the surface is unknown. Unless it affects the echoes, I am blind to it. You flickers are a mystery. You flick in and out of existence to me. The Cerik were a terror until I learned to sense the pressure waves of their leap.>

Karl took a few steps, thinking about how one foot and then the next touched the ground. If he ran, there would be a moment between each step when he was in the air. How would it be if the Cerik flicked in and out of visibility as they approached?

<I can't imagine what your world is like. What about the sun and the moon? Can you sense them?>

<I can feel the rocks expand as the day begins. It was the same on my world. The moon comes and goes over time. Each month the whole world cries in pain. I have felt mountains crack and feel the blood below stir in sympathy. Even the animals of this world are in pain. I don't think they have always been this way.>

Karl had long finished his meal, licked all the juices from his gloves and kicked the bones under the spreading tangle of the bushes. <The animals? What can you tell about the animals?>

<Stand still for a moment.>

Karl straightened himself up and stood quietly. This Ba 'saw' with sound. He listened, hoping to hear something, but if the Ba was making some signal, he couldn't hear it.

The blowhole puffed again. <You have two large limbs for walking, and two manipulator limbs with five sub-limbs on each, one of which is structured differently from the other four. You are generally bilaterally symmetric, except for some internal organs. You appeared to be covered in a second skin that is not organic to the first. You are digesting the fish that you ate, and your lungs are developing pustules. They are hurting.>

<Yes. This air hurts me. The second skin protects my true skin from it. I must stop now and heal the damage to my lungs before it overwhelms me.>

<If I had sensed the details earlier, I would never have had to ask if you were native to this world. It is plain that you are not. Go heal. I do not wish you to suffer for my entertainment.>

Karl was reluctant to stop, but he really needed the break. While his energy level was up, he needed to take care of the damage. <Tomorrow, we'll talk again.>

There was a vibration and the blowhole in the dirt vanished.

13

Tom stepped down from the boat into the Graddik courtyard. *I wish I had my cane.* But it wouldn't look good. The Cerik were probably blind to his aging posture, but a stick in a prey's hand would put the *Name* on alert. Samuel, walking beside him, had strict orders not to help him, either.

The High Perch was nearby. A few passing Cerik looked at them, but a boat landing in the courtyard was a common event.

Denton was waiting at the entrance. In his court leathers and his muscles, he almost looked as big and impressive as a Cerik, as long as a real Cerik wasn't standing beside him. Tom nodded. "Still holding up here?"

Denton stood straight and tall. "I'm doing okay."

He had chosen this position. He lived here day in and day out with the Cerik, commuting for the minor Home celebrations and when he needed supplies. Tom would never have chosen this life for any of his people, but Denton had discovered how to make himself big and strong when he was young, and always liked being around the Cerik. He even had the scars to prove it. The *Name* liked the idea of having a court U'tanse—one that was less fragile than most and in instant contact with the U'tanse Home.

This request to talk to Tom personally was a rarity. It had been years.

At the entrance to the Perch, Denton held them back, until he rattled the floor with his shoes and received the call to enter.

Protocol demanded that he kneel, hands and feet to the floor, but Tom couldn't do that anymore. He bowed as deeply as he could.

There was a disgusted growl. The *Name* said, <I will speak with Tuah alone!>

Samuel and Denton backed out.

When Tom raised his head, he saw that Tetedo, Kallu's chief telepath had not moved from his position at the *Name's* right hand. There was surely a reason for that. Tom settled his mind and kept his *ineda* tight.

There was silence for a moment as the two Cerik masters considered him.

The *Name* stirred. <Tuah, what do U'tanse do with their dead?>

Tom blinked. It was hardly a question he expected. Nor could he ask why.

<It is our tradition that when the body is available, that it is returned to the Home. Most of our food is plants from the U'tanse planet. We use the dead to enrich the soil so that these plants may thrive, and so nourish our people.>

<Do you bury them? If you dug, would you find the bones?>

Tom was a little disturbed by the questions. What was going on? The Cerik had always maintained a hands-off policy concerning U'tanse traditions. Basically, if the U'tanse did their jobs, what went on inside the Home did not interest them.

<Not exactly. There is a device, a 'cooker', where various materials, such as organic waste, old fabrics, packing materials, and selected animal parts are shredded and then decomposed. After a time, the result is added to the soil in our underground farms. With a ceremony, dead U'tanse are fed into the same device. No bone fragments larger than the tip of your claw are likely to be found after processing.>

The *Name* said nothing, but his claws made impatient patterns in the air. As far as Tom was aware, the Cerik simply dragged their dead to a trench near the settlement and let scavengers take care of the problem. Many of their dead were already shredded in battle by the time that happened. Other than rare trophy heads, they cared nothing for the dead bodies.

The three of them spent a minute in uncomfortable silence. Tetedo took the lead, to spare the *Name* from asking himself.

<Tuah, the *Name* has need of your assistance.>

...

Denton whispered to Samuel, "Did you hear that?"

"What?"

"The *Name* called Tom by his personal name! That's a pretty high honor."

Samuel leaned against the wall. He was worried about how well Tom was holding up. Cerik status games didn't interest him.

"Did you get any hint about what the *Name* is talking about?"

They waited out of hearing range. Maybe he'd be able to hear a scream from the *Name's* chamber, but not conversation. And in a case like this, it didn't matter that he wasn't a telepath. Everyone was likely locked down right now anyway. He'd read in the Book that the use of *ineda* had blossomed once the U'tanse arrived on the planet. Native Cerik telepaths were reasonably common, but not much of a threat. Power was gained in battle, after all, and telepaths might have an edge in tactics, but they were also more sensitive, and thus more vulnerable to mental distraction.

"No. Not a hint. Tetedo and the *Name* have been deep in blocked conversation for the past couple of days now. I've heard several rumors, but nothing I can believe."

Samuel sighed. "Tell me anyway. Anything to kill time."

Denton shrugged. "Okay. One is that the *Name* has a disease, and that he wants his U'tanse to heal him."

"Is that even possible?"

"I don't know. I guess theoretically. But really, no Cerik would ever admit to having a disease! That's just asking for *ssitt*. If I were a Cerik and I thought I was coming down with some plague, I'd just go find my biggest, strongest enemy and attack him. Go out with a clean strike." The big guy smiled broadly, showing his teeth. "No Cerik worth the name would choose weakness over pain."

Samuel just nodded. "Give me another rumor."

"Hmm. Oh, there was one that the *Name* of the Getterin clan had challenged our *Name* to a battle at the next Face, which is coming up soon. You know… over the loss of the shipment of pipes."

"How likely is that?"

Denton wrinkled his nose. "Possible, but the crash hardly had anything to do with the *Name's* honor. It was a squabble among the unnamed. I don't see it escalating to that level. Then, there was the one about…"

The doorway to the chamber opened and Samuel straightened up, trying to match Denton's posture.

Tom backed out of the *Name's* presence and then walked over to join them. His face was unreadable, but he couldn't hide the drain on his energy.

"Are you okay, Tom?" Samuel asked, not daring to reach out his hand to help, as he would have at Home.

"Good enough. Come on, let's get back. You and I have to plan an expedition."

Samuel looked hard at his eyes. "You and I?" Samuel had very little experience outside of the caves, and Tom was too old for such a thing. Only a direct order from the *Name* had brought him here.

Denton was likewise puzzled. "Sir?"

Tom shook his head. "Secrets. It'll become clear in a day or so. But for now, get me Home."

14

The voice rumbled up, seemingly from the ground below. <You don't appear to be healing.>

Karl coughed where he lay. Ba was still in the same place, but he was connected to the soil in ways Karl didn't fully comprehend.

<No. It may have reached the point of no return.> He held up his shaking hand before his eyes. The skin was becoming bluish. <The acids may cause the damage to my lungs, and I've been working on those, but something else is happening as well. I'm almost too weak to hunt anymore. Without the protein, I won't have the resources to rebuild.>

<You are dying? Just from the air?>

<Yes. Probably.>

<How have your people survived this world?>

<We live in caves, in old Delense burrows, with filtered air. We have masks that let us breathe for a while when we go out. And we can heal, once we reach safety.>

<But you have no safe place?>

<That's right, Ba. No place. I wish I could just crawl under the ground like you do, but that wouldn't work for me.>

<How close are your people?>

<Too far, and I can't seek them out.>

There was silence. Then, Ba asked, <Are you in conflict with your people?>

<No. But when the boat crashed, I was given up as dead. The *Name* would not like it if I survived. Many Cerik hate the idea of the U'tanse. They would fear one that was free.>

<So you must hide from the Cerik, but why hide from your own people?>

<We are telepaths. What one knows, all would soon know. Only by blocking my thoughts can I stay alive. Everyone who knew of me would have to do the same.>

<Then I am a danger to you too.>

<Perhaps. But only if they knew to seek for you.>

<I am only safe alone.>

The rumble of his voice had an odd inflection. Karl didn't know enough about the Ba to know if it was sadness, or pride. At least he had found a way to be a free... person.

15

Samuel looked at the other three in the Home's conference room. Tom had been very quiet after meeting with the *Name*, and hopefully, now was the time for planning, and that couldn't happen without revelations.

It was a group of four: Tom, Samuel, Abbie and Gem from Supplies. The thick-walled door was closed and Tom had requested strong *ineda* from everyone. That was fine by him. Without telepathy, everything would have to be spoken and he wouldn't be left out by accident.

Tom tapped the chart laid out on the table. "Officially, the *Name* has requested that we go to the crash site and salvage the shipment of pipes. The story is that the *klakr* hunters all reported that the pipes were scattered, but in good shape. We still need them, so we'll go collect them."

He looked at Samuel. "Just the two of us will go. That means that you'll be doing all the hard work. Sorry."

"I can do it."

Abbie objected, "You can't go, Tom! You're not up to it."

Samuel wasn't surprised that Abbie was distressed. She'd appointed herself his chief caregiver a few years back. She was the first one at the boat's landing to make sure that he hadn't been exposed to bad air.

Tom nodded. He had a subdued expression on his face that Samuel worried about. "I understand. However, it's a direct order from the *Name*. There is also the real reason we're going."

Samuel put down his pen, listening intently. Tom was looking down at the chart, not meeting their eyes. "We are supposed to recover Karl's body. Apparently, the *Name* can be challenged at the Face if there's any hint that a U'tanse might have escaped.

"He wants proof that Karl died. Supposedly, that's why his enemies went to the crash site—to show him up. The *Name* thinks that with U'tanse senses, I'll be able to find his remains better than Cerik hunters who were too distracted at being in *klakr* territory.

"This is my task. If I fail, if I don't bring back Karl's body, then I have been told that a significant example will be made, to make sure that all U'tanse on the globe know that it is impossible to escape their *Name*."

A significant example. What could that be? Samuel was beginning to wonder just how bad the Cerik politics were getting. Clan-on-clan raids were a fact of life. The duel that brought down the boat in the first place was hardly unusual.

The only thing that was different was the missing U'tanse. A Getterin-Graddik fight wasn't something the *Name* would want to avoid. He might enjoy it. But if the anti-U'tanse made an issue of it at the Face, then that was another thing.

If enough *Names* at the Face turned against Kallu, anything could happen. If they didn't find Karl's bones, the Cerik response was likely spilled blood. With Kallu's *Name* at stake, there might be a *lot* of spilled blood.

From the faces around the table, everyone was thinking the same thing. They had to succeed.

Tom tapped the table. "This isn't just a fly-in and fly-out, one day task. a boat will drop us off with a shouter, and then we will call when we're done to be picked up. The two of us will need food, water and air for several days, some kind of temporary shelter against the weather and scavengers. We'll need carts to load the pipes on, complete with straps. And we'll need a bag for the body, or body parts."

Samuel started making a list. Gem looked over his shoulder.

Abbie frowned. "The two of you, alone without a Cerik, in *klakr* country? We'll have to send others after you, with more bags."

Tom lowered his voice, but they could all hear. "Abbie, don't make it harder than it already is. The *Name* wants me to go, so I go."

"Then at least take more helpers. Take Denton or his brother Jerrold. They're both big and strong—and they have telepathy."

Samuel didn't meet his eyes, but he could see Tom looking his way.

"No. I have need of Samuel's special skills. If it were just the pipes, then the more muscle, the better. This is different."

Samuel steeled himself to make sure everything came together without a problem. It wasn't the first time he'd had to prove that he was just as good as any other man, even if he was a tenner. He'd been fighting that battle since he was a boy. He had to make sure Tom didn't regret his decision.

16

<Karl. Wake up.> The Ba's voice felt like it came from his chest, vibrating throughout his body.

<Yes, I'm here. What do you want?>

<Wake up. You need to be alert.>

<What?>

Karl tried to lift his hand, but it didn't move. *Am I that weak already?* He tried again, and it came free. It was half buried in the soil. Startled, he struggled to sit up. Dirt fell away. He had been sleeping in a cavity, formfitted to his body in the ground.

<Ba, what happened.>

<I have moved you. You said before that you needed food to fuel your healing. The meadow and the creek did not supply your needs. As you slept, I moved beneath you and carried you away. This is a place with more fish.>

But he was weak, barely able to crawl. He moved to a nearby rock and sat.

A Ba-sized circle of soil from the meadow had been transplanted into a new setting. There was a cliff to one side, and there was a much larger river just a few feet away.

<Where are we?>

<Another place. Stay where you are and be ready.>

The Ba shook the ground. The circular patch began to blend in with its surroundings and the Karl-shaped cavity filled in. The vibrations changed, and Karl looked over to the water. Something large was leaving a ripple in the water. Two things. There was one approaching from upstream and another from downstream.

What were they? Large fish? Predators? He shifted his feet, getting ready to move.

The two waves in the water merged and erupted. Dozens of fish leapt out of the water onto the shore, flapping on the rocks. Weak or not, Karl was on his feet, getting close enough to grab the fish and toss them farther from the water before they could escape. Nearly half were the edible kind, and he concentrated on those.

He was breathless as he panted, catching as many as he could eat into a pile.

The blowhole puffed up. <Can you eat these?>

<Yes. Thanks.>

It was all he could do to collect wood and start the fire. It was the worst cooking he'd done, but he ate them, charred spots and all.

Stuffed, he crawled back onto the Ba-spot. <Thank you. I am too weak to hunt. I would have died today without food.>

<Heal.>

<I'll try.>

Karl didn't try to think too much about what kind of sound-trick Ba had used to scare the fish out of the water, but he was grateful. He needed all the protein he could eat.

He'd never heard of anyone as air-poisoned as he was. The atmosphere was acidic when it entered the moist cavities of his lungs, and it was common that people developed damaged areas there. Everyone, other than the tenners, were trained in the process of breaking down the unusable damaged tissue and accelerating the regrowth of healthy new lung structures.

But living constantly in the bad air had added a new problem. The dissolved nitrates were binding with the hemoglobin in his blood, making the red blood cells useless for transporting oxygen throughout his body. He could repair his lungs, but still suffocate because his blood had failed its job. Normally, the effect was so slight on people living in the Home that they never had to deal with it. The body's natural regeneration of red blood cells took care of it.

Karl would have to learn how to make it happen faster. A lot faster, if he were going to survive. He settled into a trance and the outside world faded away.

...

<Are you looking for a *klakr* or the U'tanse?>

The Sakah hunter shivered slightly, and moved back from the edge of the cliff. It was the best viewpoint around, with the crash site visible in one direction, and the valley below spread out until it faded in the brown haze.

He snarled at his hunting partner. <You'll bleed if you say that again. I have seen three different herds of runners, a *hatsen*, and more *chitchits* than you can imagine on this mountain. If I see a *klakr*, I'll tell you, but don't think I would go running after fresh blood like a cub. If you aren't looking for the U'tanse, go back to your *erdan* and quit distracting a real hunter.>

<I don't think it's here. And time is running out.>

<Perhaps. It does appear that Kallu has woken up. I had hoped to find the U'tanse, still alive, with blood to show when I revealed it.>

<Our *Name* might have plans of his own. Our job it to catch it, alive—nothing more.>

<The rumor is that Kallu is sending U'tanse to find the U'tanse bones. It would be easy to take them.>

<That's up to the *Name*, but if he makes the call, I will be his Right Eye.>

17

Linda bar Franklin entered the office. Abbie looked up. "Yes?" She saw the look on the young woman's face and gestured to the chair.

Linda sat, and stared at her folded hands. "I'm sorry to bother you. I was just wondering if I could request a job change?"

Abbie scanned her surface thoughts. "The garden? Do you have any experience with plants?"

She shook her head. "Just the usual training when I was little."

"Why do you want to change from carpentry to gardening? You liked your job, the last I heard."

Linda shook her head, still staring down. "It's hard to explain."

Abbie could sense part of it. "Is it about Karl?" *If rumors have started already about the expedition to recover his body, then someone has leaked.*

"Maybe. I don't know. It's just... I had a dream about him."

"Oh?"

"Yes, last night. I dreamed he was buried in the ground, and traveling... somehow."

"At the same time?"

Linda looked up with a sad smile. "Sorry, it was a dream. I can't explain it. It was like he was buried. And I thought... maybe... I don't know."

Abbie nodded. "Actually, your request is not unusual. Sometimes, when people lose someone special, they like to work the soil to be close to the remains of their loved one. Some of our best gardeners started out that way."

Linda nodded. "It's silly. I'm sorry. Karl isn't really in the garden."

Abbie reached across the table and took her hands. "How we feel isn't silly. Let me think about it for a while. You think about it, too. In a few days, or even a month from now, if you still want to work in the garden,

I'll arrange a temporary reassignment. We'll see how it works out before making any permanent changes."

...

"Samuel?"

"Yes, sir." He put down his pen. The cargo was coming together quickly, but he kept finding additional items to add.

Tom held out a small chest. "Add this, but don't write it down."

"Sir?" He took it. It was heavy for its size.

"This is a secret item, only for the Head of the Home. Don't speak of it. Don't write about it. Don't let it creep into your public thoughts. And don't open it unless I order you to."

Samuel added it to the stack of materials already collected on a cart. The small wooden chest looked old. Had it come from the original stash of supplies from the Human home world, or had one of the early generation U'tanse created it? He picked it back up, wrapped it in cloth and re-stacked some other boxes around it to make it less obvious.

He turned back and jerked when he realized Tom was watching him. "Sorry."

"Don't be. It's more important than I am."

18

Karl sat in his form-fitted depression, his hands flat on the soil, as the Ba moved rapidly through the night. It had taken some effort to keep from rolling free when he woke up, traveling faster than a man's sprint, only a couple of feet above the surrounding land. It was fascinating to watch, but frightening as well. The Ba was too wide to follow the paths of the grazers, so they were constantly shifting direction, finding places to fit between the vegetation and the rocks. Sometimes it was impossible.

<U'tanse, lay flat.>

From experience, he did as he was told. Ba didn't have a 'front'. Rather than turn to go a different direction, the Ba just went 'sideways' or 'backwards' for that matter. Karl watched the tree line approach. There was a last instant shift to the side, and then the Ba went *over* a mid-sized tree. He could hear it splinter as it was flattened. Part of the dirt Ba was carrying shifted, and for the first time, Karl could see the back plates. The back was a maze of hand-sized segments, all showing growth lines. By the moonlight, they appeared pale, lighter than the soil that covered them.

Cautiously, Karl placed his hand on the bare plate. His own perception, mixed with the living vibration of the creature, gave him a sense of his structure.

<Ba, what do you eat?>

The blowhole was nearby. He could almost feel the breath. <The soil feeds me.>

Karl nodded to himself. *No mouth, no teeth. No digestive system that I can sense.* If he didn't have to spend all his time trying to keep his own body working, he'd love to find out the secrets of the Ba-kind.

He closed his eyes. He was dizzy from trying to watch.

Ba is tired. All this travel is depleting his energy stores. Why is he doing this for me?

. . .

Both Sakah hunters on the ridge watched as the boat settled down on the flat spot between the crash and the rotting bones of the *klakr*.

<We should call the *Name* on the shouter and let him know.>

The larger of the two snarled. <We will wait. Likely our telepath will already know.>

<I dislike having a worm crawl through my head.>

<Request *ineda* training, or learn to enjoy it. But don't gripe to me about your imperfections. We're here to watch. The *Name* will call us when he wants action.>

The smaller shut up. He'd hunted with him long enough to know that he had some plan in mind. He was ready to settle into *erdan*, but then the other growled.

<You see something?>

They were at a deliberate distance, where they wouldn't be seen except by an exceptional hunter. It was hard to make out the activity down by the new boat. But he didn't have to wait long. The boat's buzz echoed across the distance. It was taking off, leaving the U'tanse alone on the ground!

<Now we call the *Name*?>
<Yes!>

19

Samuel pushed the big-wheeled cart over the rocky terrain. "Why couldn't the pilot land closer to the crash! This ground is impossible."

Tom was walking by himself, using a cane to help him make the trek. The older man didn't respond to his gripes. He turned back to his task. The big wheels were his idea. The little ones they normally used at Home would have been absolutely useless on this ground.

But it didn't make it any easier to push the carts uphill to the crash site.

"Samuel. Help me get to the boat."

He was happy to lock the wheels and walk over to help. Tom's face was strained.

"What's wrong? Do you sense Karl's body?"

He shook his head. "I sense Cerik. All around us. We need to get inside the boat."

Samuel put his arm around Tom's back and lifted. They hurried to the opened hatch—the one with the door torn completely away in the crash.

Cerik. That can't be good. The pilot that brought them was long gone. He didn't mention any other Cerik in the area, and Tom would have picked up on it if he'd known.

They're from another clan. They want us to fail. They want us dead.

"Do you have my special box?"

"Yes, I brought it on the first cart."

"Get it. Bring it inside."

There were three carts, lightly loaded with their supplies. They would take them back loaded with pipes and Karl's body, according to their plan.

Samuel didn't need to be told to move slowly. How to live with predators was part of every child's early education. Do nothing to startle them, or to trigger their impulse to chase fleeing prey. He moved to the cart as if he had all the time in the world and picked up Tom's special box and carried it back up to the damaged boat.

Tom was already inside. He took the box as soon as Samuel set it inside.

"Start moving pipes across the hatchway. Make it hard for them to get inside."

Samuel didn't have to be asked twice. He started dragging pipes from the storage area, two at a time, and began stacking them across the opening. Tom was working on something, but there was no time to see what he was doing. Samuel had just managed stacked the pipes three rows high when a Cerik landed out of nowhere right it front of him and slammed him against the far wall.

An uncertain growl echoed through the chamber as the pipes rolled under the attacker's feet. Tom, in spite of his age, jumped at the Cerik and they both tumbled outside. By the time Samuel had gotten to his feet on the slanted floor, he was just in time to see Cerik claws rip through Tom's chest, tossing the limp body a dozen feet away.

"Tom!" he cried, but all that did was turn the murderous gaze on him, in the opening.

It was clear his boss and long time mentor was dead, and the rumble in the Cerik's chest meant he was next. Instinct turned his feet uphill, into the cargo bay. There was no escape, but it was better than standing there to be gutted.

Tom, why did you do that! Denton couldn't take on a Cerik like that!

He'd set up a lantern that gave some light. *Is there any place to hide?*

His brain said no, but he gripped one of the lids on the water tanks.

And then there was the scream of a Cerik in battle, but it wasn't right behind him; it was outside.

More screams—he crept alongside the walls, until he could see what was happening.

One Cerik was sprawled on the rocks, his torso bone white where his skin had been sliced open, and his face was ripped away. A few yards past that, a lone Cerik was surrounded by three others. He recognized one of the three by old scars on his back. He was Graddik—a pilot who often made deliveries to Home. The *Name* had sent them to guard their work!

He almost turned to tell Tom what he was seeing, the reality of the corpse outside hadn't sunk in.

Oh, Tom! If he had just waited… or if their protectors had been faster…

There was no illusion that the three-against-one battle was fair. This wasn't a duel—it was efficient slaughter. The second attacker was downed quickly. Samuel ducked back inside, just in time to hear the triumphant roars of the others.

He looked around at the scattered pipes in the room, more to avoid thinking about what he'd just witnessed than anything else. His eyes settled on the little chest that Tom had brought, its lid still open. He reached over to close it, but a folded sheet of paper caught his eyes. *To Samuel*, it was labeled.

<U'tanse!>

He unfolded the paper and scanned it quickly, before stepping over the pipes and facing his protectors. <I am here.>

<Your telepath is dead. Shall I tell the *Name* that you have failed?>

Samuel straightened up and took a breath. <No! He discovered the bones of our fallen before he was killed. I will contact the *Name* via the shouter as planned when the body parts have been collected and the pipes are ready to load.>

The pilot gave a sigh of dismissal and he and the others left quickly, vanishing over a nearby ridge.

Samuel forced himself to check on Tom's body, nearly ripped apart by the attacking Cerik's claw. Blood was splattered all over the rocks. His face looked caught in a moment of determination.

Inside, he opened the paper again and reread it slowly, making sure he really understood what he had scanned a moment before.

> *To Samuel,*
>
> *I started this expedition with no hope that we would find Karl's body, but we must not fail to provide proof of his death. To that end, I have taken a poison that will appear to be a stroke or heart attack.*
>
> *Tell the Cerik that I discovered Karl's body and told you before I died. You will have to keep this lie to yourself all your life. I know you can do it. You have an uncrackable ineda and the strength of spirit to pull this off. No one, not Cerik nor human, can ever know what happened here.*
>
> *Now here is how we can supply two corpses from one...*

20

Karl woke when Ba stopped. He sat up and stared at the strangely carved cascade, noisy with churning water, where a lake spilled down the slope to vanish in the mists. Ba was vibrating himself into the ground.

<What is this place?>

<Here is where I leave you.>

<What? Explain.>

The blow hole started puffing dust as he settled lower, even with the surrounding soil. <I will only be safe alone. You might die, but your best chance will be here. This is an abandoned dam, built by the Delense. I discovered the place long ago, when I was smaller. Fish collect near the spillway and will be easy to catch. There is also a hidden underground burrow, which you say your kind can use.>

<Hidden? Where?>

<The entrance is underwater, also near the spillway. Maybe it will not be enough for you, but it is the best I can do.>

Karl brushed the surface, until he could feel the Ba beneath him. <I thank you.>

<I will miss our talks. I will miss carrying you on my back. But I must be alone, to be safe.>

21

Samuel caught Denton's look. *I guess I have changed.* If Tom had complimented him on his *ineda* before, it must be impossibly dense now. *I don't even want to know what my thoughts are.*

He stood motionless with the two body bags as the *Name* and a dozen other Cerik came closer to inspect the cargo he had been sent for.

<Tuah was killed?>

Samuel dropped into the crouch that U'tanse used when addressed by the *Name*. <For your *Name*. Other Cerik attacked your crashed boat as we were unloading. Tom defended your things and was gutted.>

The eyes of his master didn't probe his own too deeply. It was obvious Tom was doing more than just defending some pipes. He growled. <Show me.>

Samuel moved to the smaller of the bags. He opened up the wrapping and revealed Tom's dead face. Part of his savaged torso was visible as well.

The Cerik growled. <You were his Second? What do you name yourself?>

<I am Samuel.>

<Sawuel. You also found the lost one? Show me him.>

Carefully, Samuel re-wrapped Tom's corpse and moved to the other bag. He pulled the wrappings back, and pulled out a human arm, stripped to the bare bones of any flesh. The crowd of Cerik murmured among themselves. Nothing else on the planet had the distinctive hands and fingers of the U'tanse, and the stench of death crept out for all to smell.

<As you can see, most of the bones and flesh that I was able to dig out of the carcass of the *klakr* are decomposed and broken. He was probably eaten a day or so before the beast fought that other Cerik. If Tom hadn't sensed the body the instant we landed at the crash site, I don't know if I would ever have found it.>

One of the crowd snarled with glee. <That Ruthenah pilot fought a *klakr* already poisoned by a U'tanse!> The whole crowd turned to consider the news. The greatest hunt in recent memory was a fraud! The one calling himself a new Uriko had killed a beast already weakened! It was a sensation.

The *Name* held back and spoke low. <Sawuel, take your cargo and your dead to your Home. Tuah was a valued Builder. Give him your U'tanse ceremony.>

Samuel nodded to Denton and they carried the body bags out.

It worked! Let's get out of here before the new scandal fades and gives anyone a chance to have second thoughts.

Tom had been right. It had been possible to make two corpses from one body—as long as no one thought to check to see if Tom still had his right arm.

It had been a grueling ordeal. He'd wrapped Tom's still warm body, and then conscious he might be observed, carefully cut the arm free and dropped it in a chemical bag Tom had prepared. The caustic materials from Tom's secret case stripped the flesh from the bones in short order.

The next day, feeling the eyes watching his every move, he carried the bag over to the decaying body of the *klakr* and under the guise of hunting for Karl, he managed to 'discover' the arm and harvested bits and pieces of the beast to substitute for other parts of Karl's body.

With two bags of rotting flesh baking in the sun, the one with 'Karl' packed with urine-saturated cloth to give it a distinctive U'tanse smell, he worked furiously to collect and re-stack the pipes into transportable bales. Only then could he activate the shouter and call for a boat to come pick him up.

And they arrived in five minutes. Imagine that.

No one could ever know what happened. Tom was correct. No Cerik and no U'tanse must ever know that 'Karl' was a fabrication.

22

When Karl stirred from his healing trance, Ba was gone. The pit where he'd been was smoothed, but a few marks on the ground hinted that his giant flat friend had continued on his own path. Karl called out a few times, but there was no response.

He told me he was leaving. I guess I'd better find that hidden burrow before this last round of healing wears off.

Ba's companionship and unexpected care for his well-being renewed in him a hope that had evaporated when he had hiked down the mountain. His health was on a razor's edge. If everything worked perfectly—with plenty of fish to eat and nothing to wear him out, he was able to repair each day's damage to his body. He even had a handle on how to boost his own body's ability to scavenge dead red blood cells for their iron and to generate new ones from the cellular factories in his bone marrow. But it was still just enough. He had no reserves. He'd used them all up.

He looked at his arm. It was almost skeletal, with much of his muscle mass used up. He could still walk. He could still catch fish, if they were plentiful. But he was hardly the man he was before. He made the effort not to look at the reflection of his face in the water.

His leather suit was hanging off of him as well. *I'll keep the goggles on to help me find the opening, but the rest of it will just drag me to the bottom.*

"Near the spillway" is what Ba said. He eyed the water flowing rapidly over the edge. The notch in the dam was lined with massive stones. There was a faster channel where the bulk of the water exited the reservoir, and a narrower one to the side, composed of a series of pools, that formed a fish ladder. It would be his prime fishing spot, he could tell.

I don't want to get swept away in the strong current. He moved to the edge, on the other side of the fish ladder and undressed. Goggles in place, he stepped gingerly into the water.

Oh, that feels good. He hadn't had a chance to bathe since he left on this trip. Already, places on his skin were scarred from untreated air burns. Skin had lower priority than his lungs.

He ducked his head and looked around. The water was a little murky, and he couldn't see more than a dozen feet away. He took another breath. *I can't hold my breath long. I hope it will be enough.*

He swam the surface, keeping his eyes underwater as much as he could.

Dark area. Was that it? He moved closer, pumping his lungs full of air. He'd have to double up his healing later, but he needed to oxygenate his body as much as possible now.

He swam down, and it was frightening how easy it was to go lower. He used to float better than this.

The darkness resolved into a tunnel. Already his lungs were hurting from his need for air, but he had to go inside.

He stroked the water as fast as he could, and he could feel his body straining for another breath.

Up! Up! He found air quickly, and he grabbed the unexpected railing in the dark.

He panted for a moment before pulling his goggles free. It didn't help. It was still dark.

An underground burrow—it was what he was looking for, wasn't it?

It was enough that he could breathe the air and hang on to the railing while he caught his breath.

I'll have to see without light.

He'd never gotten the practice to visualize the world with his clairvoyance as well as some of his cousins. He'd been limited to working controls and healing his body. But hunting for *lulur* and fishing, with the specter of starvation behind it, had exercised those senses.

He closed his eyes in the darkness, and *saw*.

Next to the water was a large room, a loading bay. There were wheeled carts stacked a few feet away—larger ones than they used at Home. He sensed corrosion and decay.

There was a corridor beyond. *That's too small for Ba. How much of this place did he explore?*

He pulled himself out of the water and felt for the wall. He could sense the rooms and some their contents, but he wasn't about to walk in the dark and trip over something a Delense had left on the floor ages ago.

I'll give this a few more minutes before I go back out and rescue my suit.

23

Abbie put her hand on Linda's shoulder. "I didn't expect to be here with you."

Linda gave her a small smile. Debbie was standing on her own, her little hand sweaty in her mother's grip. "I guess you can't ever expect this."

The gardens were crowded, as the dual funeral had brought everyone in the Home who could make it. Tom, in particular, had friends from all over the planet who were there in spirit, riding the senses of the locals.

The shrouded bodies were on carts against the far wall, and everyone knew there would be no last viewing. The deaths were horrific and it would be best to not think about the details. Words were said about both men's lives of service. Linda learned more about Karl's early years than she'd known before. Separated by two years, it had been enough that they moved in different circles of friends.

She heard Abbie sniffing and put out her hand to hers. She whispered, "You loved Tom."

Abbie blinked at her tears. "It was silly, I know. He had always been too old for me, and there was never any... you know."

Linda whispered, "It's not silly how you feel."

The words were spoken, the lives celebrated, the promise of a new life "around that dark corner where we can't sense" was made—and then the bodies were fed into the grumbling machinery where their useless remains could be made useful again.

. . .

Karl was overcome by the wave of grief that he sensed from Linda.

She's at my funeral. How is that possible?

He had made several trips back outside to get his suit and to fish. He also brought fire-making materials, but hesitated to burn up the oxygen in the burrow. How far back did the passages go? How much air did he have down there?

So he built his fire outside and cooked his fish under the growing moonlight. He was almost done when the waves of emotion at the edge of his perception became too strong to ignore.

Did Tom do something to…? And then he realized that Tom had died.

Bits and pieces of the story were available in people's minds. They had gone back to the boat to collect the pipes. Another clan had attacked and killed Tom.

If I had known…

But it was useless to play that game. He didn't even know where the mountain was anymore. He had ridden Ba in the night while he slept. He'd never find it again.

The grief echoing from other minds triggered his own.

I can never go home again. I'll be alone the rest of my life.

He let himself wallow only a few minutes, then tried to shake off the self pity.

This'll kill me as quickly as the bad air.

Isn't this what I dreamed about not too many days ago—a safe place to sleep, away from the predators and the weather?

He needed to explore it. If there was indeed only so much good air down there, he needed to find out its extent quickly, before he used it all up just waiting.

The bones and ashes went into the spillway to avoid attracting scavengers, and he dove in. Practice made the passage into the burrow quick.

In the dark, he checked the progress of his torch-making supplies. Perhaps they weren't as dry as he hoped, but with luck, he could get a fire started.

It took three tries, but soon he had a bundle of twigs spouting a modest flame.

The loading bay, by the wavering yellow light, looked strangely un-Delense-like. He scratched the surface of one of the carts and flakes of rust came loose. Definitely not the Delense design he was used to. The Delense coated everything, even their metal work, with a ceramic surface. The pipes he'd been transporting had been coated inside and out with a thin, whitish surface that prevented contamination. This was more like some of the experiments U'tanse metal workers had produced. Bare metal corroded.

How old is this place?

The corridor showed ruts, matching the wheel spacing of the carts, and centered in the narrow passageway. There was certainly room for a Delense to push a cart, but a Cerik might have difficulty. Certainly Ba couldn't have made his way through, unless he was much smaller then.

With a little practice, he could move quickly down the path without blowing out his flame. If he had to make his way back to the water in the dark, so be it. He needed to see what was here.

Not too far down the way, there was a control panel—not the advanced touch panels he was used to, but levers and valve-handles, much like the U'tanse had built for their own air systems.

Could this be the same?

It couldn't be a U'tanse place. He was sure of that. But it looked like the systems worked the same, whoever built it. The real question was what these valves controlled. His fingers itched to try them, but that could wait.

Then something caught his eye. He moved the flame closer.

There were markings. Delense markings. He was sure of it.

One more thing I didn't study enough. U'tanse more scholarly than he had made a study of the few remaining examples of Delense script discovered since the Arrival. Supposedly, they were mainly technical.

That's what he needed right now. One more thing to 'listen' for on his long nights.

And what is this? The lever had a scale. It was dark at the bottom and pale at the top. On impulse, he pulled the lever upwards. Surprisingly, it moved. There were squeaks, but it moved. He listened, both with his ears and with his clairvoyance, but there didn't appear to be any action anywhere.

Oh well.

He turned one of the valves. It stuck at first, but then moved.

Water. He could hear it. Somewhere water was moving through a pipe.

He waved the torch around, but there wasn't any visible leak. The burrow was below the lake level. He'd have to make sure he didn't accidentally flood the place.

Thunk. A deep sound came from somewhere nearby, but on the other side of the wall. "What was that?"

A metallic creak followed, and then two things happened at once. A vibration started in the walls, and the corridors filled with light.

24

It was only after the funeral, when the last possible hard evidence of the fake body was gone, and he could finally relax, that Samuel started noticing the looks. By the time he had walked back to Tom's office, he was sure that something was up. Telepaths were discussing something, and since none of them had let him in on it, he had to be subject of discussion.

It wasn't hard to figure out.

"Gem, could you get Abbie and meet me in the conference room?"

She looked startled, but nodded and walked out. He went to the rack of books and unrolled the most recent family tree for the Graddik's U'tanse clan. He'd transcribed it himself not two months earlier, folding in all the new births and marking all the deaths. There had been an exchange of young women from the last Festival. Moving them into the family tree had been his motive for refreshing the document with new black ink and freshly rolled paper. He hadn't considered he'd be needing to consult it so soon.

The two women entered the room and sat down across from him. It wasn't a good sign. Perhaps being without telepathy made him a little more sensitive to other ways to read people's thoughts. If they had sat down beside him, where they would all be looking at the paper together, that would have been more hopeful. As it was, there was a strain in the air.

He waited a little for them to speak, but he had to break the ice.

Samuel tapped the tree diagram. He spoke simply. "We three, and six others reported directly to Tom when I drew this out. Who do I take orders from now?"

Gem glanced at Abbie. Abbie stared down at the paper. The funeral was still fresh on her face. He said softly, "I'm sorry to bring this up so soon. I just have a feeling that we need to let people know."

She nodded, not meeting his eyes. "Denton said the *Name* asked you to name yourself. Doesn't that make you the leader?"

He shrugged. "I suppose I'll have to answer to him, but that's just Cerik relations. I can't be the leader of the Home. I'm not a telepath. I don't have the people skills." He took a breath. "And I'm too young. I'm not sure people would accept me, especially after having Tom to look up to all these years. We are more than just Kallu's U'tanse. We need a leader that we can count on."

Abbie said, "You are right. There has been some discussion about who should be the leader."

Gem shrugged. "Some say it's perfectly natural. You were Tom's closest assistant, his right-hand man. He was always giving you special jobs. It was like you were his Second. The *Name* probably picked up on that. So when you brought back Tom's body…"

Samuel snarled, "Like I had killed him? To take his place? Is that what people think?"

She winced. "No… It's not that. It's just… you've been very closed up. Nobody can read you. We believe what you said. "

He was horrified. Some of them *did* believe that. Deliberately, he called back the memory and dropped his *ineda*.

He was just piling the pipes up three rows high when a Cerik landed out of nowhere right it front of him and slammed him against the far wall.

An uncertain growl echoed through the chamber as the pipes rolled under the attacker's feet. Tom, in spite of his age, jumped at the Cerik and they both tumbled outside. By the time Samuel had gotten to his feet on the slanted floor, he was just in time to see Cerik claws rip through Tom's chest, tossing the limp body a dozen feet away.

"Tom!" he cried, but all that did was turn the murderous gaze on him, in the opening.

Abbie and Gem cried out, living that moment though his eyes. Samuel snapped his *ineda* shut. He reached across the table and took each woman's hand in his own.

"I'm sorry. I hadn't intended to force that memory on anyone, but I can't let people think that we have so lost our humanity that we are killing for position like the Cerik. I loved Tom! He died to save me. I don't want to be Leader."

Abbie squeezed his hand. "I know." She raised her eyes to his. "We didn't think you killed him. But you are the logical one to lead the Home. You have been intimately involved with everything that Tom did for years now. You know how this place runs. The other men old enough to step into the role have already specialized in other jobs. Tom was training you for this."

He shook his head, "But I'm not a telepath. I can't feel the people like Tom did, like you do. All the other Homes are led by telepaths, and for good reason. Like this unvoiced suspicion that I killed Tom. I had no idea that people were thinking that. Unknown, and unresolved, something like that could tear a Home apart."

Abbie said softly, "Father was a tenner, and he led us for decades after the Arrival. You don't have to be a telepath to lead. You sensed *something* was wrong, and took the steps to quell it."

Samuel sighed, "You would be a much better leader."

She chuckled. "I doubt Kallu would take kindly to that. I don't think any Cerik has talked to a woman since Mother, and then only because she scared them. No, our masters can only deal with men. Their females don't even have voices. That's a fact we must face."

Gem chewed her lip. "Abe and Sharon led the original home as a team. She was the telepath, and kept him linked in to the people."

He smiled. "Are you volunteering?"

She held out both hands and looked horrified. "Oh, no! I've got a storehouse to run. I was just thinking out loud."

He sighed, "That's what it would take for a tenner to lead—that's for certain. We are so blind in many ways."

Abbie nodded, "So, it's settled, then. We find you a partner. Have you had an eye on anyone?"

He rubbed his forehead. "Let's go slow. Why don't you be my partner for now?"

She dimpled. "Ah, if I were fifteen years younger, I might be tempted. But long term, you're going to need someone your own age. Gem is right—a *close* couple like Father and Mother—that's a leadership our colony, and the others, will accept. For a time, I'll help, and that's what we'll announce, but we really need to find you a long term mate."

Gem rubbed her hands together. "Matchmaking, I love it! Don't you worry Samuel. We'll find the perfect girl!"

He sighed.

25

Karl allowed himself three hours to wander about the abandoned burrow. He still had to fish, collect and dry firewood, eat and then spend hours in a trance to keep his body running properly. But at least, he was out of the elements and didn't have to worry about predators discovering him while he was deeply into the workings of his cells.

In Father's Book, there had been a mention of hydroelectric plants on the human home world, complete with diagrams. This was obviously a Delense version of the same thing. Water flowed through pipes to spin a generator. With electricity, the chambers were lit with light bars that were similar to those in the Home.

Delense machines we use today are all powered from energy cells brought down from space. Nobody uses plants like this one. They moved beyond hydroelectricity before we came around.

But this one still worked after being idle for hundreds of years, at least. The Delense were master builders. He hesitated to change the settings—just in case there was a fatal weakness somewhere—but at least there was light everywhere. There was also no sign that the air was growing stale, although he didn't sense any breeze that might have pointed to an air pump.

By the third day of exploration, he was still finding new corridors. The place was larger than Home.

There were markings everywhere. He'd taken to mentally visiting each of the Homes, hoping to luck onto a scholar studying Delense script.

Unfortunately, his random samplings were not bearing fruit. There were too many U'tanse to count, and most were concerned with day-to-day life.

But what is that?

The doorway was marked with stripes, and had a large clamp to secure the way. He hesitated. Most doors, even the ones that sealed off store rooms or working areas, had simple latches.

What's behind there? If there was water, he could flood the area, even drown himself.

That's not how I would do it, though. Access to a water tunnel should be through an overhead hatch, not through a doorway. That would be senseless. And the only senseless thing the Delense did was to bomb their bloodthirsty masters.

He found a metal tool and came back to bang on the striped doorway. At least it sounded normal—not at all like water on the other side.

Timidly, he unsealed the door. There was a brief puff of air when he opened it up, but nothing horrible happened.

Inside was an open fabrication area. There were dozens of workbenches and hoists with hooks, chains and pulleys. The only strange things were the metal latticeworks hanging from the hoists. Below them were piles of dust, as if the lattice grids had been coated with something that fell off.

He avoided touching anything, but walked the length of the area. There were metal-working tools. They were not like the human ones at Home, but the designs were similar. Only these were designed for Delense hands to work them.

Another odd thing. Some projects had been left abandoned. There were half-cut metal sheets, and templates only partially completed. And the metal was shiny, un-tarnished.

How could that possibly be?

He picked up a polished piece of copper or bronze. There was a slight patina on it, but he knew from experience that anything made of copper had to be kept coated in oil or at the very least, kept in filtered air, or it would rapidly decay and be covered in blue crystals. But not this piece.

Were the Delense in the process of discovering their ceramic coatings? Somehow this one had not decayed over all this time.

Like a flash, the idea came over him. *Perhaps this chamber uses filtered air?*

He hurried back to the door and closed it. He sniffed the air. There was the usual tang of the poisonous nitrates, but that could have come in when he opened the door. Was there a filtration system here?

He kneeled down to the pile of powder below the lattice grids. He fingered the dust. *Maybe, just maybe.*

26

In the hallways of Ruthenah's Perch, the pilot lovingly stroked the tusks of the *klakr* head. <The Graddik will suffer for this! I will not bear the lies!>

The ridicule that was growing at his victory over the 'sick' *klakr* had turned his triumph into ashes.

His *rettik* echoed the anger. <But how? The Face is upon us. We are bound to observe the *katche*. If we attack Graddik, then all will turn on us.>

The pilot moved his claws in controlled circular patterns as he thought. His righteye was right, as distasteful as it might be. An attack during the Face would be suicidal, even if he could get in, cause some damage, and get out un-cut.

But revenge delayed was revenge that grew.

He looked back at the *klakr* head mounted on the wall. There was certainly room on that wall for more heads. He just had to plan this out perfectly, so that the display of heads was a work of art.

27

Karl breathed deeply through his mask's filter. There was no tang. It was just like the filtered air of Home. It was almost too wonderful to believe. He'd still monitor his healing daily, but if this gray powder did the job as well as the white concoction invented by Father back at the Arrival, then he could look forward to making some progress in his life, get really healthy, and not just hold off death from day to day.

The Delense had made a metal working chamber, and had filtered the air to allow them to work with metals that would corrode too quickly to be useful. Karl had examined the setup and had puzzled out how it worked. There was an electric oven that baked the powder and vented the gasses that were produced. The baked powder was made into a paste and coated onto the lattice grids and then supported in the air. Over time, the powder soaked up all the nitrates in the air and would have to be heat-treated again, but for as long as he could keep it up, he had a chamber with good air where he could sleep and live. And now, he was satisfied that the powder would work in his gas mask as well.

So many questions. What is this powder? Can I make more of it? Will I be able to filter the air of the whole place?

He had a Home of his own now, but a Home with no one living there but him.

The Delense lived and worked here, but then they abandoned it. There was no disaster that he could sense. They had turned off the generator, closed the doors, shut down the perfectly working equipment, and then left, never to return. But the technology was old, for the Delense, much closer to what the U'tanse had been able to create for themselves. Had the Delense invented something new, like the ceramic coatings or the power from space, that had made the whole place obsolete?

They certainly didn't leave me a note. It might be a mystery he'd never solve.

But obsolete or not, this was a valuable resource—a Home that was not under the control of any *Name*.

If I had a few cargo shipments—seeds for human food crops, furniture-making tools, and colonists, we could make the rest. We could have a whole clan out of reach of the Cerik. A free Home!

Of course, grand thoughts were immediately followed by reality. Cerik would not tolerate such a place. They had tracked thousands of Delense ships across the stars to wipe them all out. And this place was hardly a fortress. Its only defense was secrecy. Everyone would have to live like tenners, with constant *ineda* to hide their thoughts from the Cerik. And babies weren't born with the ability to block their thoughts. If there were ever to be a totally free place for U'tanse to live, then it would have to be out of the range of Cerik claws.

And for now, that was an impossibility.

He shook his head. *Live day-to-day. Don't overreach. I still have to catch today's fish.*

28

For a planet with an extensive coastline around its single large continent, there were very few coastal cities. The legendary original City of the Faces was built at the foothills of a large western mountain range where it opened up to vast grasslands. When the ancient clans gathered, often once a generation, it was the ideal place to host normally warring tribes with plenty of room to hunt for food.

In modern times, when the Delense invented rapid transport, the Faces became more common, every two or three years. It was also the perfect time for the Delense to attempt a fatal blow to their Cerik masters—when every *Name* was at ground zero.

It wasn't enough. Seconds and warriors-in-waiting quickly stepped in to fill the power vacuum, and their revenge was complete.

But even with the City of the Faces destroyed, ancient tradition could not be denied. Within ten years, a New City of the Faces was built near the ashes of the first. With no craftsmen Builders to create grand Perches for them, the New City was little more than a collection of tree-houses for many years.

Then the U'tanse arrived. Tenthonad's City Perch was re-made with the finest materials the old Builder factories could supply. Ghader's City Perch was next to be crafted. Soon, even anti-U'tanse clans were happy to pay for an upgrade, as long as it was done out of their sight and completed well before the Faces.

Although no U'tanse were allowed within sight of the City during the Faces, many craftsmen had been all through the place and shared their memories with everyone.

These days, each clan's party was less than twenty-seven. There was the *Name*, perhaps his *Second*, along with the necessary pilots and prey-handlers to insure a comfortable feast.

Kallu was getting a better feel for the new perch. He had it rebuilt after the last Faces. It was sturdy and did not creak like the one before.

There was a clatter of claws.

<Enter.>

Tetedo asked, <Getterin will be demanding payment for the pipes.>

Kallu didn't reply. He had expected that. Right now he was dealing with his own starvation. The Faces was a rotating feast, with each *Name* providing prey for his round. There was honor in devouring everything offered, and often poor clans only had enough prey for some of the *Names*. He wanted to be able to chase down everything quickly, and leave his slower peers to envy him. Hunger gave spice to the chase.

He asked his telepath, <Have you sensed anything from Sakah?>

There had been no response when his guards had killed the Sakah hunters that had killed his U'tanse. Of course there was no honor in claiming a failure, but that didn't mean Sakah's *Name* didn't have some scheme of revenge, waiting to spring on him.

<Nothing yet. Sakah has no telepath, but his *ineda* is strong.>

They discussed all the potential enemies. He valued Tetedo. It was a shame telepaths rarely made good *Seconds*. If there were a battle, he was confident Tetedo would rely on him for protection rather than attack him to take his place.

He just wished he had the same confidence in all his workers.

29

Karl's muscles filled out, his lung capacity returned, and it felt good. Each day he went swimming with a spear he had fashioned in the metal-working shop. A little practice, and he managed to chase down all the fish he needed with disappointing ease. He'd never thought of himself as a hunter—not surrounded by Cerik—but there was something satisfying in a successful hunt. Sometimes, he swam out deeper into the reservoir, careful to avoid the spillway. He just needed to expand his horizons.

There was something down below, corroded and buried in the mud. It was unlike anything he'd seen before. He could only make out its outlines when the sun was high. It was down too deep to reach. When the water ran clean, rather than murky after the rains, he could make out some details. There were fins and what looked like a propeller—one designed for water rather than air. The only thing he could imagine was that it was something like a boat, only designed to move through water, rather than through the air.

It makes sense. If the only way into the burrow is under water, they'd need some enclosed craft to transport things that water would harm. And one of them crashed, or leaked or something.

But it was off limits for now; a puzzle for later. Still, it made him think. Passages from the Book mentioned human boats in the water. It sounded common. But that was another difference between the U'tanse and the Cerik. The Cerik never went into the water.

Almost never. There was that fable about the Far Island.

The Cerik had their Tales, stories of hunters and great leaders. One dealt with the Delense discovering a new island forming off the coast. Some legendary hunter had gone to conquer it, but found only bare lava rocks, with no prey to chase. He ended up eating half his Delense Builders before they brought him home.

They had to make the trip in a water-boat, didn't they? That was before flying boats and space ships.

Maybe his new home was from the same era.

The Far Island still existed, and was now covered with vegetation. Some Cerik had surely taken it over and populated it with runners, now that flight was easy.

It was a shame, really. If the Cerik could be stuck on land, the U'tanse could all escape to the Far Island and live their lives in peace. It was a nice fantasy.

30

The conference room was geared for a long stay. Samuel's hand worked constantly, copying down what the telepaths were saying. The Faces was a time when anything could change, and they had to be ready.

Kallu's feast of *ooro* was well received, with the lizards moving fast enough to keep the other *Names* jumping. There was good humor all around—up until the moment when it was Kallu's time to face the others.

Each *Name*, after his feast, held court. Praises and public complaints, mainly complaints, were aired at this time.

"The boat crash is being mentioned. Kallu is being charged with letting a U'tanse run free."

Samuel snapped, "Who is making the charge?"

"Ghader."

He frowned. "They're pro-U'tanse. Can you read the speaker?"

Ken bar Daniel, the young telepath shook his head. "No. Strong *ineda*. I'm getting this from one of his nameless standing beside him. Kallu is replying."

Lu bar Will, sitting beside him, spoke. "I'm getting a surge of anger from Getterin. They think Ghader is being too easy on Kallu."

Ken said, "Kallu said that he knew the U'tanse was injured and could not survive. When there was concern expressed among the *Names*, he sent U'tanse to search for the body, and they found it."

Lu frowned, "I'm getting a lot of noise. I can't tell from which group. Anger."

"Kallu is shouting. He's describing his plan. There was..." Ken went pale.

Samuel tapped the table. "Report! What is being said?"

Ken nodded. "Kallu said he had a party of his hunters resting at the gates of the U'tanse burrow... I think he means here... Home. If the body wasn't found, they had orders to enter and... *take* the youngest half of the U'tanse colony. <If my Builders harbored wrong thoughts, I'd rather grow a new set who know better.> As an example."

Lu was wresting with the minds she searched. "Some of the anger is turning to hunger. Someone is yelling that it should be done anyway. Another is demanding to see proof of the body."

Samuel wrote furiously.

Ken continued, "Kallu is challenging them. No one has the right to take his property. He dealt with the issue. It's done. If they need proof, ask their own telepaths. He saw the body. The U'tanse know that the body was found."

Abbie moved quietly around the table, doing something that Samuel couldn't sense. But the two telepaths, calmed visibly when she put her hand on each shoulder and handed them a cup of water.

I could use some of that calm. The news is surely out now. Until today, a good percentage of the people here thought of the Cerik as stern, but fair overseers. Maybe not those who worked outside and dealt with them day to day, but those who lived their lives inside and never turned their thoughts outward had little to fear.

The idea that the *Name,* their *Name,* was ready to send his hunters into the corridors to slaughter all the infants and cuties wasn't something many would be able to deal with.

Abbie put her hand on his shoulder. She leaned over and whispered, "I have ordered the nursery workers to go double-shift. Young mothers are starting to panic and we're going to have to calm everyone down, one-on-one."

He nodded. Kallu had his example, even if no one but Tom felt a Cerik claw. If he wanted fear, he had it.

. . .

Karl was outside exploring below the dam when the wave of distress hit him in the stomach. Linda was hurrying through the corridors. She'd abandoned her work in the garden and was racing to the nursery, where little Debbie was playing with the others. She had to *see* Debbie, to hold her.

It took him two minutes to puzzle out her panic. He traced the rumors through other minds. It was the *Name.* Kallu, the one who used to be his master. He was at the Faces, snarling at his peers. His mind was open, making it clear to the Cerik who had telepaths that he had been prepared to sacrifice half his U'tanse if there was a hint that any U'tanse had escaped.

He would have killed Debbie, if he thought I lived.

The wrench in his gut almost brought him to his knees. He looked fearfully toward the sky, fearing a boat would drop down any second and discover him.

One man can't be free, as long as the rest are held hostage.

But how could he change it? How?

. . .

It was two days later, on the last day of the Faces, that Graddik and Getterin agreed to a settlement over the pipes for *ooro* exchange. Kallu had demanded payment for his crashed boat. The Getterin *Name* wanted the original promised *ooro,* that he was now due since Graddik had collected the pipes. Kallu agreed to a half-payment, but Getterin would have to come get the *ooro* using their own boat and water tanks.

Ken reported the news to Samuel. "We should hear about the schedule soon."

Samuel looked over the reports from the *ooro* hatchery. "Not too soon, I hope. We're down to forty percent of the harvestable adults after supplying those for the Faces. Let me know as soon as you hear a date."

He regretted the popularity of their farm-raised *ooro*. They weren't ready for the demand, especially now that all of the *Names* had tasted them. They would have to install more tanks and he would have to recommend that Kallu demand higher prices.

I'm not ready to demand anything of him. Not yet.

It was going to be hard to deal with a master that was plainly ready to kill half your people.

Abbie had reported to him the smaller-scale panics had happened at the other Homes. They had all been living under the illusion that the U'tanse had become valued partners of the Cerik clans. They were valued maybe, but not partners. Valued like the *ooro* he was soon to send off to be devoured.

31

Linda was back at her new job, watering each of the bean plants and checking each for pods ready to harvest. There were also the clawlets that had found their way into the gardens. The tiny little beasts had discovered that they liked earth-crops, and they seemed tolerant of the filtered air. She plucked each one she found from the plants and deposited them into a jar she kept tied to her waist. One of the other gardeners was experimenting with them. If they ate earth-plants, and breathed earth-air, could they be a new food item? The word wasn't in yet. Supposedly they weren't poisonous, but they were too crunchy and bitter to be rolled into the menu just yet.

After that scare the day before, she was more aware than ever how far away the garden was from the living quarters. Home was strung out along the face of a cliff, just under the surface. She looked up to see Samuel walking through the area, heading toward the outside hatchway that led to the *ooro* hatchery. The only worse place to work was there, outside the protected passages among the tanks in the sun.

He looked angry, walking rapidly. She *listened*. Samuel was opaque as ever, but the word was out. A Getterin boat was coming in before it was announced, to pick up the *ooro*.

Barely had she puzzled it out when one of Samuel's assistants came running, chasing him.

"Samuel! The boat is landing at the inside landing bay!"

"What? Did you tell them they needed to load at the tanks?"

"They don't seem to be listening."

Linda could hear the overhead hatches from the next chamber over, where normal shipments were loaded. She glanced at her belt automatically, but she hadn't brought her breathing mask to work today. Normally, it was unnecessary.

That'll be a pain if they take too long. Her way back to the living quarters wound through the landing bay area, and if they still had the overhead hatches opened, she'd get an unwanted dose of outside air.

A psychic shock sent both her and the young assistant reeling. Samuel looked at them, alarmed.

"What happened?"

"Attack... a Cerik just killed Jesse."

Samuel started running. He yelled at his assistant, "You stay here. Notify Denton immediately! If there's a fight, stay out of it and keep the *Name* informed!"

Linda dropped her bag of beans and began running after him. There were attacking Cerik between her and Debbie!

Samuel glanced her way as he paused at the door. "Contact the nursery. Tell them to get everyone in suits and masks. Get them out the front door, even if they don't have a mask."

She didn't understand, but she did as he said. Everyone's mind was in a whirl, as if surrounded by endless screams. Only a few minds were sharp and clear. She forced herself to be one of them.

Daylight poured through the open door. She peered past Samuel, seeing three massive Cerik, each with a large *dul*, a hunting sack, at their waists. One was putting a severed head into his sack.

Samuel whispered, "Stay out of sight. Go hide in the garden."

She shook her head. Debbie was the other direction.

Samuel watched in horror as the three hunters converged on a cluster of people trapped among the shipping carts. He started running, straight toward the boat. Linda didn't hesitate, she followed.

He dashed into the opened door. She followed on his heels.

Inside, there were two Cerik, their faces ripped away, lying on the deck.

Samuel looked at her. "Tell Ken, back in the garden: Unknown hunters have killed the Getterin pilot and picker and took the boat inside. It's a Trojan Horse. Get the information to the *Name*."

She nodded, not understanding any of it. But she sent the words. Ken's thoughts picked it all up.

Samuel triggered the door to close. There was an angry Cerik shout outside.

"We can't keep them out forever. Hang on. I'm going to seal the tunnel to the living area."

"Yes!" She knelt against the wall. Samuel was tapping controls. The boat started making loud warning noises. He grimaced and slapped a control.

The world shook as the boat lurched forward, far too rapidly for the confined space. On the screen, the doorway to the living area zoomed at them. It was deafening and she flew across little space, hitting her head against the wall.

Samuel looked dazed as well, but he reached out his hand to her. "Are you okay?"

She shook her head. "What's going on? Is it the *Name*, coming to kill the babies?"

"No." He looked around the room, hunting for something, anything, to use as a weapon. "Enemies of the U'tanse, maybe. I don't know. We have to hold out until the *Name* sends his hunters to protect *his property*." His voice was bitter, but even now, she couldn't sense a whisper of his thoughts.

"But they can't get through to the nursery?"

"I hope not. We just have to hold out."

There was a roar outside that echoed through the metal walls.

There was a buzz, and the hatch opened up. A nightmare of a face snarled at them. Samuel jumped at him. A Cerik claw caught him in the belly. A second later, another slashed his head from his body.

There was a satisfied roar. Linda watched in horror as the beast cradled Samuel's dead head for a second in his claws and then dropped it in his sack. Then he turned his eyes on her. She screamed.

32

Karl curled up on the ground, shaking in agony, having ridden in her thoughts until her head left her body and her thoughts drifted around a corner, where he couldn't follow. For just an instant, she had sensed him.

Unable to turn away, his thoughts followed the battle through the eyes of Samuel's assistant, watching from the garden door. Workers in the landing bay fought, but even with make-shift weapons, they were no match for Cerik. No spike could penetrate the armored plates beneath their skin. Wounds bubbled and sealed themselves in seconds in the nitrated air. One, a pilot, managed to back the boat away from the opening, but the force of the original impact had collapsed the supports, and the tunnel instantly collapsed, sealing it again.

The leader was angry that he couldn't fill his *dul* with the heads they had. By the time they noticed the passage to the garden, Kallu's forces were arriving. The mauraders piled into the boat, and lurched aloft, only to be blocked by a Graddik boat.

Karl lost interest as Cerik battled Cerik. He wept, his eyes blurry.

How long had he held onto the impossible hope that they might meet again? He'd dreamed, especially the past couple of days, of meeting her again and carrying her off to his new home.

Just a few minutes ago, he'd imagined what she would say as he showed her his newest discovery, this Delense city, a dusty and long-abandoned harbor, plainly designed for the vanished aquatic Builders. Clearly constructed out of sight, invisible even to overhead boats.

"A treasure trove," he'd imagined telling her. Rooms full of round platters marked with Delense script. If there was any place that held the secrets of the Delense, this was it. Much of it was filled with Delense gadgetry—powered down, but maybe functional.

For just an instant, his heart had been full of hope. A secret fortress, where the U'tanse could gain power in secret, where a true plan for freedom might be created.

Hope was now dashed. Linda was gone. He had no reason to live.

Senseless cries of thousands of U'tanse filled his head, too many to allow any clear thought. He absorbed their pain, not trying to understand. He struggled to bring Linda's face to memory. He'd felt her thoughts alone for so long now, without seeing her. It was hard to focus.

But there was a whisper. **Mommy!** And as if he opened his eyes, he could see Linda's face again.

He zeroed in on little Debbie's cries. She was being hurried across the open ground, getting away from the battle cries. Strong hands pushed her along, to safety.

Okay. For her, I'll live.

Festival Girl

1

"Debbie! You get in here!"

She ducked her head and glanced down the corridor where Pulu and Betty were waiting for her with pity on their faces. She knew it was over. Her best buddies, late cuties like she was, knew it too.

She sighed. "Yes, Scar. I'm coming."

Go on without me. I'll get away next time.

They turned and left, heading off to the pool to watch the boys bathe.

Scar was taking off his normal hand. Actually, she didn't know which one she liked least. The one with a right hand and fingers was pretty creepy, especially since it still looked like it was carved out of *dlathe* wood. At least it didn't make her wince like his metal blade hand.

He grinned, sensing her thoughts or maybe just reading the expression on her face, "But I like my claw best."

She shook her head. "I know you do, but then, you like Cerik, too."

He chuckled, and it was deep in his broad chest. "It does no good hating them. We're both living here on this world."

"You killed one."

He nodded, thoughtfully. "But that makes no real difference. It was in battle."

She didn't pursue it. They'd had this argument for years. The same attack on Home that had left her with no mother had given Denton bar Simon the opportunity of his dreams, to battle with Cerik, against Cerik. He'd been reporting to Kallu, the *Name* of the Graddik clan when the telepathic alert spiked in his head—the U'tanse Home was being attacked! Kallu had collected every available hunter in sight. Denton had stepped up to join them and Kallu had let him come.

In the melee that erupted when they arrived, Denton had jammed a sharp-pointed, metal saw blade into a broom-handle sized pipe and attacked one of the head-collectors.

No U'tanse had ever studied their masters closer than he had during his years stationed at the Graddik Perch. He'd observed the way they moved, both with his eyes and his clairvoyant senses. He'd watched a dozen fatal and near fatal battles from the sidelines. He'd speculated about some weak spots between their subdermal plates—even chatted about it with his nameless Cerik co-workers.

Years of speculation was resolved in thirty seconds of real battle. Cerik claws and musculature were built for a powerful sideways slash. Their instinctive defensive moves were meant to divert those slashes or at least redirect them to tough, protected areas of the body.

His home-made spear, coming straight in, penetrated a weak spot on the attacker's chest, the serrated edge of the saw holding it in place even after the powerful Cerik knocked the shaft free. With hate-filled eyes, he slashed at Denton, taking off his hand at the wrist.

But the saw blade kept the wound open wide, and in spite of the bubbling and rapidly congealing blood, the Cerik weakened rapidly. He hesitated and tried to brush the blade out of his chest. His claws were superb weapons, but inferior tools. With a bellow of surprise and anger, he fell.

A few feet away from where he collapsed, Denton struggled to bind a leather strap around his arm to keep from bleeding to death himself.

Soon, the attackers were all down, and Kallu bellowed his victory. Through the pain, Denton wondered what would happen to him—a slave who had killed a master.

But Kallu was in a good mood. He called him *kede*, a Broken Hunter, and collected his other hunters and left to celebrate.

. . .

Scar rubbed the stub of his wrist. Debbie was getting harder to control by the day, and he wasn't really the best parent for her. They had bonded in the days after the attack when she was tiny. He was healing from his lost hand, and she was the first orphan child the Home had ever dealt with. Her father had been lost on an expedition, and then her mother, taken in that attack. There were several volunteers to be her substitute mother, and at loose ends, having lost his job at Kallu's perch, he volunteered to be her father.

He had three sons, but no biological daughters. Living alone among the Cerik for so long, he had fewer children than most. He wasn't experienced, and Debbie was a trial—especially so with her studies slipping.

He hadn't always been there for her either. Twice, he tried to go back to Kallu and resume his job. That's why he had the claw made. Cerik slash at each other all the time, and he wanted to be one of the crew. The first time he came back to heal a slash across his chest, the people started calling him Scar. He liked it, and didn't take the extra healing effort to erase the mark.

The second time he returned, missing an ear and with a matching slice across his cheek, Howard and Abbie had a long talk with him as he healed. He agreed to spend his time Home, training other men who would be working closely with the Cerik.

He looked at Debbie, pulling out her study materials. She didn't hide the a sullen look on her face.

I'm going to miss her.

...

Debbie heard his snores, and calmly set aside her memory sheets. Pre-Arrival history had nothing to do with her. She kept her thoughts cool and calm. *Ineda* lessons had come in very handy.

She slipped out into the corridors and walked quickly toward the pool. Several adults gave her the eye, but privacy rules kept them quiet. That was one thing about Graddik Home rules that she was grateful for. She knew of other Homes that had a more communal parenting environment. From what she heard, the strictest adults took it on themselves to make all the cuties toe the line.

Pulu must have been listening for her.

Debbie, hurry up. Alex bar Ira is thinking about Melody REAL HARD.

She sampled his thoughts lightly, briefly. Oh, was he ever ready!

But she firmed up her own barricades. Scar had not ever had kind thoughts about 'emotional leeches' he called them.

He just doesn't understand. He's old. He lived in a different era.

Back in the 'good old days', supposedly everyone was happy to let their elders give the girls a list of good gene stock, and the boys were happy to do their duty when asked.

She doubted it, and if so, then they must have been a passionless lot.

Not me. When I come of age, I won't let anyone tell me which boy. I'll find the right one. Someone who feels about me the way I'll feel about him.

The inspirational stories she'd been raised with never sat right with her. Okay, she could see that they were a colony of prey in a world of predators, and that they needed to work together to survive. Yes, they all had to take orders from the *Name* to earn their protection.

But I'm not going to raise babies just so they can be sold off at a profit to the next Cerik who wants them.

Her thoughts were interrupted as she entered the pool area and spied three of her friends whispering together near the clothing rack.

When she was close enough, she asked, "Where are they?"

Pulu pointed. "Over there, just past the rock outcropping. I hope Melody says yes. She's been trying to find the right sperm for months now."

Debbie could feel the excitement leaking through the *ineda* of her group. She just hoped her block was stronger.

They could all strip and swim out to get closer, where they could watch, but they'd been caught before, and she still hadn't worked off her extra gardening chores. She was content to wait, and sample the thoughts from beyond the rock.

Melody had only been with them for a year and a half. She'd signed up for a pregnancy, and as luck would have it, she pulled a tenner slot in the lottery. That meant another month of classes on how to pick the right genes, and by then she was out of the mood.

I would have made a good tenner. I like math and science. Unfortunately, she was a girl and no girl was ever given the chance to be born a tenner. Nothing was fair in this world. All women were expected to have babies and needed the psychic genes.

Waves of excitement and anticipation were peaking from the hidden couple. Other eyes started turning in that direction as well. Sex was never a secret. Betty was breathing hard, her eyes glistening.

The peak came quickly, and then not too much later, a wave of disappointment. A minute or so later, a male body began swimming away from behind the rock. Melody was still in her trance, making her decisions about which sperm were to be killed off.

Pulu sighed. "That was a short one. I would have thought…"

Debbie was distracted from the whispers as a strong thought, marked for her, caught her attention.

Debbie bar Karl, please come to the conference room. It's time we had a talk.

"Abbie," she whispered, frightened.

Betty asked, "What?"

"Abbie just called me. I've got to go, now!"

The other two girls looked at each other fearfully. If Abbie caught Debbie, then they'd be next.

2

Howard bar Jonah found Abbie resting at the conference table, her head resting on her hand. He rapped on the table gently.

She jerked. "Sorry. Dozed off. It's been a long day. Any news?"

He sat down beside her. "Why don't you go on to your bed? There's no need to work long hours at this."

She smiled. "Hey, I'm wrinkled, but I'm not senile yet. Besides I've got one of the girls coming for an interview—as soon as she builds up enough nerve to show. I caught her slurking with her friends down at the pool."

"Late cutie?" He sighed. "I guess it's to be expected."

She chuckled. "Like you weren't watching down at the pool at her age?"

He looked affronted. "Well, yes, but I'm a guy."

She poked her index finger down on the table. "And that's why I'm still in charge of people, and you run everything else."

He nodded thoughtfully. "That reminds me. We have the *Name's* approval for the Festival."

"You don't sound happy."

"The numbers. Minus three."

Abbie shrugged. "He's doing it again. It's pretty clear he doesn't want the Home population to grow beyond what it is already."

"Yes, but it's a bad trend."

"Every colony loses people. That's how new colonies are formed, after all."

He shook his head. "Not this way. Not by a constant drain of our young girls. We're already the first Home with more males than females."

"Don't worry about that. The first few generations selected for gender in births. We could too. But we'll discuss this later. She's approaching."

...

Debbie hadn't been in that area of the Home before, at least not that she could remember. She'd passed by the turn-off to the conference room regularly, on her way to the gardens, or to go visit the *ooro*, but she'd never gone this way.

It was strange. The corridors changed from the round tubes she was familiar with, to square, with rectangular doorways. The walls began to have decorations. There were maps and charts, some of them the first she'd seen, outside of examples in her studies. There was a closed door, labeled Conference Room.

She hesitated, then reached for the door.

"Come on in," came the voice from the other side.

She worked the latch and entered.

"Close the door behind you, please."

Debbie tried to keep her composure. Abbie was the oldest person she'd seen, and she couldn't get over the lady's wrinkled face and the veins in her hands. After a moment, she couldn't hold her gaze on her eyes and looked down at her own hands.

Her voice was old too. "I knew your mother—Linda."

"Oh?" She was puzzled. She had expected some kind of lecture.

"Yes, when she decided to change from carpentry to gardening."

"She was a carpenter?" Debbie knew little about her mother. She had heard that she worked in the garden—that's why she was at the wrong place when the Cerik attacked—but little else.

Abbie smiled. "Oh, yes." She stood, and Debbie could tell that it was an effort for her. "Come with me."

They left the conference room and walked down to another room, where three men were working over charts. They paused and watched as Abbie went over to the large rack where the books and scrolls were stored. The top shelf was too high for her to see, and the shelves covered the whole wall. "This is your mother's work. She built this about a year before you were born."

Debbie moved closer and fingered the fine-grained wood. She'd never spent any time paying attention to how furniture was made, and now, when she looked at the way the shelves attached to the verticals, it looked like it must have taken a lot of work to fit it all together.

"I know that she built quite a few pieces around the Home, but I couldn't tell you which ones were hers." Abbie watched Debbie's serious examination of her mother's work for a couple of minutes, then nodded to the men and escorted her back to the conference room.

When they were seated, Abbie said, "Your parents were skilled workers. I heard that your father was gifted at complex projects. It's one of the reasons he was often sent on expeditions.

"What I need to know now is what your skills are. Debbie, what are you good at?"

She was caught a little off-guard. "Ah. I don't know." She was well aware that she was behind in her studies. That's why Scar was constantly pestering her to work on it. "I passed Women's Biology."

Abbie's mouth gave a hint of a smile. "But in spite of your recent interest in sex, you don't have any strong desire to have a baby."

The floor dropped out of her composure. *She knows!* Any hope that she had kept her feelings secret was gone.

Nobody would understand. Scar certainly wouldn't understand. He was all duty. And a woman's first duty was to have babies. Even Abbie, who ran the whole place, had her babies when she was young. Everyone back to the Arrival had a duty, to keep the U'tanse alive.

"I see you understand."

Debbie looked at her fearfully. She whispered, "I'm not of age yet."

She nodded. "We all understand that. But you have to understand that certain things must be done, whether we are ready for them or not. But let's forget about babies for just a moment. I asked what you were good at, and

I wasn't asking about how well you'll be as a mother. None of us knows that ahead of time.

"I want you to tell me what you know about the Festivals."

Festivals? She felt a twinge of fear. *What does that have to do with me?* A quote from the memory sheets came to mind. "Um. It's a regular thing where different Homes trade people, so that no Home will become in-bred. There's an East Coast Festival and another one here on the West Coast, and every ten years, there's a Grand Festival where people come from all over. Melody showed up recently from some other Home. Lots of the women, or their mothers, were from other places."

Abbie tapped the table. "And another Festival is scheduled in a couple of months. Four of our girls will leave to find new lives in other Homes. Of our young women and late cuties, there are six that are eligible to participate. You are one of those six."

She leaned a little closer, her face serious and stern. "So, Debbie, I'm asking you again. What are you good at, other than your genetic stock? What skill do you have that will make you more valuable to keep with us, rather than one of the others?"

3

Scar walked through the corridors to the landing bay. There was no boat there today, and it looked empty, although there were people moving around, packing and unpacking shipments.

He smiled at his first impression. *Just spoiled. The only time I'm here is when I'm going some place, or returning.* Not many people had spent as much time away from Home as he had. Everyone had their place, and his had been unusual. Not that he would have traded his experiences for that of the engineers or the farmers or the administrators. It took all kinds to make the Home work.

Next to stacks of fresh-cut *kel* logs, he found the airlock to the gardens. Someone had propped the garden-side door open. He knew enough to know that wasn't safe, so he kicked the prop aside and let the door close behind him.

The gardens were one of the largest chambers in the Home. It had high ceilings like the landing bay, but these were crisscrossed with light bars to simulate daylight. And not just regular daylight, but the blue-tinted light of the human home world. There rows of tall corn stalks, and square patches of green wheat, not yet ripe. The Graddik's Home was lucky to have so much space for gardening. They even exported some of their produce to other Homes in exchange for U'tanse-manufactured electrical motors, paper rolls and other items.

Farming was the most common task of the Home-bound, which meant most of the workers he saw were women.

He walked slowly through the rows, until he saw Debbie down on her hands and knees, elbows deep in the soil, culling out the roots left over from some previous crop.

She didn't look his way, but grumbled, "Don't just stand there glaring at me. I'm working here."

He toyed with the idea of getting down on his knees with her and helping, but he saw the mud dripping from her hands and the impulse passed.

"I'm not glaring. I was worried about you."

She ripped out a long root and stuffed it in her bag. "You know, don't you? I've asked around. Parents are told when girls are considered for the Festival."

He nodded. "Yes, I was informed."

She glared up at him. "Then why didn't you tell them I wasn't ready to go?"

Scar sighed, considering what to tell her. "I guess I wasn't ready to lie about it."

"What?"

"About a month ago, the committee contacted me and asked about you."

"Five weeks! You've know about this for five weeks and you didn't even hint about it!"

He grumbled. "If you recall, it was about then that I started checking up on your studies. You need to be as prepared as possible."

"You don't even care that they're taking me away, do you?"

"Of course, I care. I'll miss you."

"You should have told them no!" She stared down at her fingers as she dug black out of her nails. "You could have stopped them."

"No, Debbie. I couldn't. The pick is up to the committee. All I could do is tell them about you."

"What did you tell them? That I'd just love to be shipped off to some other Home and make babies for their young men?"

He made an effort to keep his voice low. "No. I told them that you were strong and independent." He sighed. "And that's why you're sure to be picked."

"Why?"

When she looked his way, he had trouble meeting her shiny eyes, and the tear-marked face.

"Maybe… maybe they would make a rare exception to keep an eligible girl from the Festival if she had a particularly valuable skill—someone who was likely to invent a new product, or someone who had already found their place in a strong working team. Certainly not someone who just worked hard in the gardens.

"No, the real exceptions come when a girl is too weak to take the stress. No one wants to send a girl to Festival who will promptly curl up and die of homesickness. The Festival is for the good of us all, and not for just the strong ones like you. I've known you'd leave for some Festival since you were little. You had to put up with the loss of your birth parents, and none of us volunteers were ever the rock you needed. I'm sorry for my failures, but it has left you strong. I don't have any fears for your future. You'll do fine."

He was on the verge of too much emotion himself. He turned and walked away. He wasn't any good at that kind of stuff.

Debbie watched him until he was out of sight. She brushed at her face with her upper arm and sniffed. After a moment, she pulled a small pouch out of her belt sack and filled it carefully with fresh clean soil.

4

It was the day.

Pulu held her right hand. Betty held her left, and carried her travel bag.

Debbie was still getting used to her new white woman's outfit with trousers. She was still two months from being of age, but the committee had decided to send her off in style. She was afraid to touch anything that might get it dirty.

Pulu said, "We could still make a run for it. I know a place behind the looms where you could hide out of sight."

"They'd find me."

"Well, yes, but it would take time, and you might miss your boat."

Betty shook her head. "I don't know why you'd try to hide. This is a great opportunity. Just think of all the boys at your new Home. You know how they all drool over the new girls who arrive from Festival. That'll be you in just a few days. I wish I could go."

Debbie had done everything she could think of in the three weeks since she'd been told she was selected, including checking her family tree. It was clear why she was on the list. She had one great-grandmother that had arrived from Festival, but the others all were born here. Betty, whose own mother was from the Tenthonad Home, wasn't really a candidate.

Several people called out good wishes as they walked through the corridors. Up ahead, she could see Omary and her own circle of friends making their way toward the landing bay. Omary and Henna were both more popular than she was. She was grateful that Betty and Pulu had stuck with her.

As they entered the bay, she saw Clara going up the ramp. That made her the late one. *Oh, well. Late and the only cutie.* She only had an instant of self-pity before the crowd of adults that were there to see them off moved in and gave their own good-byes and words of advice. It was a swirl of faces and she was so awash in voiced and projected feelings of goodwill that she could barely make sense of them all. Betty forced the handle of her travel bag into her hand, and she was abruptly walking up the ramp into the boat.

You look wonderful, Debbie. Smile for the boys. The parting thought echoed in her head.

She didn't have time to linger and get a last look at her friends. The girls weren't the only passengers, and she skittered to the side as she saw the Cerik pilot snarling at the lot of them. Omary patted a spot beside her on a bench.

She sat. Omary leaned closer. "Count your blessings. You didn't have to deal with the boys."

Debbie nodded wisely. She'd heard. Once a woman was chosen for Festival, she wasn't supposed to get pregnant by any of the local boys. That didn't stop some of the friskier ones from making their last play at forbidden fruit.

The boat was packed. There were the four of them, Howard the Home's Leader, and a half-dozen others, men and women, all concerned with the crates of goods that they were taking to the Festival.

Howard was at the doorway, watching the pilot. He said, "Hang on, there'll be a slight shift as we lift."

She gripped Omary's hand, and they lifted off. It wasn't bad, but it was disturbing. She hadn't ridden anything other than a garden cart in her whole life. There was another shift, and although she couldn't see anything outside, there was a change in the light, coming from up front where the Cerik pilot controlled the boat.

We're outside.

She smiled at Omary. The woman, really only a year older than she was, smiled back, but her eyes were teary. The emotions leaking from her were full of deep sadness at leaving.

Why don't I feel that way?

She reached out and connected briefly with Scar, who had not come to the boat to see her off.

I'm off!

He was sad, but trying to restrain it. **You'll have a wonderful experience.**

And she found herself agreeing. **Yes!**

They separated.

She forced herself to breathe deeply. It was all too exciting for words.

. . .

Howard leaned against the wall and held a scroll. Just moments after announcing that the trip would take another hour, he began reading:

"Abe, the Father of us all, instituted the Festival when the very first new colony of U'tanse was created. When the *Name* of Tenthonad finally agreed to sell a three-fold group of his new Builders to form a separate Home, under the control of the *Name* of the Kakil, certain rules were established that must be followed by all Cerik and all U'tanse.

"No colony would be established with less than a three-fold, that is twenty-seven adults. All colonists would owe their allegiance to the new *Name* and forsake any duties to their previous Home.

"In addition, a Festival was established, to be held no less than every three-fold lunar months, where females of bearing years would be exchanged among the Homes.

"It is binding on all exchanged women that they will owe their allegiance to the new *Name* and forsake any duties to their previous Home, just as if they were part of a new colony."

...

Debbie had read the history of the Festival herself, once it had become real for her. There was a lot more to it than this change of allegiance to the new *Name*, but the Cerik were firm that it be made clear to all.

If she understood it right, the Cerik didn't really care about the females, other than as breeding stock, so this idea of keeping the breeding pool mixed was reasonable to them.

She looked at the two women who were coming along for other Festival duties. It hadn't occurred to her that there was a chore that would let a woman travel outside the Home. All the expeditions that she'd heard about were always done by men who went to exchange goods with other Cerik clans or repair Delense factory machines. The idea of seeing other places was a new, exciting idea. What would it take to be chosen to be one of them? She'd need to find out.

Omary whispered to her, "Do you know which Home we go to?"

Debbie shrugged, "I think we go to a separate Festival place, several Homes meet and the exchanges are done there. I don't think it's decided yet."

She had a worried look, "So, we may not all go together?"

"That's right."

"Oh." She looked even more abandoned than before. "I thought we'd all be sisters together in the new place."

Debbie didn't know what to do. She took her hand. "Who knows what will happen then? But we can be sisters now."

Omary managed a little smile.

She's like a little cutie. It was a shock. Omary was the older. She'd been of age for months now, a woman. She may have already had sex.

It was a little dizzying, even more so than the shifting and swaying as they traveled through the air. *I'm still a cutie, in spite of the dress.*

So much was made of a woman coming of age, even more so than the men. She'd thought that something magical would happen, like switching on a light, or the first time her *ineda* exercises actually worked. There was all that training on how to manage her bleeding and how to prevent a *random* birth. For the past three years it had seemed like the Home had concentrated all its efforts on making her ready for coming of age. There was a day, even marked on the calendar, when it was all supposed to come together for her, and she'd be a woman.

And yet, Omary beside her had been through all of that, and she was acting like a mid-year cutie, in need of comfort.

Will anything really happen to me, when I come of age?

5

"We'll be landing in five minutes." Howard smiled, trying to put them at ease. "There is no indoor landing bay like we had at Home. Because of that, we will need to walk a short distance through the outside air. I want you all to pull out your breathing masks. Go ahead and put them on."

Debbie had been pleased when she saw her very own mask in her travel bag that morning. She'd played with Scar's mask since she was little, but since she never went outdoors herself, she'd never needed a mask of her own. She slipped it on easily. It smelled like leather, rather than like Scar, and it fit her head shape. Scar's had never really fit.

Omary was having problems with hers.

"Here, let me show you." Debbie turned the mask right side up, and showed her where the straps adjusted for a snug, but not too tight, fit.

"Thanks." Her voice was a little muffled, and her eyes were a little frightened.

"No problem. It's okay if it's not a perfect fit. A little outside air isn't going to kill you. Even if you didn't make the effort to repair the damage, a little exposure would heal itself in a day or so."

It was what Scar had told her a long time ago.

They landed and the Cerik pilot growled at them. She knew a little of the language. She hadn't studied, but Scar used it all the time. She whispered to Omary, "He's just telling us that we should unload."

Omary nodded. "He sounds so angry."

"They always growl that way."

They all stood and Howard led them out into the bright daylight.

None of them had ever been outdoors before. Henna stumbled at the edge of the door, but Howard caught her arm. Debbie linked hands with Omary. It was hard not to stare at the world around them. An unexpected surge of panic threatened to choke her up. She shoved it away.

Howard led them down the ramp. "Step carefully. The ground isn't quite level."

Omary mumbled through her mask, "It's so big."

Debbie only nodded.

There were three boats on a leveled patch of soil, with room for several more. Off in the distance, the ground went on, seemingly forever, with tiny little trees in the distance, blending off into a brown haze. In the other direction was a mountain, just like the drawings in her worksheets. Only this was real and alive, with trees and water flowing down a channel in the distance.

Even the air was alive, blowing steadily from the side. She could smell something, like in the garden. Some plant was scenting the air with a sharp tang, but she didn't recognize it.

And the big red sun... It was hard to look away. There were patterns. Dots and streaks. It was all too much.

Howard came to join them. "Don't look at the sun too much. In just a moment, we'll be back inside, and you eyes will have to adjust to the dimmer light. Now follow me."

They walked together towards the large, wide double-doors extending outward from the cliff face. Debbie glanced back, and saw the others moving the carts out of the boat.

Off to the side of the big, windowed doors, there was a smaller hatchway only wide enough for people and carts. They headed for it. Another man was there to greet them.

"We're entering through the airlock to keep the filtered air from getting mixed with the outside contaminants. We'll be entering in groups of three."

Not in a hurry to leave the outside, she moved to the back of the line to take the second group. Omary looked her way, but was eager to get inside.

Quickly enough, they had all cycled their way through the small intermediate chamber.

"Greetings to the West Coast Festival!" A large, pleasant woman was there to take them by the hand as they exited the airlock.

Inside was a huge expanse, with both overhead lights and daylight entering through the double-door's large glass windows. It was larger than the gardens of Home, but this one was open floorspace, with several groups putting up tables and small tents. At least a dozen dark, open corridors led deeper into the mountain.

"First order of business is to take off your masks and put them back into your travel bags. Every Festival, we have some girl who loses her mask, and it's very embarrassing for her when it's time to leave and the whole group has to hunt this big place for it."

There was more information, and Debbie listened halfheartedly. This new place was fascinating to see. She didn't worry about missing the information. What could they do to her? Send her back Home?

There were people watching her as well. There was a woman with a green dress that sported a wide collar. She was watching all of them and taking notes on a flat slate. There was one man in decidedly worn clothes that was leaning against a wall, watching with a grin. He noticed her watching him and gave her a slight nod. She returned it.

Both of them were locked down under *ineda*.

I guess if they're making their decisions on who to take, it makes sense to start now. I guess the girl who's not paying attention gets marked off.

She wasn't really certain what the decision was based upon. If she were in charge, she'd assign numbers to the girls' ancestors and make up a magic formula to choose which ones were likely to share the least genes—not that she was sure how to make such a formula.

But as long as they had a choice, giving points for behavior made sense too. You were likely to have to live with the person you chose for years and years.

Not my job.

Willfully, she turned her attention back to this not-quite-a-Home.

On her second look around, she noticed one of the larger tunnels seemed to be blocked with rubble. Quake damage that they'd never gotten around to fixing?

"And now, I'm sure you'd like to see the rooms where you'll be staying for the next three days. The girls who arrived earlier from the Sanassan Home will show you the way.

A group of six girls were waiting for them, with the slightly superior look of those who had already heard the introduction speech.

Six from Sanassan? Are they a bigger Home?

It hadn't occurred to her that each colony might be different. In the back of her mind, one Home was probably just a duplicate of the others. Didn't they all eat the same food and live under the same rules?

Debbie picked out a girl at random and walked up to her.

"Hello, I'm Debbie bar Karl."

She nodded. "And I'm Sandra bar Abe. Not the original Abe."

Debbie chuckled. "I bet you say that a lot."

She sighed. "It's so automatic, I don't even think about it anymore. But I'm going to ignore any boys with famous names!"

Sandra was one month younger than she was, for which Debbie was grateful. She'd hate to be the youngest one in the whole group.

They picked out one of the sleeping chambers close to the main room, and close to where Sandra had unpacked her bag. The room was bare except for a bed and blanket. No one lived there. Sandra told her that when her group arrived, they were still filtering the air so she had to wear her mask for a couple of hours.

"Meals are announced, and it'll be a while. Tell me about Graddik Home."

6

Outside, new boats arrived. Workers set up cooking stations, and began haggling with their counterparts, trading spices and foodstuffs that were rare in one Home and common in another. New girls in their white Festival outfits arrived and mixed with the earlier ones. The most common conversation was, "What is your Home like?"

The second most common question was, "Are the boys cute?"

The only idle person in the place, the man with the shirt that had an open seam and was frayed around the edges, watched the proceedings with barely disguised glee. Late in the afternoon, the men he had marked as the Leaders of their respective Homes came to greet each other and share drinks from the kiosks. He tested their thoughts, but every one of them had unbreakable *ineda*. That was to be expected.

When the six of them began to move as a group towards one of the lit corridors, he picked up his bag and followed. One of the Home Leaders glanced back his way, but said nothing, until they reached a conference room.

He turned. "I'm sorry, but this is a closed meeting."

The worn stranger nodded. "I am aware that this is a meeting between the Leaders of the respective Homes. Everything said behind those doors is verbal only, and forever secret among you. That is why I request to make a statement, inside, with the doors closed."

"Who are you? What colony are you from?"

He smiled broadly. "I'm afraid that information must wait until I am behind those doors."

The men inside looked at each other. One, just taking his seat at the far side of the table, said, "We have a great deal of work to do, but we can give you five minutes or so."

The others were willing to go along with the eldest Leader of them. The stranger followed them in and closed the door behind him.

"Go ahead and make your statement."

"Thank you, Will bar Matthew of Ghader."

He addressed them all. "Respected Leaders, since the Arrival, all of Humanity has been composed of the different colonies under the control of the *Name* of various clans. There have been a few excursions, where selected U'tanse have gone on short trips, only to return when their task was completed.

"The Festival, in its turn, has evolved from a simple exchange of young women, designed to keep us a unified people, into something much more. It has developed into a marketplace among the U'tanse, trading goods that are particular to our people. Outside, in the main area, I saw workers from Sanassan trade leather goods for bales of woven goods from Graddik. I saw a cluster of cooks gather around the Kakil tables as a new spice was unveiled. Foods, materials, and of course gossip, are freely exchanged or haggled over. This is another way we have been able to stay one people even though the vast majority of us are unable to travel and a majority never leave the Home of their birth."

He gestured to the seated men, "And if there is a leadership of the U'tanse as a whole, it is here, in these secret meetings, spoken in English, by men who have developed the tightest *ineda* on the planet, behind tightly closed soundproof doors where what they speak cannot be repeated by others.

"Separate Homes connect in a common culture through the Festivals. And although it was designed by the Father of us all, based on a human culture long before the Arrival, it is marvelous that it is in may ways similar to the Faces time of the Cerik."

He shook his head. "But apart from that, we are all alike. We live in Homes, all designed after a common model, all started with twenty-seven brave colonists, and all served by the Festival."

He held up one finger. "With a noticeable exception." There was a puzzled look on a couple of faces.

"The Festival itself is different. Here we are in a habitat similar to the Homes—after all, they were all originally Delense cities. But there are no gardens, no nursery, no workspaces, no corrals, not even a landing bay for the Cerik to land their boats. And the people here—this isn't really an expedition either—we're all from various Homes. The Festival is an exception to all the rest, and the only one—until now."

That caused a stir.

A voice asked, "Who are you?"

He bowed back, "Respected Leader Hannibal bar John of Kakil, I must, for now, identify myself only as Aaron.

"I am a representative of a working group of U'tanse similar in many ways to the Festival itself. Some of us are from one Home, and others from another. I am not allowed to identify which. Secrecy is highly valued. *Names* will be quiet for their own political reasons and even Respected Leaders of involved Homes are not allowed to reveal what they know.

"Unlike the Festival that comes and goes within days, we will exist for a long time, certainly for years. Due to our secrecy, our lines of supplies are limited." He held up an arm and tugged at the frayed cloth. "As you can see, we are poor on the basics. Our diet is limited. We can't produce our own clothes. We aren't a *colony*. We have no nursery, for example, although our people are both men and women. We are all workers at this secret task.

"We beg to be allowed to participate in the Festival marketplace."

Will of Ghader asked, "How did you get in here in the first place?"

"I walked in the front door. No one expected anyone but you and your groups, so everyone expected I was from one of the other parties. But of course, being here is one thing. Trading is another."

Quinn bar Scott of Dalla frowned. "How can we tell if what you say is true? This might actually be a scheme by one Home to gain resources from another."

Aaron nodded. "Sadly, with secrecy comes the possibility of lies. You already have that problem among you. Leaders have the most secrets to bear."

Hannibal asked, "What is it you want? What is worth sacrificing your secrecy?"

Aaron shook his head. "I'm hardly sacrificing secrecy in this room, speaking with the strongest locked minds on the planet. But as to what I want, this Festival? Ideally, a few bolts of cloth, seed grain and whatever foods I can carry, and hopefully, one of the Festival women who has shown that's she's more interested in gardening than in bearing children."

Will fingered his beard. "Cloth, and seeds should be no problem. Turning one of the women in our care over to a totally unknown group—that is not a light thing, not a light thing at all. We will have to discuss this among ourselves. Come by tomorrow and we will talk again."

Aaron bowed, "Certainly. However, let me leave this with you, as a token of my group's intent. I was mentioning trade, not gifts."

He pulled his bag up from the floor and removed six thin cylinders in leather pouches, lining them up on the table. He passed one to Hannibal to his right. "This is a book, written on a thin metal scroll—we don't have a paper supply."

He pointed, "Remove the strap and unroll it carefully. The edge is sharp and can cut." He handed the rest of them around. "They are all identical."

Hannibal gasped. "This is… Delense script?"

"Yes, it's a Delense to English dictionary—only five hundred icons as yet. The work is still underway." The room filled with excitement. In the generations since the Arrival, the Delense written script was a persistent enigma. The Cerik had never been interested in any script. Their minds couldn't even grasp such things, and the Delense had never left many examples of it around.

Quinn asked, "What *metal* is this? How did you get sheets of it?"

Aaron smiled, "It is pure copper, and we can make large rolls of it. And a warning, it will corrode quickly in the outside air. Keep it in the pouch. At the bottom is a filtration chemical—not the usual one we use for gas masks—a different one."

He picked up his bag, and nodded. "Until tomorrow, then." He walked out, closing the door behind him.

7

"What is this?" Debbie mumbled, in between sweet chewy bites from the bowl. It was evening, and when the outside light started to fade from the large windows on the door, the place seemed to change too. It felt more like a Home with all the light coming from the light bars hung from the ceiling.

Gabrielle looked her way, "Oh, that's *janji* fish in the stew. It's my favorite."

Debbie nodded. "Thanks." Gabrielle was from Ghader. Ghader has *janji* fish. She noted it down in her mental list. She chewed again. It actually wasn't bad.

The meals were being supplied by each Home in a rotation. *Showing off their best, I'd bet.* She wondered what Graddik would serve when her Home's turn came around.

There were about thirty of them, all in white, seated at a common table. The rumors were that this arrangement wouldn't last. Some of the girls, before they came here, had step by step information about what to expect from the girls that had been to the previous Festival. Debbie had thought about asking, but she'd never gotten close enough to the new girls at Graddik.

She looked over at a smaller table where the workers were eating. The man in ragged clothes seemed to be a lively center of attention. His clothes didn't seem to bother him. It would bother her. What Home did he come from? There weren't any others dressed like him. Did non-participating Homes send observers or something?

The woman who greeted them when they arrived stood up on a small platform and spoke, loudly enough to attract attention away from the tableside chatter.

"Good evening. I won't take too much of your time. I just wanted to let you know what to expect over the next day and a half."

She held up three colored cloths, draped over her arm. "Over the course of the remaining time, each of you will be approached by a representative of your new Home, and as you are selected, you will be given a sash like these to wear. Each Home has its own pace at choosing people, so don't worry if you aren't one of the first."

The girl sitting next to her whispered, "Tomorrow, they'll separate the tables so the chosen girls will sit with their new sisters."

There was more of the speech, telling them when the events would be taking place the next day. Other than managing their own beds, there were no chores for the girls, just time to get to know each other, and a chance to visit the workers of the other Homes to get an idea of how the other U'tanse colonies lived.

The speaker sat down, and Debbie made sure that she had eaten all that was available to her. The *janji* stew was really quite delicious.

The girls were already wondering what it meant to be chosen early or later. "How about you, Debbie?"

"It makes no difference to me." She even meant it. The picking and choosing was done by others. She had no say in the matter. Her only chance had been back at Home when Abbie asked her what she was good at, and that had fallen through.

The Festival was an ordeal for all of them, but someone had gone to a lot of trouble to make it pleasant. So, she'd eat the good food and enjoy the pretty new dress and appreciate the opportunity to see what the other Homes were like. If she had to cry, she'd do it in her bed, where no one would watch. And she kept her *ineda* up.

That strange man kept his mind closed all the time as well. She *listened* to the conversation over at the workers' table from time to time. The man called Aaron loved to talk, but didn't seem to talk about himself much. He must have been on a lot of expeditions, because he was describing the differences in the East Coast mountains and the ones near the West Coast.

"The quakes are bad everywhere, but because the mountains near the West Coast are taller and younger, the sides are steeper and the avalanches are more noticeable. That's partly why there were fewer Cerik clans in the interior, even though there are hunting plains in among the ridges. It's harder to build a perch that will stand the constant quakes. There are several abandoned Cerik cities, villages really, in the mountain valleys. With the Delense gone, their support system collapsed and they died out or were absorbed by the other clans."

Something about what she heard made her think about Scar. She was suddenly horribly lonely.

Making contact with another telepath at a distance wasn't easy, when they weren't expecting it. Telepathy isn't shouting, it's listening. When she was little, she'd learned the trick of forming a mental image of Scar, not what he looked like, but more like the feeling she got when they talked.

She made it as real as possible and then listened across the distance. She was lucky, he was open and receptive, and sensed the echo of himself.

Debbie?

Hello, Scar. I was just wondering. Have you heard about abandoned Cerik villages in the interior mountains?

There was a mental chuckle. **Yes. Old clans that died out. What's going on at Festival—history lessons?**

Oh, just people talking. I thought of you.

And I'm thinking of you. There was a warm comfort in his thought.

He asked, **How is it going? Are you okay?**

Fine. It's wonderful. Eating new foods, meeting nice people.

That's great. I love you.

Love you, too. I've gotta go now.

Bye.

Debbie hurriedly put aside her bowl and stood up, facing the other direction, so the others wouldn't see the moisture around her eyes. She made sure her *ineda* was back up.

She walked closer to the worker's table, until she could hear the voices.

"Yes. It's a full, Large Moon tonight, and there ought to be a running of the *chitchits*."

One of the cooks asked, "Can we go out and see them?"

Aaron pointed, "They should be visible through the windows. Is the moon up yet?"

"It should be, but it would be behind the mountain."

He stood. "I'll go check for activity." He walked over to the large doors. After a moment, several people got up to follow. Debbie trailed the group.

The large doors had windows down to waist-level, and there was room for all of them to look outside. The sun had gone down, but there was a glow in the sky.

Aaron said, "The shadows leave plenty of places for the *chitchits* to hide. Once the moon gets higher, they'll start to make for the water. We're just a thirty minute walk from the closest brook. They'll stream down the mountainside and choose safety in numbers to get to the water where they'll mate. They go all the way to the ocean. In the weeks to come, they'll return to the mountains in dribbles. The young, when they hatch, will swim upstream and move to land when their legs get larger."

Someone said, "I see something."

"Where?"

He pointed, "In the light, near the ridge."

Aaron nodded, "Good eyes. Yes, some of them are starting early."

There was a rush to get better directions. Some could see them, but Debbie kept looking on her own. After a few minutes, she was rewarded. "By the landing field."

"Where?" "Where?" There were several girls at her side that had come to see what was going on.

She pointed. "Little. Smaller than an *ooro*."

"Oh, I see them." "Where?" "What's an *ooro*?"

With legs wide to the side, they scurried from one shadowed area to the next with a swaying motion, almost like they were swimming.

A few minutes later, Omary edged her way up close to her side and squeezed her hand. Debbie could see the excitement in her eyes. Maybe Festival was just what the shy little girl needed.

To their side, there was a noise.

Aaron looked over, and shouted "No!" Hampered by the crowd, he was slow to break free as three of the girls, all decked out in their breathing masks were entering the airlock.

Debbie pushed away from the window. *What's happening?*

She hurried in his footsteps. Aaron was too late to catch them. They were already opening the outer door, and he slapped at the controls in frustration.

"What's going on?" She asked.

He carefully punched the controls to open the door. In a low voice, he said, "The Cerik pilots. They won't be in *erdan*, not with lively prey just outside the door."

She nodded, and slipped into the airlock with him.

"No. Stay inside."

"I'm Scar... Denton's daughter. I know Cerik better than most. And they'll listen to me quicker than some strange man in ragged clothes." She tapped the cycle control.

He took a deep breath. "Okay, but keep everyone calm."

"I know." The one thing they didn't need was panicky prey in bright clothes running around in a hunting field. Scar had mentioned, probably to keep her from being nervous, that the pilots taking girls to Festival were some of the most even-tempered of the lot. There didn't need to be an incident. But then, they were Cerik.

The outer door opened. The girls were already on their way over to the landing field. Fighting her instincts, but desperate to catch up, Debbie started running. "Wait," she said. "Wait for me."

They paused. In the shadows, she could see Aaron taking a different route. In his darker clothes, he was nearly invisible.

She hurried up, and was relieved to see someone she knew.

"Clara," she said, breathless from the run.

"You don't have your mask!"

"No time. You know who my dad Scar is?"

The others were puzzled.

"Um. Yes?"

"Well, let me say he would be very worried about us right now. We need to calmly walk back to the airlock."

"Aww. Why?" asked one of the others.

Clara got it. "Um. Amy, I think maybe Debbie is right." She looked around, fearfully at the dark shadows, made even darker by the moonlight creeping over the mountain ridge line.

"But we're not close enough to get a good look," complained the other.

Debbie took her hand. "All of us, link hands. We're walking, calmly, back to the airlock." Reluctantly, they did as they were told.

They made it half way back, before there was a snarl that echoed off the rocks, and a blaze of motion ended in the moonlit sight of a Cerik tearing one of the *chitchits* to pieces.

Clara began a squeal. Debbie shushed her. "No! Make no sound. We're *walking* carefully back to the airlock."

They moved together. Debbie kept her eyes on the doorway, more to keep her own panic under control than anything. She barely heard footsteps slightly behind and to the side of them. She hoped it was Aaron.

As they neared the doors, she could see a line of faces in the windows, silhouettes against the inside lighting. Were they watching them, or the Cerik?

"There is a man with us outside. He'll meet us at the airlock."

And he did. He appeared out of the darkness and tapped the controls, just as they walked up. When the door opened, he said, "Inside, all of you."

"There are four of us."

He gave her a push. "You'll fit."

Clara laughed, nervously, "You breathe in while I breathe out."

Stern faced men, including Howard, were waiting on the other side.

He took her hand as they all spilled out. "Are you okay?"

"Yes, they're a little scared, but no problems."

"You didn't wear a mask."

"A little outside air won't kill me—I know how to heal."

"Still, come on and we'll check you out."

She looked around. Maybe half the people had seen what had happened. Some of them had realized the seriousness. The girls at the window were still watching the funny animals outside, oblivious to it all.

She looked up at the man who ran the Graddik Home. He used to be in charge of everything she did. "In a minute or so. I'm waiting for Aaron to come back in."

Howard hesitated, then nodded and walked away.

The door opened a second later. Aaron's face was cloudy. She hadn't noticed before, but there were streaks of gray in his hair.

"Everyone is back and safe," she said.

He nodded. "No thanks to me." He gestured to one of the other workers and whispered to him. The man nodded and then typed an involved command on the control pad, probably locking it for the night.

She walked over to the window and saw that the running of the *chitchits* was in full stream. The animals were dashing across the field in large numbers. The crowd was chatting appreciatively at the spectacle. Many had never seen much of the outdoors at all, and this was really amazing. In the distance, by the landing field, she could see three of the pilots having a great time. But for the bulk of the *chitchits*, sheer numbers gave them safety. They would make it to the ocean and breed.

8

Clara came into her room after the lights dimmed.

She asked, "Tell me true, were we in danger from the Cerik?"

Debbie patted the mattress beside her. She sat and Debbie gave her a hug.

"Our pilots were all chosen because they were the least likely to hurt a bunch of girls. Scar promised me they were the best, slowest, and most careful pilots available. Still, you can never trust a Cerik, especially when there is prey around. You know how we teach the infants to behave themselves and to be calm and obedient? Well, the Cerik teach their cubs to jump on prey, instinctively."

Clara's eyes were wide. This was stuff she didn't really know.

"You know those *chitchits* outside. There's a market for those. Clans buy them up in bulk as pets. But pets mean something different in the Cerik world. Cubs jump on them and learn to kill that way. They're trained to get excited by the smell of blood.

"Scar lost his ear by accident that way. He was just too close to an excited Cerik at the wrong time. They were even friends. But if you aren't careful, all the time, you'll get slashed.

"I don't know if we would have been killed, but it wasn't worth the risk just to get a better look."

Clara leaned closer. "I'm still scared. I can't stop shaking."

Debbie held her, and could feel the shivers. She had an idea.

"You know all the things we're told not to do, to avoid Attachment?" Clara nodded. "Well, you're a grown up woman now, and you're too lively to want to give up being you. But for tonight, why don't you reach back Home and sleep in Flora's thoughts?"

Clara sniffed and smiled. "Maybe not Flora."

"Oh?"

She nodded. "She's got a boy she's sleeping with."

"Really? I hadn't heard."

Clara took her hand. "Not to be curtish, but you haven't been very friendly the past few weeks."

She sighed. "I know. Festival hit me hard."

"But you're better now?"
"Yes. Better."

...

Cerik nightmares hadn't bothered her in years, but Debbie woke with sweats and a dissipating sense of sharp claws and blood. She sat on the side of the bed and felt around with a flash of her clairvoyance. It was still early. Most of the others were still asleep. But she was awake, and rested enough. She'd not do anything more than worry if she laid back down.

She dressed and went looking for a pool. Staying quiet, and with no one to question, she quickly got lost in the corridors. This used to be a much larger complex, until quakes had collapsed many of the tunnels. If there was a pool, common in the old Delense burrows, then it was lost to the rubble a long time ago.

But surely there was a place to wash up?

She found it, clearly U'tanse in construction. There were eight shower heads in a narrow room. The walls, ceiling, and floor were surfaced in enamel to catch the water and channel it to a drain.

There was a shower back at Home, in the nursery, for cleaning up the infants who were too small to take to the pool. This would have to do. She was brushing the water out of her hair not twenty minutes later, when Clara stumbled in.

"Hi," she looked confused. "No pool?"

Debbie pointed to the showers. "Why are you up so early?"

She had a little smile, "I got chosen. I'm going to Ghader." She fumbled with the blue-striped sash. "Did you get picked already, too?"

"No. Just couldn't sleep."

Clara nodded. "Me neither. And now I'm too excited."

Another girl appeared, this time with a solid red sash. Debbie left a minute later and headed for the breakfast table.

This time, there were several tables. The big common table had been broken down and was now half the size. Surrounding it were six small tables, each with a little flag corresponding to the sash.

What if I just missed the person with a sash for me? She sighed and shook her head. *Who am I kidding? I'll be the last one chosen.*

9

Outside the closed door of the conference room, Aaron waited patiently. The Leaders of the Homes had been up early, working with their staff to get their first round picks notified. About half the girls had woken with a sash to go with their outfits. The easy decisions were all made, and now came the hard choices.

The door opened. Hannibal of Kakil said, "You can come on in now."

Will of Ghader spoke, "We were just discussing that episode last night. We understand what happened; high spirited girls, excited by something unusual, and then you going to get them. What is puzzling is why you let Debbie bar Karl go outside with you. Could you explain?"

Aaron nodded, solemnly. "It was an urgent situation. When she followed me into the airlock, I told her to go back. She understood the danger, and was as intent on getting them back to safety as I was. She let me know that she was the daughter of Denton bar Simon, who is known for living among the Cerik, and that she was familiar with their ways."

He spread his hands. "All this happened in a second or two. Faced with a delay of forcing her back out, or letting the airlock cycle us through, I went with speed. It turned out that she had judged the girls well. Better than I would have, probably. She had them turned around quickly and kept them from displaying panic. I did nothing but run around in the dark, prepared to head them off if there was a problem. But she brought them back, and I did little more than open the airlock."

Howard of Graddik asked, "I notice you don't seem confused that Debbie bar Karl had claimed Denton as her father. Had you talked with her before the incident?"

"No, but I was aware of her, and her story. The headhunter attack on Graddik was a blow to all of us everywhere. Maybe not many paid attention to the orphaned infant, but when I began surveying this Festival's candidates, I had made the connection.

"But no, I had not spoken with her before she met me at the airlock door. As you suspect, she is one of my preferred choices for the gardener position. Her initiative and bravery is a surprising bonus."

Hannibal asked, "Who are you? The group, I mean. We've been fumbling along, calling it Aaron's Group. It's annoying. Do you have a real name?"

He was silent for a moment. "We study historical records, as you might have guessed. I would call us the Delense Analysis Group. We haven't actually named our group, but that will serve."

Howard spread his hands flat on the table. "Debbie is of Graddik, and I feel a special concern for her safety. We had promised her a new future in one of the Homes, and I'm very reluctant to break that promise. To be blunt, your small group with limited basic resources may not be the best place for the girl. If we can't be sure of adequate nutrition, clothing and care, not to mention the psychological burden of being a new girl in a limited pool of females, I would have to object to your request, for Debbie, or for any of the other girls."

Aaron nodded. "I would expect no less. Consider this offer:

"Our group, while secret, could allow regular contacts between Debbie and a person of your choice, with the communication limited to her wellbeing. If she decides to leave, I can transport her to Sanassan, Dalla or Kakil or back to the next Festival here.

"I would hope to speak to her about this job, and to let her make a choice. If she prefers to proceed to another of the Homes, then I wouldn't stand in her way.

"If she does take up this opportunity, I might suggest, that since Sanassan currently has an excess female population, that she be officially assigned there to keep the records straight, and just consider this a temporary excursion of indeterminate length. That way her absence would be of no hardship to anyone."

Hannibal chuckled, "And your Delense Analysis Group stays off the records."

Aaron smiled, but said nothing.

Will nodded. "We will consider this now."

. . .

"What is this spice?" Debbie asked the worker from Kakil, holding the remnants of a pastry.

The lady smiled, "We call it mint, after an Earth seasoning. It's from this plant." She visualized a low, ground-hugging plant with wide leaves. "We pulp the leaves while fresh and soak them in a soda wash to remove the bitters."

"Debbie bar Karl?"

She turned. Howard and the mysterious Aaron were standing there.

"Um. I'll get back to you about the spice. It sounds interesting."

They left the flow of traffic around the food tables and walked over to a little cluster of chairs by the big double doors.

"I know I shouldn't have gone out last night, but…"

Howard put up his hand, "No, that issue is over with. Don't worry about it. "We're here to talk about… an unusual offer." He nodded to Aaron.

"Debbie," Aaron began, "I know you came here expecting to move on to a new Home. I have an alternative, but before I can explain, I need you to understand that what I say has to be kept under strict secrecy, whether you accept or decline the offer."

She firmed her *ineda* and nodded.

He smiled. "Good. I am from a small research group, detached from any of the Homes. It's like a long-term excursion. The group is small, and our resources are few. Right now, we need a gardener more than a girl seeking to become pregnant. I think you would be the ideal candidate."

She listened with a slightly open mouth as he described the unusual conditions and what would be expected of her.

Howard added, "We would expect that you contact Abbie once a week, just to let her know that you are doing okay. At any time, you can decide to leave, and Aaron will deliver you to Sanassan."

She looked first at Aaron, then at Howard. "And you trust that he'll turn me loose?"

Aaron chuckled. "As much as we need a good gardener, we need to be able to trade during the Festivals much, much more. I intend to stay on good terms with the Leaders of the Homes and keep all my promises."

Howard nodded, "I believe him."

She didn't know what do say.

A secret group. That means what?

But seeking her out to be a gardener—the only gardener, it seemed. Wanting her for what she could do. That sounded nice.

And she'd travel more, not just hop into a boat with the other girls and step back into daily routine. And if it didn't work out, there was always Sanassan.

Howard mumbled, "We can give you some time to think about it."

She took a breath. "Um. What would that mean? Would I get a red sash?"

"Well," Aaron didn't quite meet her eyes. "I think it might be best to stay without a sash today, and then leave early tomorrow morning."

"And miss the goodbye ceremony?" she asked.

Aaron clearly hadn't thought it out. He looked at Howard, who shrugged.

"Fine with me," she decided. "Play ignorant today, and skip tomorrow's tears." She sighed. "I just wish your group had a sash of your own, but you're secret. I get that."

10

The only thing that kept her from panicking during the day, and running to Howard to call it off, was her determination to pick the brains of all the cooks in the place. Cooks knew all the tricks, like that mint plant. If she were going to be a Chief Gardener, then she had to know which plants to grow.

Omary saw her and made a straight path across the lunchtime crowd. The red sash and her bright smile told Debbie all.

"I got Sanassan! Can you believe it? I hear they have animals, big ones, that you can feed by hand and everything." She was fingering her sash, smiling down at its color.

"That's great. Have you made friends with the other red sashes yet?"

"Yes, there's Uma and Lillian and Dori so far. I hope Sanassan picks you too. I really do."

"We'll just have to hope. I know the decision hasn't been made yet."

There were other greetings and hopes throughout the day. Debbie silently said her goodbyes, knowing she wouldn't be there for the final ceremony. It was a constant reminder to keep up her *ineda*. If she was to work for a secret group, then she'd need it all the time, just like Abbie and Howard and all the Leaders. Important people had secrets to keep.

...

"Debbie?" He whispered in the dark of the morning.

"I'm up and dressed." Her heart was beating rapidly.

"Follow me."

She grabbed her travel bag, a little heavier than when it arrived, with some food and spices and a couple of plant cuttings she'd wheedled from the cooks.

At the airlock, Aaron picked up a large backpack and a wheeled tote and looked her over seriously.

"We'll be out in the air for several hours. Expect air-burns. I'm sorry I can't supply you with a skin suit. Secure your collar and apply this salve to exposed skin. Anything you miss will have to be healed later."

Several hours outdoors? Air burns? What's going on?

She applied the salve to her arms and face. He had ties to keep her leggings secured tightly against her shoes.

They went through the airlock and she had to hurry to keep up, in spite of his heavy load. The Large Moon was bright enough that they didn't have any worry about stumbling over the rough ground, but they were not heading to the landing field. Instead they were following an animal trace that paralleled the cliff.

Maybe he hid his boat away from the main landing field because of secrecy. Why was he so quiet? All business.

After a couple of days of pretty speeches and fancy meals, this was feeling a little harsh. They were a mile or so away from the Festival burrow when she felt someone calling her. It was Howard.

"I'm being called."

Aaron stopped, frowned, and then nodded. "Go ahead and answer. Just don't tell them where we've gone. I need to take a break anyway."

She could see the sweat on his face and neck in the dawn light.

Hello, Howard.

Ah, Debbie, I was just checking to see if you got off okay.

Everything is fine. We're… heading out.

Good. Remember to check in with us regularly.

I'll remember. Thanks. Bye.

Good bye.

She pulled her *ineda* up tight again.

"Howard was just checking on me."

He nodded, taking a sip of water from a bottle. "I've got water for the both of us." He offered the bottle, and she drank a little. It took a little practice to lift the mask, sip and reseat the mask as one easy motion like he was doing.

Seeing his heavy breathing, she asked, "Is there anything I can carry? That's a big load."

"I'm used to it. I don't want you to sour on the job before you get started."

"Really, I could pull the tote."

He nodded. "Okay, but we shouldn't be too much farther."

Shortly, the animal trace crested a rise, and she could look down on a river valley below. The tote was harder to handle than she had imagined, the wheels catching on every rock and stick in their path. Downhill was in some ways harder, as it made the handled, two-wheeled cart difficult to steer. It was frustrating, but she wasn't going to give it back to him.

They headed down to the river.

"Take a break," he said, peeling off his heavy pack. She wheeled the tote up next to it.

"Water."

He handed her the bottle, then took a drink himself when she was done.

"That's the hardest part of the trip."

"Oh?" she looked around. The vegetation had gotten thicker, and even the animal traces looked impossible to navigate, at least while hauling the bags.

"Rest here a moment. I'll be right back." He slipped off into the bushes.

She looked around for a place to sit, and settled for leaning up against the tote.

A place on her arm was starting to itch. She looked *inside*, down at the cellular level, and found the patch of skin already dying from the air burn.

She'd deal with it later. She snapped back alert to the outside world, suddenly very conscious of the life around her. There were dozens of plant types, and every one of them was hosting little crawlers. Down at her feet, something was creeping over the ground-covering ferns, moving between the twigs just as she was moving between the trees. She checked her leg straps, just to make sure she didn't collect passengers.

Aaron pushed a large branch aside. "Pull the tote this way."

He held the branch until she passed, and then he went for his pack.

At the water's edge, there was a large, dark-colored cylindrical tank. It was lashed to a tree, and there was a man-sized hatch held open with cords.

"You get inside first, and then I'll hand you the bags."

She moved closer, uncertain about the tank that appeared to be floating in the water. "What is this thing?"

He chuckled. "Did you know that the original definition of the word 'boat' was a craft that moved on the water? Back on Earth, of course.

"This is a boat, only one that travels on water, not in the air."

She gripped the side of the hatch and pulled herself in. There were lights inside, and places to sit. But the constant motion underfoot was unsettling. She poked her head back out. "Okay."

"Here's the tote."

After some struggle, both bags were secured and Aaron untied the rope securing the water-boat to the tree and they drifted off into the current.

He gave a sigh, and closed the hatch.

"That was a lot easier than when I arrived."

Debbie gripped a handrail and felt queasy. "Is it going to move this way the whole time?"

He looked at her face and took her arm. "Come with me."

They stepped to one end of the interior. "Sit down in that seat."

She sat, and was pleasantly surprised to find that the chair was human-shaped, and comfortable.

He sat in the other seat beside her and flipped a switch, a mechanical clicking type like U'tanse used for their machines in the Home. With a smooth, silent motion, something opaque moved aside and she found herself looking out a curved glass window at the flowing water.

"We're going under power now. Do your best not to get sick. You'll quickly get used to the motion, I hope."

He adjusted more controls and she felt a surge as they began moving quickly through the water. Aaron could change their direction with the twist of a large dial.

He grinned and looked her way. "We'll be on the water for awhile. You can relax."

She asked, "Is the air filtered?"

"Partly. There are filter canisters on the walls, but the inside air isn't pumped through them."

He peeled off his mask and sniffed. "I'd say it's about forty percent better than the outside air, and it'll get better over time. You can leave your mask on, if you wish."

She hesitated, then removed her mask as well. A little air wouldn't kill her.

"Um. Is this Delense technology, or U'tanse?"

He smiled, "It's a little bit of both. The facility where we live was built by the Delense, back before they had spaceflight and boats. Home-grown U'tanse technology and Delense machinery of that era are close cousins. The hull and motors of this water craft were Delense. The electrical and steering systems were entirely rebuilt with human hands and human designs. We are the only ones with water craft technology on the planet."

She nodded, Scar had mentioned that Cerik were strictly land animals— they even hated to walk through mud. As far as they were concerned, the world ended at the shore. Spaceflight was easier for them than crossing over to the Far Island, the only land mass other than the large continent.

"Is that what your group does? Uncover old Delense stuff and make it work?"

"*Our* group. *Our* group." He smiled. "That's part of it, I guess. When we get to our destination, a lot more will make sense."

She nodded, closed her eyes and tried to keep her stomach from embarrassing her.

A minute later Aaron looked over and smiled to see her asleep.

11

The girls were lined up, all with their blue-striped sashes proudly displayed.

"Now, dig out your masks."

Clara leaned over to her new best friend, Jillina, "Did you see Debbie, one of the girls I arrived with? I wanted to say goodbye, and I haven't seen her."

"The serious one? No, but it's too late now. Here, let me help you with your mask."

Over to the side, Will of Ghader was saying his goodbyes. "Well, it's been an interesting Festival."

Hannibal chuckled, "I can't remember an uninvited guest before. Did you really buy all of his story?"

"He didn't tell us all that much, but this metal book says volumes. Did you notice that all the copies were identical, down to the smudges? He has some kind of print copier, in addition to metal sheeting and the new air filtration chemical. I'll take his word until I have reason not to."

Howard shook Will's hand. "I have to trust him. And I'll be checking up on him. But I'm afraid to ask too many questions. He seemed pretty serious about the secrecy."

Hannibal nodded. "I don't even think he gave us his right name. Probably worried we'd dig into the family tree archives and figure out where he comes from."

Will said, "Aaron." He looked thoughtful. "Not a common name, but I've heard it. It's in the Book."

They all nodded.

. . .

Debbie woke, startled by the noises. She grabbed instinctively, and snagged Aaron's sleeve.

"Sorry," he said. "I had to make some adjustments." His face looked serious.

"What's wrong?" She sat up in her chair.

He didn't look up from the water-boat's controls. He didn't answer for a moment.

"Debbie, don't be startled, but we're going to go lower into the water."

"What?"

He applied some power and the river water started splashing up on the window.

"We're sinking!"

"It's a controlled dive. There is no danger."

Debbie could hear noises that hadn't been there before—rhythmic pumping. The light changed as their view went below the waterline. She held her breath.

And then let it out as a new world opened up before them.

The sunlight through the water showed that they weren't alone.

"Fish."

"And more. Look over there."

Where he pointed, a slowly moving giant snake moved its body side to side. There were fins every foot or so, and the snout showed respectable teeth.

"He can't get inside?"

Aaron chuckled, "No."

They slowed to match the current. He snapped a few controls and many of the noises went silent. They were several feet below the surface.

"Now, Debbie, hold your *ineda* solid for a little while."

She made sure she was tight, and asked, "What's going on?"

"The Ghader boat with the returning Festival girls will be flying over this area in a few minutes. While I don't expect the pilot would ever notice us in the river, I don't want to take any chances."

"Why?" She pulled her gaze away from the fish to look at his face. It was still serious.

He gestured at the water-boat's controls. "Look at us. Two U'tanse, moving wherever we want to go, without a Cerik to watch over us. Two U'tanse not under the control of the Cerik. If we're discovered, we're in great danger."

Debbie frowned, "Why? What's so dangerous about it?"

He looked down at the controls, drumming his fingers, thinking about what to say.

"Debbie bar Karl. Your birth-father was on an expedition in a boat that crashed. However, he didn't die instantly, and that caused a major political stir among the Cerik. All because there was a U'tanse, walking free without a Cerik.

"Kallu, the *Name* of Graddik, was in danger of losing his position, and maybe his life, because he hadn't immediately rescued or killed that U'tanse. To save himself, he sent Tom, the Leader, to find Karl's body, and Tom lost his own life in the effort.

"Kallu survived, but another Cerik, in the Ruthenah clan, was embarrassed in the process. To regain status, he attacked the Graddik home, killing your birth-mother Linda in the process, leaving you orphaned."

He spread his hands. "All that loss and carnage, because one U'tanse walked free. This is serious business to the Cerik. The U'tanse have been valuable to them, but only if they can be controlled, down to the last individual. And what they can't control, they will kill, quickly and ruthlessly."

Debbie's chest was tight, and her eyes watered. Aaron's example cut far too close to home.

Maybe this is all a mistake. I should be off on one of those boats, with a sash, heading for a new Home.

A safe Home.

Somehow, even as the thoughts came, it didn't feel right.

"But what's wrong with being free?"

Aaron stared out into the water. "Nothing. There's nothing wrong with being free. It's just not safe."

. . .

They surfaced a few minutes later, when the flying boat had safely passed by on its way. Debbie dug out snacks from her stash in the travel bag, and soon the river brought them to the ocean.

The waves got bigger. Debbie found herself gripping the side of the chair.

"Do the animals get bigger too?"

"Yes, but there aren't many that would be interested in us, if that's what you're worried about. Many of them hunt by taste, and the hull tastes wrong."

"They don't try to swallow it, do they?"

"No, they just taste the water around us. Some day, I'll take you out where some big ones live and show you."

Her eyes were strained, "No hurry."

He looked at her. "The waves too rough?"

"I can handle it."

"I could take us below. It would be calmer, but we can't go very fast underwater."

"I'll manage."

"Just another hour, I promise."

She nodded, staring out the window.

12

The mountain seemed to dive straight down into the water. She watched in fascination as it grew nearer, and green patches became clusters of trees. Everything was new. Every mountain was a different thing, with its own shape, watercourses, and vegetation.

Aaron pointed off to the right. "There's an ancient Delense village hidden in that cove. It's obscured from sight, both from the mountains and boats passing overhead."

"Is that where we're going?"

"No." He adjusted the control wheels again.

Debbie gripped her seat. She recognized what he was doing—taking them under water.

The ocean water was much clearer than the river had been. The fishes and the underwater terrain were more sharp-edged, and the colors were different.

Aaron steered them straight toward the mountain, following a channel that was deeper than the surrounding area.

The tunnel opening under the water was clearly artificial, built with a supporting arch made with large slabs of stone. Aaron flipped a switch, and a beam of light illuminated the darkness. They slowed to a drift as they entered.

"I don't want to move any faster than I need to," he grinned. "I'd hate to ram the sides."

When they broke the surface inside, Debbie could see a couple of men, waiting next to the water. She let out a breath, pleased that one of her secret fears, that Aaron's group was just a myth, had proved false.

Outside they secured the water-boat with ropes next to the edge, while Aaron began shutting down all the systems.

When he released the hatch and opened it up, they were waiting.

"Aaron, we were worried you would be late." A tall man held out his hand and one by one, took the bags that Aaron handed him.

Debbie snatched up her travel bag, suddenly worried that she'd lose it among the others.

Aaron frowned, "Problem?" He grabbed the edges of the hatchway and pulled himself out.

Debbie followed, gripping her bag, trying to do the same, but the tall man gave her a hand.

Then he turned back to Aaron.

"Sakah just ran a boat out of juice and had to abandon it near the Third mountains. They tried to recharge it with the rescue boat, but they had totally drained the downed one. The charging circuits wouldn't even work. Sakah's *Name* just wrote it off. He still has more boats than he uses."

The other man, normal height, but gray-haired and a little stoop-shouldered, said, "It's not common knowledge yet. It doesn't appear on any of the traffic reports. Plus, Sakah is a political problem. It would be risky for one of the other *Names* to move a U'tanse repair team into Sakah territory."

Aaron nodded, "So we might have a window of time. Can we reach it?"

Tall one said, "Only overland. The maps show a route."

Debbie listened, standing with her bag as the men talked. She puzzled out a little bit. From her Graddik history lessons, she remembered that Sakah was the clan that had killed Tom bar Abe, when he was looking for her father. They were one of the couple of holdout clans who had not accepted U'tanse.

But what were they going to do with a stranded boat? Strip it for supplies? Repair it?

Aaron turned to the tall man. "Lemm, can we transport a power cell all that way?"

Ah, ha. Lemm. I have a name now.

He shrugged. "We brought it here from the old crash site. It'll just take longer. We'll have to..." They started walking away.

Debbie raised her hand. "Ah, Aaron?"

He glanced back. "Oh, sorry. Gentlemen, this is Debbie, our new gardener. Debbie, sorry, but I can't take the time to show you around. Just ask someone." They hurried off. The older man gave her a nod, but they were all too focused on the news for introductions. After a minute, they were out of hearing range and she was standing by herself, listening to the water-boat brush up against its mooring post. She was on her own.

13

She looked at the two big bags, and moved over to the wall to set her travel bag down, where no one would get it confused with the others. Her travel bag contained her only possessions. If she were going to have to explore this place on her own, she didn't want to be carrying it around, but she dared not lose it either.

There was a long corridor leading away from the loading dock. Aaron and the others had turned off at one of the side branches, but she hadn't paid enough attention to be sure of which one of the six it was.

She walked over to the wall and put her hand flat on the smooth, cool surface. Closing her eyes, she expanded her perception. Like a fast-expanding bubble, she sensed the scope of the place. And like a popped bubble, it was gone, leaving her with an awareness of the maze of hundreds of tunnels and chambers.

"It's huge!" Much bigger than Home—the entire mountain must have been hollowed out. It would take days to walk the whole of it, but the glow of human activity was one level up, and off the second branch.

With more confidence in her step than in her head, she started down the side branch, quickly reaching a broadly-curved ramp that took her up. All the tunnels seemed wide enough to move carts in both directions easily. All had the characteristic curved walls and ceilings of the Delense.

All her life, she'd been told of the Delense factories, but details had been sparse. They were automated facilities that produced some machine or parts or building material. Scar had told her of the ones he had seen, and she'd gotten the impression that there was barely space in the passageways for the Delense that had built them, and that sometimes the U'tanse repairman would have to crawl through tunnels to reach the broken piece.

This was entirely different. She could almost feel thousands of the Delense, ghosts of the past, walking about the corridors, doing some great task. But it was just an illusive fantasy, a leftover from her psychic flash. Her eye went to the floor, where dust had gathered. Human passage through here had disturbed the traces, forcing long-settled particles to the side. The center was clean, but no one had swept, perhaps in a thousand years.

Her memory of Cerik history was poor. She had blown off those study sheets as too boring. How long had the Delense been gone? This place felt even older than that.

She peered into the side passages, some with their dust undisturbed. There were darkened tunnels and rooms, some empty and some with… things she didn't understand—machines of some kind.

A few minutes into her walk, she noticed, with a shock, that an old woman was watching her. Up ahead, standing in the passageway, she waited, standing still like one of the cold machines. Debbie picked up her pace.

"Hello?" she called.

The old lady tilted her head. There was a smile on her face.

Finally, as Debbie drew close, the stranger said, "A Festival dress. How lovely they are this year." She waved a finger in a circle. "Show me."

Debbie hesitated, then spread out her arms and twirled slowly under her inspection, letting her take in the look and construction of the white pants and shirt.

Old eyes seemed in heaven. "Do you mind if I feel the cloth?"

She chuckled, "No. Go ahead." Debbie moved closer and the lady's thin fingers tested the weave and thickness of her sleeve.

"They even gave you white shoes. But you've gotten them muddy! I hope the cloth doesn't stain."

Debbie sighed. "Aaron and I hiked for a long time. I'm glad they held up to the rocks we went over."

She sighed. "That boy never paid any attention to clothes. Did you see that rag he wears? Ah, well. I guess there's no help for it."

She looked up into Debbie's eyes. "You're the gardener?"

Trying not to confess her limited experience, she nodded. "I'll try to be."

The lady took her left hand in both of hers. "I'll be so grateful for anything you can produce. I have pestered Aaron for a garden since we came here. My name is Sally. Come on in and meet Edgar."

She pulled her into the next room.

A man, maybe about Sally's age, was asleep on a bed. He was emaciated, and only his easy breathing let her know he was alive.

"Edgar, this is the new girl, come to make us a garden."

She turned to Debbie. "Edgar has been asleep for three years now. I care for him."

Sally's story was simple. "When the quake collapsed Dalla Home, there were so many deaths. It was all screaming and confusion. Luckily, the people in the nursery and in most of the living quarters were able to evacuate, but dozens were killed outright, and some of us, in the back tunnels, were trapped."

Old memories brought tears to her eyes. "The *Name* evacuated the whole Home, everyone but us. We were left, too deep in the tunnels to dig out, and not worth his trouble. There were ten of us. The power was cut, so we could only stumble in the darkness, those of us who don't have the sight.

Edgar found me and led me to a safe place next to the pool. He brought us all to safety, my Edgar."

She sat on the bed and took his hand. "We were married, the two of us. He found some words in the Book and back when we were young, we brought all our friends together and told them the news.

"They said it wouldn't last, but we showed them, didn't we Edgar." She smiled down at the peaceful face.

Debbie knew of others that had married. She hadn't realized it was a Book thing. Reading the Book was one of those massive study chores she kept putting off.

"Anyway, it was a long wait, in the darkness. We were in contact, of course, with the rest of the colony, being hauled off to another old Delense burrow to rebuild. It was hard, for them and us, knowing we were abandoned to die, and at the same time, they were having to work around the clock to get the new Home habitable for the infants and the cuties.

"And soon, our air began to go bad—not from an outside leak, but from our own exhales. Three of the ten simply lay down and died, whether to save us more air, or from their fears of suffocating, we don't know, their minds were blocked. Edgar suggested we all go into *ineda*, to shield the survivors from our fate."

Her tears were flowing, as she gripped his hand tightly. "That was the last time I shared his thoughts."

She sniffed and straightened up. She smiled at Debbie. "Sorry about that."

Debbie put her hand on her shoulder. "It's okay."

Sally took a breath. "So we began to fall unconscious. I was so intent on not shaming Edgar by my weakness. I spent all my efforts in trying to stifle my panic as the breaths came harder and faster.

"I was the only one conscious when the waters of the pool began glowing with a light from down below."

She smiled. "It was Aaron, of course. His underwater boat had found a passage between the nearby river and the pool in the Home. He loaded all five of us that were still alive into his metal fish and carried us off to this place.

"Gordo didn't recover. He was dead before we arrived. Lemm and Powell recovered with the good air. Edgar... lingers."

"Is Powell the older man who was with Lemm when I arrived?"

Sally looked puzzled. "No. Powell and Lemm were nearly the same age. That must have been Idiot."

"Idiot?" Debbie laughed.

Sally's lips curved up mischievously. "Aaron has told you about secrecy here?"

She nodded.

"It is important to all of us that the Cerik never find us. It is also important that the Cerik never learn our identities. The ones we love that still live in the Homes could be hurt if it were discovered that we still live.

"So, we go by first name only around here—no bar this and bar that. Should a Cerik catch our thoughts when our *ineda* is weak, there is less information they can use. And any of us are free to choose a different name entirely. So, when he arrived, he called himself Idiot, and he seems pleased to stick with it.

"What's his story?"

Sally shook her head. "No. Everyone owns his own history. Should Idiot decide to share it with you, be grateful, but no one else will tell it, if they know."

Debbie nodded. "So… everyone is thought dead?"

Sally grinned. "Everyone owns his own history."

"Ah. I get it. I guess."

"Well, I'm Debbie. I come of age shortly, but I'm here to grow a garden."

14

While Sally gave her directions to the chamber that had been fitted with lights for the garden, it was plain that she never wandered more than a minute or so from her sleeping, dreamless Edgar. Sally sewed up ripped clothing and bleeding limbs for the group, but she was frail and her interests were focussed.

"Come by and talk. Everyone does. I'm always here."

Debbie found her 'garden'.

How am I going to grow anything here?

It was a sizable room, and a quarter of it had been fitted with the bluish lights that Earth plants preferred, but other than a few dried-up plants sitting in metal tubs, there was nothing but dust.

I'm going to need soil, and seeds.

She hiked back to the water and retrieved her travel bag. The first order of business was to change clothes. She carefully folded the white Festival outfit, and slipped into her normal work clothes. She had only that one set, and some work gloves. From the looks of the place, and some things Sally said, it wasn't likely there would be replacements when these wore out.

This place is bare. The corridors were empty. Sally's room had a bed, but no chair or other furniture. She had mentioned other people, but they were nowhere to be seen. Even Aaron and the other men had vanished.

She closed her eyes and took a deep breath. She had snacks to keep her going for awhile. Someone had to be feeding Sally and Edgar; even if Edgar seemed skeletal, he had lived there for three years. She could breathe. There was food. There was water. The place was illuminated.

"Don't panic over the small stuff." Scar had told her that. *Concentrate on work. I'm Chief Gardener here.*

She grinned and walked over to the other storage bags. If Aaron wanted her to stay out, he should have told her. She opened them up, and was relieved.

The bags of seeds were all on the wheeled tote, so she balanced her travel bag on top and wheeled it all to the garden.

If food is scarce, I'm going to have a struggle to keep all of this from being eaten before I can plant it.

She immediately unpacked the bag into the smaller sacks. There were thin metal bars that had been brought in to build the light scaffolding. She used them and some tubs to build a shelf, where she stored the seed sacks, separated and up off the ground.

With the unloaded tote, she went back and loaded up the big pack.

Sally was relaxed on the bed, sitting beside Edgar, talking about someone named Cyclops, and stitching a small blue garment of some kind.

"Sally?"

She looked up, and smiled. "Do you need something?"

Debbie patted the pack. "I thought you'd like to see what Aaron brought back from Festival."

She rolled out of the bed and set aside her repair work. "What is it? Aaron promised to try to get supplies, but when he didn't say anything...."

Debbie opened the pack and brought out a bolt of white cloth.

Sally was overwhelmed. "Oh!" She took it in her arms and cradled it like an infant.

"There's more." The second bolt was of a dark gray, and the third one was blue. Debbie dug into the bottom and held out several of the various colored and striped sashes, made for Festival girls.

"Oh Edgar, I'm going to be very busy!"

Debbie looked around the room. "You need a work table, and a chair."

"I know. I've been asking for them, but Dennis told me Aaron has assigned him other jobs."

"Where is Dennis?"

Sally shook her head. "I don't know. It's different here, with everyone using *ineda*. When Cyclops brings me dinner, I'll ask him."

"Umm. That reminds me. How do meals work around here?"

"Are you hungry? Did Aaron forget to feed you? He gets distracted."

"I'm okay, for now. I ate really well at Festival. I'm just concerned about the future."

"Well, Cyclops will find you, when it's time."

"And Cyclops is…?"

Sally looked back at her bolt of cloth. "Oh, I'd better let him introduce himself."

. . .

The tote had developed a squeak in one wheel. She didn't know what to do about it, but at least it still rolled fine. She was particularly grateful for the broad slow curve of the ramp, especially by the time she'd wheeled it up three levels.

The control center was plain to see. It was messy, with three different maps spread out over a table. There were several chairs and it looked as if people had been deep into a planning session, and then walked out.

"Who are you?"

She jumped, and turned to see the man who had walked up behind her. He had white hair and a matching beard, but wasn't old.

"Ah. Debbie, the gardener. I brought some supplies that had been left down at the dock."

He frowned and then nodded. "Okay. What have you got?"

She pulled the pack off the tote. "It looks like paper and…"

"Paper? You've got paper?"

She handed him the pack and he dug inside, pulling out the fat roll. "And pens!" He began stacking the materials on the table, beside the maps.

"We can really use these." There were also some drawing tools and a cutter for the paper roll.

He laid them all out, neatly arranged. Then he noticed her.

"Oh, sorry. I'm Powell."

"I'm glad to meet you. Sally mentioned you earlier."

He nodded. "So, you are new here?"

"Just today. Aaron brought me here, and then ran off as soon as we got out of the water-boat."

"I'm not surprised. Lemm was about ready to explode when he discovered the abandoned boat and found out that Aaron wasn't here. So, you're the gardener. Good luck with that. We need a better diet here."

She smiled, "That reminds me. I have no soil to work with. Can you tell me where the exits are so that I can go collect some?"

"Sorry. There are no exits."

"What?"

"This place is entirely sealed off with no access except by water. Well, not exactly. We have air circulation pipes that go to the filtration station and a fresh water supply from the lake up in the mountains. But if you want out, it's swim or take the submarine."

"The what?"

He smiled with the look of one who knows something rare. "The water-boat. It's mentioned in the Book. It's a craft that can travel on or under the water. They were common on Earth. The Delense may have made this one, but we humans invented it a long time before the Arrival."

"So, I guess I need to talk to Aaron then, about taking me out to collect soil."

"Can't. He left just a little while ago. He and the others took the submarine to go off on their repair excursion."

"Well, how long will they be gone?"

"That's hard to say." He scratched at his whiskers. "From the looks of the maps, it'll be a week or more at best."

"But I've got to get started!"

He reached over and rested his hand on her shoulder. "It's your first day. Nobody expects miracles here. Take some time to settle in."

Debbie didn't reply. His words were comforting and kind, but what she heard was, *"You're a little girl. We'll take care of you, and when you're older, you'll make a nice mother."*

She took a deep breath. "Do you know where Dennis is?"

"Dennis? He's with the repair excursion. But if you don't mind, with all the people gone, I'm on double duty. I've got to go up to the lake and check on a metal fabrication run. It was Lemm's job, and somebody's got to do it."

He started back down the corridor.

Debbie called out, "How are you going to get out?"

He kept walking, "Swim, and don't ask me to haul you back some dirt underwater while holding my breath. I can't do it." He turned the corner and was gone.

She sighed. *They gave me this job, and I can't even do that.*

With her hands on the tote, she considered hauling it back empty to the dock where she found it. *I might just leave it here.* She looked around, amused at the evenly spaced row of pens, flanked on either side by little flasks of ink. Powell liked things orderly.

Suddenly, she grinned.

...

Squeak. Squeak. Squeak.

Sally looked out her door. "What is that?"

Debbie pulled the chair off the tote. "None of the men will be using this for a while. I saw it in the corner of the control center. I can't see any need for it to gather dust, do you?"

Sally rubbed her hands and took the chair. Debbie rolled the small table off the tote and began scooting it side ways into Sally's room. Quickly, they had her sewing table set up.

"This will make it so much easier. Thank you, Debbie."

"We girls have to stick together. Are we the only ones?"

Sally nodded. "For now. Aaron is always showing up with new people. I've been hoping for someone I could share things with. Girl things."

"I'll come by and talk some more soon. But I've got a job to do. Right now I need some more directions."

Sally listened to her plans, wrinkling her nose. "Better you than me."

15

"What is that smell?" The voice echoed down the corridor.

Debbie hurriedly took her home-made stirring paddle out of the basin and put a lid on it. She quickly checked her hands and washed them in the water pail beside her, placed there for just that reason.

"Hello? Who is there?" she asked.

A young man walked in. He wore a cloth strip, colored a faded black, over his eyes. He seemed to have no trouble navigating the doorway.

He nodded her way. "I believe you are Debbie, the new gardener?"

"Yes. And the smell is fertilizer. The homegrown kind."

He nodded toward the basin. "It reeks all the way down the corridor. I hope it doesn't stay that way."

She gave a slight smile. "It will be much better when I have soil. Unfortunately, I appeared to be locked in. Aaron took the submarine."

He chuckled, "You've been talking to Powell. He's the only one who calls it that. But, I came to bring you to dinner. And may we leave now? I want to air out before I eat."

"Certainly."

Debbie moved a little closer, and as far as she could see, there weren't any holes in the cloth. "Are you Cyclops?"

"How did you ever guess?"

They began walking back towards the dock. "Sally told me Cyclops would come for me at mealtime."

"Not from the legend?"

"What legend? Is the name from a legend?"

He laughed again. "Yes. And once you read it, I'll explain why I chose it as my name."

"So… you weren't born with it?"

"No. Come on. Walk faster so I can breathe."

He was moving rapidly down the corridor, and she had to hurry to keep up with him. "It's a Book thing, isn't it?"

"You haven't read the Book?"

"Er. No. I hadn't gotten around to it. I can read just fine, though. The Book sounded… long." She felt very young and stupid.

He shook his head. "The education of modern youth." He began to slow down as they turned the corner and sighed. The smell was gone. The air circulation in the place was more complicated than she had expected.

"Is there a copy here?"

He nodded. "Yes, from the Dalla collapse. Aaron took a moment to raid anything he could find. He found the Book and a few maps. They've all been invaluable. When you get time, check out the Mythology section of Father's writings."

While Debbie's nose had gotten saturated with the manure smell early on, a new scent caught her attention. "I smell dinner."

They walked out onto the dock area, looking very empty without the submarine taking up its place at the water's edge. Powell was standing over a wheeled stove, with a fat black cord running from it to an opening in the wall. Several fish were sizzling over the heating elements. Another young man, naked, was squatted over some nets, facing the water.

Cyclops raised his voice, "Robert. You may not have been told. We have a new member of our community."

The naked man turned and faced them. His eyes went wide and he grabbed up the nets to hold them in front of him.

Debbie chuckled. "Don't worry, Robert. My friends and I used to go down to the pool to watch the guys all the time. You don't have anything I haven't seen before."

Deliberately, she turned toward Powell. "I thought you had left."

He sighed, rotating another fish. "It's taken me this long to get ready. It'll be a hike up in the dark, as it is."

Cyclops said, "I'll keep a watch out for you."

"Thanks. I'd hate to be stuck out there with a broken leg."

He transferred one of the fishes to a platter. "Sally's."

Cyclops took one of the knives and expertly separated the bones and plates from the meat and scraped the bones off onto the discard pile.

"Everyone," Debbie said, pointing. "I'm collecting table scraps and any leftover vegetation as part of my soil-building program."

Powell sniffed, "Is that what that stink is? It about knocked me over on the way down."

Debbie smiled at him sweetly. "It'll be under control as soon as I can get some outside soil to mix it with. It's a necessary step. I'm here to make a garden."

Cyclops said, "Play nice, you two. I'll be back in a minute." He took the deboned fish platter away to Sally.

Powell sighed, "I still can't bring you dirt. I'm not that good a swimmer. Get Robert to help you. He's our fisherman, and he can out-swim them, I suspect." He plopped a fish on a platter and handed it to her. "Watch for bones."

She walked her platter over to where Robert sat, now magically clothed in damp trousers.

"So. You catch the fish."

He looked to be two or three years older than she was. "Yes." He glanced at her, but quickly looked back at his nets.

"Robert, do you think you could swim to land and bring back sealed containers of soil?"

"Maybe. Why?"

"I'm going to grow a garden, and I'll need soil for the plants to grow."

"There's mud. It's closer. Right out there." He pointed at the middle of the water.

She considered it. "Um. Probably wouldn't work. This is salt water, isn't it?"

"Yeah."

"The plants wouldn't like the salt, and I'd have to rinse the mud to get rid of the salt, and I'd probably wash away all the mud doing it."

He chuckled.

She pushed, "But would you try?"

"I guess so."

"I'd appreciate it."

He was quiet for a moment, then he looked at her for more than just an instant. "Debbie?"

"Yes, Robert."

"Are you of age?"

Powell groaned out loud.

She looked over his way and saw that Cyclops had returned and was listening as well. She blushed.

"Robert. No, I'm not. And I definitely won't be until I get my garden!"

He nodded. Abruptly, he stood up and walked over to pick up a platter.

I guess the conversation is over.

She picked cautiously at her fish, at first. It was tasty. She wondered how long she could live on a fish diet.

16

"Here's where you sleep." Cyclops tapped a flat plate on the wall and the light came on in the little room. "I apologize for the bed, but we've all had to use it when we first arrived. Dennis will build you a better one when he gets the time."

Debbie kneeled and gripped the coarsely woven pallet. "This is *shash*. You have that near here?"

He nodded. She was having a little trouble reading his expressions with the cloth across his eyes. Maybe it was something in his voice, but he seemed irritated. He pointed off at a blank wall. "Powell is walking beside a patch of them right now."

She nodded slightly to herself. Cyclops was "seeing" using his clairvoyance, rather than his eyes. Was he blind? In any case, he was very good at it—extremely good at it.

"That's good. I've used *shash* back at my old Home for a lot of projects."

He looked back at her. "That's lucky, because it's one of the few easily accessible building materials we have."

"This bed will be fine. I can build my own later. According to Sally, Dennis is kept pretty busy."

Cyclops sighed. "We all are. There's only a handful of us, but we're used to the environment a Home with hundreds of people could supply."

She looked up at him. "So, what is your job, other than calling everyone to meals, delivering Sally's plate, monitoring Powell, and helping me out on my first day?"

He shrugged. "Mostly monitoring. We are secret, even from our own people, and because we must live with *ineda*, we can't even whisper mind to mind. But in every Home, U'tanse spy on their Cerik, and keep records of excursion flights and rumors exchanged, like at the Leaders-only meetings at Festival. My… gift is clairvoyance, as you've probably suspected. I can read the secret notes in all the Homes. It gives us an edge. It may keep us alive."

He sighed, "And I have been getting behind today, so I'd better get back to my job."

"Goodnight. And thank you."

He dipped his head. "Um. One last thing. Take it easy with Robert. He's not used to girls. I can't tell you his story, but he doesn't have the Home-life experience you'd expect."

She listened to his steps dwindle with a lot of new things churning in her head. This group, *her* group now, was monitoring the whole world, all though through his amazing perception.

She had clairvoyance. Everyone other than the tenners did, to some extent. Every woman needed it to control her body. But it was usually a trance thing. For her, it could also be a burst of insight. But reading text from across the continent? That was unheard of. Had his blindness enabled this?

And what was Robert's story? He'd struck her as acting younger than he looked. She sighed. So much to learn.

But for now, I need sleep. She crunched the stiff *shash*. *On a lumpy bed.*

. . .

Debbie could barely see the rocks tumbled randomly on the bottom of the pool, but she grabbed the biggest one that she was sure that she could get back up to the surface and started kicking strongly. With a gasp she shoved the rock up onto the lip of the pool and grabbed hold of the edge to catch her breath.

"What are you doing with those rocks?" asked Cyclops.

She panted as she rubbed the water out of her eyes. "How long of you been there?"

"Not long."

"Sally told me about this freshwater pool this morning, so I came over here to see if there was any sediment at the bottom that I could use for my garden."

"That doesn't look like dirt to me."

She nodded. "The pool is pretty clean, but there is a bunch of rubble at the bottom that I could use as edging. I thought I would retrieve some of it."

He hadn't moved from where he had propped himself against the wall since he had spoken to her. She suspected it was because she was naked. "Cyclops? Is there a nudity rule in this place? It's kind of strange, the way people act."

He nodded. "There isn't a rule. But with the particular exception of Sally, we're all just a bunch of guys, and it hasn't been an issue. I'm wondering if starting one would be a good idea."

Debbie rested with her head propped up on her crossed arms, just a little grateful that only her head and arms were visible—not that it would really made a difference to him.

"Back at home," she said, "there were some little rules. For the cuties that didn't have parents that wanted to live with them, girl rooms were collected on one corridor and boys on another. Of-age men and women were assigned pretty randomly in another section. There wasn't really a rule against peeking into other people's rooms while they were dressing, but it was frowned at. You'd get a lecture, and everybody knew."

He smiled. "I think I remember you mentioning that you went to your pool with a bunch of girls to watch the boys."

She ducked her head down and muttered, "Yes, and I got a lecture for it, too."

He laughed. "So don't get too uptight if some of us sneak a peek."

"I wasn't. Robert was asking..."

"I don't think we know what he was asking. He's rather quiet. But my question—do you think we need some new rules? This is a different environment than a Home. We're all under *ineda*. Everybody *doesn't* know what everyone else is doing. And you're the only available female."

"Semi-available. But I know what you mean." She sighed. "But what's the future here?"

He smiled. "That's the question isn't it? Aaron changed the game when he went to the Festival. Not only do people know that we exist as some kind of non-Home group, but he also is bringing in ordinary people."

"Not rescues, you mean?"

"Um."

"I know. Everyone owns his own history. I got the lecture. But it looks like it, from the sample I'm seeing. The Dalla collapse, Robert's mysterious upbringing, your eyes—I'm thinking everyone here was rescued, except me. I was recruited. That makes me an 'ordinary person', doesn't it?"

He looked a little uncomfortable. "But you see what I'm getting at, don't you? Twenty years from now, maybe a lot sooner, we'll have the magical twenty-seven that all the Homes start out with. Most Homes have rules like you described. Should we be any different?"

Her eyes glazed in thought. "I don't like the idea of changing things, just because I showed up. And if there were new rules, different from the way Homes work, then it would make it even harder for the next girl who shows up." She shook her head. "No. I'd rather make adjustments myself than make everyone else change to suit me. Besides, I'm here to make a garden, and as soon as people understand that, the embarrassment should go away."

I'll just find out when the guys bathe, and set my schedule differently.

He smiled. "We can hope everything goes smoothly."

She gestured at her pile of rocks. "You want to come in and help? I need about twice this many to help build up the edging of my first plot."

He winced. "Sorry, but I don't swim."

"Oh, well. I'll get it done."

He turned to go, then asked, "You are a strong swimmer. Why are you pestering Robert to go get the dirt for you?"

She looked puzzled. "But… that's outside. I'm…" She took a breath. "Is it allowed?"

He tilted his head. "This isn't a Home. There are no Cerik guarding the gates. If you go outside and get yourself killed, we'll all be pretty upset about it, but it's not our place to stop you. If that's what it takes to get your job done, then that's what you need to do. I would advise talking to Robert about how to get it done easiest, but that's up to you."

17

She fingered the metal circles.

Robert said, "It's a chain. They corrode fast when we use them outdoors. I have to replace it every couple of months, but the machine on the mountain can make new spools pretty easily, so I use it."

It had taken a couple of days, but Robert had gotten used to her, especially when she described what she needed to be done.

They already had two waterproof tanks that were perfect for the job. "But don't try pushing them through the water," he suggested, "Swim pulling a tow line, and then when you've got ground under your feet, tow it to you."

Low tide was early that morning. "It has to be at low tide, otherwise we're not going to be able to get the empty tanks out the gate."

She held the tanks while he partly filled them with water to get them near to neutral buoyancy.

"It's time," he said, as he pointed to the water level, as it showed much lower on the marked post at the edge of the dock.

"Okay," she nodded. She tugged off her clothes. "You aren't going to get weird about this, are you? I've got a job to do."

He shook his head as he peeled the rest of his clothes off as well, but his eyes were wide and he couldn't break his gaze away from her chest.

She slipped into the water. "Come on, let's get this done."

It wasn't the first time she'd navigated the gate. She'd tried it the day before, just to make sure she was up to it, but it was different this time, swimming with a spool of the chain. It was heavy and weighed her down, but it was getting lighter as it unspooled.

Swimming in salt water had its own differences. The taste wasn't un-pleasant, but it felt wrong, like there were poisons in it. She'd sampled enough of the odd plants in her old Home that she recognized some of the distinctive bitterness that signaled danger. Salt was one thing, but there was more in this water than just salt. She resolved to let as little of it as possible get into her mouth.

The inside of the gate was marked. When she reached it, she put her hand against the stones, took three quick breaths of the inside air and swam down and through the opening. The wall separating the inside and outside worlds was twenty feet thick. She swam hard, tugging the chain behind her.

Surfacing, the world outside was dim. The sun was not yet up and the moon was still behind the mountains. She breathed deeply, aware it was outside air. That had to be dealt with later.

Robert popped up beside her. "Here." He handed her his chain. "Don't drop this. It's too deep here to swim down to recover it." He took a couple of breaths. "Give me a minute and then brace your feet against the rocks and start pulling. Let the ends dangle. Don't try to wind them up, or they'll drag you down. I'll try to guide them through the gate."

She nodded. He took another deep breath and ducked down below.

Her nose itched, whether from the outside air or the salt, she didn't know. She sneezed and began pulling, hand over hand, keeping a firm grip on both chains. There were snags, but they quickly released. Shortly Robert popped up with one tank, and a second later the other one appeared.

He panted. "Over there." He waved to the shore. "See where it's darkest? A stream empties into the bay. That's what you want, right?"

She nodded. "Right."

"Swim for the shore. Let the chain slip through your hand, but don't lose it! It will be shallow when the chain is at the end, but it would be a pain to try to find it in this light."

The novelty of being outdoors added to the excitement when the tanks scraped up on the beach. But that didn't last. The tanks were heavy, even when they emptied the water, and she discovered that walking on rocks was painful.

Robert didn't seem to mind.

"You find your dirt. Look for the high tide line if you want it to be free of salt."

He laughed as she walked gingerly over the stream bed, moving upstream.

"Why don't your feet hurt?"

He didn't hear her the first time. He looked up. "Oh. Used to it."

She stared back at him. He was getting too distracted again, and when he realized what she was looking at, he turned to the side and began looking at the bank. He tapped a little of the dark mud to his tongue. "Doesn't taste salty."

It took several hours to get the tanks filled, and then they had to partly empty them to keep them buoyant enough to float.

They rested before attempting the swim back. In spite of working together, she could feel questions and confusion leaking through his *ineda*.

Finally, she said, "I'll answer all your questions, if you tell me your history."

He looked startled. "Not much to tell."

"Well, you obviously haven't been around girls."

"Oh, that. Yes, I was sold to the Keetac clan when I was little."

"The Keetac, I haven't heard of them."

He shrugged. "They're a small clan, with no U'tanse colony of their own. They harvest *po* eggs and sell them when they're ready to hatch. They're pretty rare and they can get a good price."

She remembered the claws on the pilot that had brought her to Festival. "I take it they don't harvest the eggs themselves?"

He laughed, "No. The eggs are up in *dlathe* trees. Delense had a way to retrieve them, and when they were gone, they used Uuaa to get them."

"What are Uuaa?"

Robert's face settled into a peaceful smile. "They are the nicest people. They can't talk, but they took me in and treated me like one of their own, until I got too big."

"Let me get this straight. You were sold, so that you could harvest eggs with these other people?"

"Right. Only, they're not people like us. The adults are half the size I am and they can breathe the air with no problem. They've got long, flexible arms, too. I was never able to jump around in the trees as well as they did."

"They can breathe the air? So... they are from some other place?"

"Right. Some planet or another. I think they're plenty smart, I could understand their thoughts well enough, but they never used words, not even thinking them. I think the Cerik captured a bunch of them and brought them here."

She nodded. "Like the Arrival for us. So do they only use them to collect eggs?"

"Mostly, but although Cerik can jump up to a tree branch if its sturdy enough, they can't really climb, so Uuaa do all the chores that are up in the trees. I think they were trying to see if I could do all that too, since the numbers of the Uuaa are shrinking."

"Oh."

"Yeah. The Keetac were worried their Uuaa would die out and they'd either go back to the Uuaa planet and get more, or else stop harvesting and selling *po* eggs."

"How did you do?"

"Oh, I was okay for a couple of years, but then I got bigger, and I couldn't go up in the thin branches anymore. When I fell out of the tree and broke my arm, they just left me."

"The Keetac just abandoned you?"

"Yeah, they were tired of buying the powder for my mask and having to haul around my sleeping egg."

"What's that?"

He stretched out his arms about three or four feet. "It was a little place with filtered air where I could sleep. The Uuaa were amused by my giant egg that I hatched out of every morning."

"So, you were... where?"

He shrugged. "I don't know. The Keetac took us from one grove of *dlathe* trees to another. When I was hurt, the pilot just loaded up all the Uuaa and flew off. I knew he wasn't going to come back for me."

"Let me guess—Aaron came and rescued you."

"Only after five days! I was starving and sick, and my arm wasn't healing well. But Aaron and Cyclops showed up and patched me up. Aaron did some extra healing on me, and fed me. We camped in the mountains for a few days before I was well enough to hike back here."

She nodded thoughtfully, "But other than that you're perfectly normal."

"Sure. So I got to ask..."

She sighed. "Yes. Ask."

He looked down. "I, ah... When I look at you I want to touch you. Can I feel those?"

She shook her head. "No."

He sagged.

She explained, "You see, I have a job to do, and if I get pregnant, I won't be able to do it. So no. And its not just you. 'No' to all you guys."

"I wasn't trying to make you pregnant! I just wanted to touch."

"And you didn't grow up in a Home like I did, where I could watch all the boys and girls grow up and get those urges. The thing is, it never stops with one touch. The boy really believes he will be satisfied by that one touch, but it never happens that way. And the girl never intends to let the boy touch her more than once, but things change for her too."

She shook her head vigorously. "No. Not now, not for a long time. I've got a job to do."

He sighed. "Do you think Aaron will bring us more girls?"

She chuckled. "Maybe, and believe me, lots of the girls will be more interested than I am."

18

Taking a big breath of inside air tasted sweet. Before they were totally exhausted, they used the dock pulleys to get the tanks up onto wheeled carts. Cyclops was sitting on a chair near the dock, but he didn't react as they worked.

"Is he asleep?" she whispered.

"No. He gets like that sometimes. He's watching something important far away, and he can't afford to pay any attention to us. It's okay. He'll wake up in a bit."

She dressed and was grateful she'd brought a comb this morning. As she struggled with the tangles, she asked, "Do you want to help me prepare the soil later, when we've rested?"

He curled his nose. "Not with that stink. Why do you have to do that?"

She stared off into the distance. "I don't know all the reasons. There are nutrients, of course. But the woman who trained me said that in our gut are thousands upon thousands of microbes, created on Earth like us. We have brought a part of Earth across the stars with us, and mixing it with the alien soil allows us to tame it and make it into Earth soil—the best environment for growing Earth plants."

She shrugged. "It makes sense to me. I'm starting from scratch here. I have to do everything I can."

He nodded. "I'm going to take a nap."

"I'll see you later." She smiled. Robert was okay, in his own way.

She glanced at Cyclops, still in his trance.

Memories of her gardening teacher reminded her of another chore she needed to do. With a deep breath, she closed her eyes.

Abbie?

Across the distance, she felt a wisp of though, reacting.

Debbie! It's good to hear you. How are you doing? I was a little worried when Howard told me that you'd not gone to one of the Homes.

I'm fine, Abbie. I would have made contact earlier, but I'm very busy. Are they treating you okay?

Everyone is fine. I had to say 'No' to a boy a couple of times, but we're okay now.

Abbie's mental chuckle across the void gave her a twinge of homesickness, but she shrugged it off.

Well, I have chores to do, so I'll be going. Tell Howard I'm okay. Please contact me again. We will always worry about you. Bye.

. . .

She pulled the carts to her garden and made a lot of noise when she dumped the damp soil out in the middle of her first plot. It was discouraging how shallow the pile of dirt was. It would take many more tanks of soil to build it up high enough to handle some of the plants' root systems. She revised the list of which plants she could start with as she raked in her manure.

Can I plant them wider apart, and let them have a broader base of roots?

Robert came in, wrinkling his nose. "Emergency meeting in Sally's room."

"What is it? I'm in the middle of this."

"I don't know. Cyclops said to come. Everybody."

"I'm going to wash first!"

He nodded. "Thank you."

She rinsed as well as she could. Her clothes still were smelly, but there was nothing she could do about that.

She hurried down the corridor. It was crowded in the little room.

Cyclops nodded as she stopped in the doorway. "We're all here."

He looked around the room. His eye bandage was getting so familiar to her that she realized she hadn't thought it was strange until his gaze had moved on past her.

"A volcano has erupted down the coast from us. You may have felt the quakes."

She had, but quakes were common, so she hadn't placed any importance on them. Now that she thought about it, there'd been a nearly constant rumble recently.

Sally asked, "Are we in any danger?" She looked down at Edgar.

"No. This place was built on an old basalt outcropping and the Delense intended it to last. The problem is a control systems factory owned by the Dalla Clan."

"Dalla?" Powell said. He and Sally shared a look. That was where they had come from.

Cyclops continued, "The Dalla *Name* sent a boat with a crew of U'tanse to salvage as many of the control modules as possible, before the lava flow reached the factory. The pilot landed the boat near the factory and stayed with it while the U'tanse were sent in with carts to load up product."

He shook his head. "The Cerik shouldn't have tried to play it safe. A lava bomb struck close to the boat. It smashed the side in and tumbled it. It appears the pilot did not survive. The *Name* has written off the whole group. He's unwilling to risk another boat."

Robert whispered, "What's a lava bomb?"

Debbie had actually paid attention to her geology studies. She whispered back, "A big lump of molten rock blown out of the volcano. They sail through the air and can smash anything they land on."

Sally asked, "So, the workers? What of them?"

Cyclops had a very remote expression on his face. "With no rescue, they are stuck there. It appears as if the lava will soon cover that whole peninsula."

"Aaron! We need to contact Aaron." Robert spoke what Debbie was thinking.

Cyclops shook his head. Powell sighed. He said, "We're not in contact. They have their *ineda*, and we have ours, and we can't open up. It's too risky for all of us."

"And I can see," said Cyclops, "that they're still deep in the interior, in Sakah territory. Even if they know about it, they wouldn't be able to reach the water-boat in time to do anything."

"Submarine," corrected Powell. "We can't count on them. Not this time."

Debbie asked, in the silence, "What can we do?"

"The tub! We could use the tub," said Robert suddenly.

Powell frowned in thought.

"What's the tub?" Debbie asked.

Robert spread his arms wide. "It's a big metal thing, like a stretched wash tub, only large enough to carry a dozen or more people. It floats on the water."

Powell said, "It's also slow. Half the speed of the submarine."

Sally asked, "But could it reach them in time?"

Cyclops sighed. "That depends on the volcano."

Sally said, "We should try."

Debbie agreed. "I'll go along."

Powell shook his head. "That's the thing. We don't have the people. Debbie, you're just not trained on this thing. I can't go. I'm the only one keeping the factory running and I can't just let it run unattended, not without ruining it forever."

Robert said, "I can run the tub. I've done it before."

Cyclops said, "You're needed here. You feed us all. Sally, and Edgar wouldn't last the days you'd be gone. I don't swim. Powell isn't good at it, and Debbie has no training in catching fish. If we had supplies for a few days, it would be one thing, but we don't. That's one of the reasons Aaron decided we needed a gardener so badly."

Debbie said, "Cyclops, I heard you went on at least one of these rescue missions before. Why can't you do it?"

He hesitated. And none of the others seemed to take up her suggestion.

"For one thing, I'd have to swim to get out of here. The tub is docked over at the Delense village."

"But could you pilot this tub if you were there?"

"Yes, probably, but you overestimate what I can see. Unexpected obstacles, bad weather, and other things that would be obvious to you would catch me by surprise and I'd likely sink the craft. And again, I can't get out of here to reach it in the first place."

"You say you don't swim, not can't swim. People will be burned alive if we don't do something. Can't you make the effort?"

Sally shook her head, "Debbie. Don't."

Cyclops was distressed. "You don't understand. It's... not a choice. If I tried, I'd freeze up. I'd drown before I even reached the gate. I can't help it."

Powell nodded. "It's impossible. We can't help."

Debbie knew she was missing something. But she wasn't ready to give up.

"Robert, couldn't we stick Cyclops in a tank, and haul him out, like we did the dirt." She turned to his bandaged face. "You wouldn't have to swim. Just rest in the tank while we get you to the other side. Once you're in the tub, I'll go with you and watch for the hazards you can't see. Please. We have to try."

Sally looked over at Cyclops. The bandage obscured so much, it made him hard to read.

He sighed. "I'll try."

19

Debbie had never seen him so pale and shaken.

She patted his hand. "Just go into a trance. We'll turn on the valve so you can get fresh air once we're on the other side. Okay?"

He nodded. She closed the seal and gave the chain a couple of quick tugs.

Robert was already on the other side of the gate and began pulling the chain strongly. Debbie pushed and kicked. The tank was riding a few inches above the water, more buoyant than Robert had wanted, but they needed a safety margin. It was a lot more risky with a person inside the tank than a bunch of replaceable dirt.

Sally had come down to the dock, just to whisper some encouragement before he had gotten in. She had said to Debbie, "Take care of him. He shouldn't be doing this."

But people's lives were at stake, and they all knew it.

The chain began to bind as they approached the gate's edge. Debbie climbed up on top of the tank, holding onto the stone wall for stability. With her own weight added, she wedged the leading edge of the tank into the gate. The first few inches went slowly.

At this pace, we'll never get him through in time.

She pushed harder with her feet, and it began moving. After painful seconds of indecision, she swam ahead, through the gate and grabbed the chain next to Robert. With the both of them pulling, it scraped through, foot by foot.

Cyclops was frantically banging on the inside by the time she opened the valve.

"We're clear! We're on the outside. Hang on, we'll get to shore as quickly as we can."

His hoarse voice, reduced to a tinny whisper through the pipe, said, "Hurry."

When they scraped up on the beach and unsealed the tank, he struggled out, weak and gasping. "I'm not going back that way," he whispered.

Robert asked, "Can you walk?"

"I'll try."

For the first few minutes, Robert and Debbie held him upright as they made their way toward the Delense village. She was grateful she'd stowed her clothes in the tank with Cyclops, along with their breathing masks.

Without these shoes, I'd be the one needing help.

Gradually, he straightened up, and shook off their hands.

．．．

The village was in constant shade, overshadowed by high cliffs. With no sunlight, even on hot days it was cool.

Debbie gave a passing glance at the tunnels that went deeper into the cliffside. Robert noticed. "I've explored a little. Mainly just living quarters. Everything's covered in dust. Lizards and things live in there."

She nodded, but her attention was drawn to the tub, docked at the side of a narrow inlet. It was nearly as long as the submarine, but it was wider, and over half its length was open to the air. There were thick cables running from one of the tunnels out to it.

"Robert," asked Cyclops, "would you check on the power levels?"

As the craft was being brought to life, and the charging cables removed, Debbie asked, "Is there anything we need to bring along?"

He shook his head. In the walk over, he had mostly recovered from his experience in the tank. "We don't have much of anything to take with us. If we had time, I would have collected more food and brought something to sleep on. We'll be almost a day just getting there. At least there is fresh water to drink. But we'll be hungry and if we get any sleep, it'll be on the hard deck."

Debbie thought about her stashed stockpile of grain. It could have been sacrificed for short-term food, if she had been willing to give up the seed stocks.

This trip was going to be quite different from the journey to Festival, with new clothing, and a travel bag full of everything she needed. At least she had her breathing mask.

"It's ready," Robert said, looking despondent that he couldn't come along.

They climbed in, while Robert went to the dock and began unhooking the ropes that held it in place. The hull, under her hand as she gripped it, felt textured. "This feels old."

"It is," he whispered, as he took the controls and tested the steering and gripped the power lever. "It was mostly buried at the bottom of this inlet. Aaron discovered it before my time. How he managed to raise it is a marvel in itself. The engines are new, however. The originals were long corroded away. The factory was already set up to manufacture the components." He shook his head, "I don't think we'll ever match the Delense ability to automate factories—but don't ever tell Powell I said that."

He yelled to Robert, "Ready?"

"You're free."

Cyclops whispered to her. "Come up here beside me and watch carefully as we move out. Warn me if we get too close to the shore or to the stones at the entrance to the inlet."

She found a place to sit and scanned the water. "I'm watching. You can start."

He applied power, and they began moving.

20

"I remember this," she said as the ocean swells moved them up and down and side-to-side.

"You'll get used to it."

She looked at the mountains along the shoreline. The farther out into the water they went, the smaller they looked. "Do we know where we're going?"

He chuckled. "That's why I'm steering."

"Well, help me out here. You'll need to sleep, eventually. I need to know how to do it too."

He nodded. "Probably." He pointed off in the distance. "What do you see in that direction?"

She frowned. "The water and the sky just sort of blur together in a haze."

"That's not what I see. That's the direction of the volcano. Can't you see anything?"

She looked again. "Not really. There are clouds. It's a little red."

"That may be the glow of the volcano you're seeing. Can you see the red in any other direction?"

A quick survey showed her the difference. "I can see that it's redder than the other directions. If that's the volcano, why aren't we going directly there?"

"I'm trying to stay reasonably close to shore, for our safety."

"You could be a lot closer, you know."

"And risk being seen by a Cerik, on land or in a boat. A Cerik isn't going to be looking out this far. There are dangers all around."

She remembered something Aaron had said. "What about creatures below us?"

"I don't see anything of any size."

She moved in her seat, trying to get comfortable. "Is that how Robert catches fish? Can he sense where they are?"

He shrugged. "I don't know. He probably just sees them. He swims among them and spears them."

"Do we have a spear on board?"

"Not that I know of. Hungry already? We don't have a stove to cook with either, and the *jenna* we eat have to be cooked first. Just don't think about it."

Three hours later, she put her hand on his shoulder. "The red is getting stronger."

By sunset, the mountain with red flows marking its shape was clear, in spite of the distance haze.

She took over the steering, while he rested, propped up against the side. "Are your eyes closed? I can't tell whether you're awake or asleep."

He didn't answer for a moment. He sighed. "You never read the mythology story, did you?"

"I've been busy! I haven't had the time."

"That excuse came very smoothly. I bet you've used it before."

She flushed, glad that he couldn't see it. "Well, maybe once or twice."

He sighed. "Are you ever going to go read it?"

She spoke meekly, "Maybe. I've got to get the garden going."

He shook his head. "Promise me you'll read it when we get back, and I'll go ahead and tell you."

She was puzzled by why she had to read it if he was going to tell her, but she promised.

"Okay." He stretched his neck to one side, and then the other. "The story goes that the hero was trapped by a giant with one eye in the center of his forehead named Cyclops. The hero got the drop on him and managed to blind him with a red hot poker."

"Ouch."

He nodded. "But the hero was still trapped in a cave, and the blind giant guarded the entrance. But Cyclops had sheep, which is some kind of grazing animal with a thick coat. The sheep needed to graze, so he let them go one at a time, feeling the sheep's back to make sure that his prisoner didn't get free. But the hero clung to the underside of one of the sheep and made his escape."

"Who was the hero?"

He shook his head. "The Book is written from Father's memories, and he wrote that his versions are incomplete and contain mistakes. He obviously didn't remember the name, so he didn't include it."

"Hmm. I thought Father was infallible."

Cyclops chuckled. "If you read the Book, you'd know better. He is always warning the reader that his memories are imperfect."

"So, why did you choose the name? Because you're blind?"

He took a deep breath, and removed his breathing mask. Then, he slipped his eye bandage up to expose his face.

She stared silently in horror. There were no eyes. Unmarked skin covered the space below his eyebrows.

"I was in an explosion, and my eyes were destroyed... burned away. I've healed the scars, but I've never been able to regenerate the eyes."

He tugged the bandage back down. "I've found that people are more comfortable with the mask. They can imagine eyes that aren't really there.

"So to answer your question, you can make up your own mind whether my eyes are open or shut. I don't know."

"I'm sorry."

He nodded, fitting his breathing goggles back on. "I'm always reluctant to tell people. Especially when they've gotten used to the mask. It sets everything back."

She let her mind swirl for a moment. "Kakil. You were from Kakil. James or John or something like that."

He tensed. "I'm Cyclops."

"Okay! Don't have a fit. It's just that there was this story, a few years ago, I was too little to remember all of it, but the older girls were so caught up in it. A handsome young man was burned and was despondent. Then he... committed suicide. He snuck outside and walked into the sea. They never found the body."

She saw him breathing hard.

"Cyclops, are you okay?"

"My eyes are closed. I'm getting some sleep. Watch where you're steering."

She adjusted the tiller. She had let it drift a little too close to shore. Her face burned under her mask, and her eyes ached.

I talk too much. I shouldn't have told him that.

. . .

Passing around the point, the heat was so strong it beat against her skin. Rivers of red crashed into the water, blasting great plumes of steam. An acrid smell, even through her filters, told her there was more than just steam in there as well. She steered farther away. The clouds obscured the moonlight, but the lava and the red glare off the clouds was enough to steer by.

Cyclops was indeed sleeping, and from the whimpers, caught up in nightmares. She would have woken him, but awake, what would it mean to him, to stare into this burning landscape and feel the heat on his face? She didn't want to risk it.

According to what Cyclops had said, their destination was the next peninsula over, and she wanted to be farther from the lava flows before she needed more precise directions.

This was what Sally was warning me about, wasn't it? He's been pushed too much. He doesn't swim. Was that related to his suicide attempt? Was he almost drowned before Aaron found him?

Oh! What must it have been like to have been trapped in that tank under-water with his air running out? I should never have pushed him into coming.

Only a few minutes later, the mists ahead resolved into low hills. There were three streams of red at the base of the peninsula, and in a flash of her own clairvoyance, she saw that any escape was already impossible overland.

She pushed the power level to off. Leaning down to where he slept, she put her hand on his shoulder. "Cyclops. Wake..."

He reached up and pulled her down, wrapping her in his arms and holding tightly. She resisted only an instant, letting him pull her close.

Then, he shook and released, "Sorry. I was asleep. I didn't mean…"

She just breathed evenly for a few seconds, it had been surprisingly nice being held, even if it was just a mistake.

"We're close," she said softly. "I need better directions."

"Oh." He nodded. "Okay." He released his grip on her and they both stood up.

"You're right." He pointed. "The survivors are over that way, on that highest hill."

"Okay." She applied power and steered in that direction. The lava flows were a hotter red. It was obvious that not all were coming from the volcano's peak. The molten rock was oozing out of multiple fissures in the ground.

"I'm sorry about that. I know you've made your position clear…"

She laughed. "You talk too much. Let's get back to business."

21

The red light made Jace, the foreman of the team, look demonic as he strode up with fire in his eyes and struck Vance in the face, knocking him to the ground.

"Don't you ever do that again! Shut down. I don't want to hear a thought out of you, not even if you burst into flames—got me?"

Vance rubbed his cheek and nodded. His *ineda* firmed up, covering up his panic and fear.

Jace turned to the others. "That goes for the rest of you as well. The *Name* isn't coming, but if anything would change his mind, it's some crazy thing like Vance just pulled. Only he wouldn't be coming to save us. He'd be coming to rip us open with his claws for betraying him."

Hugo said, "It was a plan, at least. Do you have any way to save us?" He was resting against their equipment bags.

Jace sighed. "That will save us." He pointed to the rows of carts, packed to the brim with the touch-panel control boxes that were so ubiquitous in Delense systems. "We're on the highest ground. If the lava flows stop soon enough, and if we can survive our own foolishness." He glared at Vance. "The *Name* will eventually risk another boat to collect this treasure."

They both looked up in the sky as another flaming bomb arched across the sky and smashed down in the valley next to them.

Hugo muttered, "If. If. Eventually. I'm not feeling the brilliance here." He was Jace's main assistant, and years of working side-by-side gave him a little more leeway to question his boss.

Jace spoke softly. "Hugo, just hang on. We don't control our fate, others do. That hasn't changed since the day we were born. Let's just play the odds, and hope for the best."

He nodded. "I know. Just... go talk to Kadel. He's hurting."

Jace put his hand on his shoulder and then walked over to where the injured man was lying on the ground.

"Hey Kid, how are you holding up?"

It was difficult for him to form words, with the pain from the burns saturating his nerves. "Not. Fun."

"I know. But if we can just hold out a little longer, we can concentrate on getting you healed. If you want, we could even leave some scars, to impress the girls."

Kadel tried to laugh, but it became a cough. "Sorry. Breather's not working right."

Jace nodded, reaching down and unclipping the filter pack. "It's this ash in the air. It's clogging up all our masks." He scraped at the filter grid and then re-attached it to Kadel's mask. "Better?"

He nodded.

Jace patted the boy's good arm and walked over to where Patrick and Darion were bring up the last of the carts.

"Is that all of it?" he asked.

Darion grumbled. "All that we could reach. The base level of the factory is already gone to the lava, and those support beams flare up brighter than the sun when they catch fire. How is the kid?"

"Bad burns on his right side. He'll have to be carried, if we move. Nothing a team of healers at Home couldn't fix."

Darion nodded, aware how likely that would be.

Jace asked, "Did you two catch my rant a moment ago?"

Patrick asked, "Partly. What did Vance do?"

He sighed. "He tried to send out a mental offer to the other *Names*. 'Come rescue us, and you can have the control modules.'"

"Uh, oh," said Darion.

Patrick said, "I don't understand."

Darion explained to the younger man the facts of Cerik honor, and what they did when they felt betrayed.

"So... it wasn't a good idea?"

"No. Even if some brave *Name* took the bait, he'd not likely keep us, once we'd loaded the carts. We still owe our allegiance to the Dalla *Name*. We'd be betrayers—not tolerated."

"So what now?"

Jace shrugged. "We wait. Keep the ash out of your breather filters and keep our water tub covered. Patrick, if you can keep a cheerful face, go talk to Kadel and try to keep his spirits up."

Darion pointed to a rock, "You've been up too many hours. Go over there and close your eyes."

Jace nodded. The ache of pretending they had a future was grinding his soul down, just as the heat was draining his strength.

22

Debbie gasped as the lava bomb arched over the hill and smashed into the valley.

I hope Cyclops is still okay.

She steered the boat a little farther from the shoreline, aiming for the cluster of massive rocks that stuck out of the water like the spine of some great dead sea-creature. They looked twenty to thirty feet tall each, poking straight up out of the water. Maybe she'd feel a little safer behind one of those.

Cyclops had won the argument, for which she was grateful. He was the one best equipped to crawl around in the dark and to avoid stepping on molten rocks, and to make contact with the stranded workers. She was capable enough to handle the tub, as long as he came back to navigate them home.

Just so long as none of those lava bombs come my way.

She would prefer to move the tub much farther from the volcano, but she had to be close enough to see his signal when it came.

"It's annoying not being able to signal with our minds," she muttered to the wind.

He had taken an electric light beamer. Its color was very different from the constant red of the lava. As long as he was back before dawn, she would have no trouble seeing it and then getting close to shore to pick them up.

She smiled. Cyclops had braved the water, getting waist-deep to wade to the shore, and she could see the effort it took from him. Whatever his personal demons, he was able to push past them when he had to. It was a shame he was so old, maybe eight to ten years older than she was. Robert was older too, but not that much.

She sighed. "Gardening comes first. When I can feed people, then I'll think about the other stuff." She sighed again.

23

The lava bomb arched high overhead. Cyclops could hear it and sense its heat, but it was not coming down on them, and he tried to ignore it.

From his hiding spot behind the rocks, he watched the crew work out their issues. He agreed with their leader. Inviting other *Names* to come poach off of Dalla goods was probably a dumb move.

He watched as the leader talked to the injured one.

I will not think about it. Burns were his nightmare, even more than drowning. Having the heat sear away parts of your body...

I will not think about it. He took a slow, deep breath.

When he read the Book, in the Bible section, he'd wondered about the references to the Lake of Fire, where the bad people went. It couldn't be much worse than this place.

When one of the others pointed toward the rocks where he was hiding, for an instant he thought he'd been seen, but no, it seemed that Jace, the leader was just finding a place to rest.

Sorry Jace, there's no time for rest.

He waited until the man settled against the rock and the other two walked off in different directions.

"Keep your *ineda* if you want to live."

"What? Who are you?"

"*Ineda.*"

Jace nodded, and it was clear he had his mind under control. Cyclops moved to the side where he could be seen. Jace frowned at the mask under the mask.

"I can take your men to safety, but only if you and all of yours can keep your minds from leaking."

Jace nodded. "I'm glad you're here. I didn't see a boat land. How close are you?"

Cyclops kept his tone low and level. "Be aware of what I'm offering. Do you know Sally and Edgar, Powell and Lemm?"

"I knew them. They're dead."

"And if you take my offer, you will be as dead as they are—unable to contact friends and family—dead to all who love you."

Jace gasped, "You mean... they're still alive?"

"Just as alive as you can be, if we all can keep the secret."

He stared at Cyclops for a moment. "Show me."

He shook his head. "I cannot. I have lost my eyes. I have no images to show you, but...," he recalled a moment around the table, one of the rare times Sally had come to eat with them. Lemm had told a joke and she laughed and scolded him.

Jace sighed, as he plucked the memory from his temporarily weakened block. "Okay, I believe you. What do you want?"

Cyclops relayed the plan.

"You'll have to take as many of our control modules as possible. They're too valuable to leave behind."

"Okay, but our first priority is to get people to safety. We aren't Cerik. We believe that people are valuable."

24

The blue-white light flashed on the shore, and Debbie, lost in her own daydreams, almost didn't recognize it until the third flash. Shocked awake, she pushed the power lever and raced in.

As she approached the shoreline, she eased off the power, trying not to crunch up on the beach quite as hard as she had the first time. There were several dark figures on shore, and a couple of them in the water.

The first one aboard looked at her and smiled. "Hi. I'm Patrick."

"Debbie." She nodded.

"Help us with Kadel."

Three men were carrying a third, hoisted high to keep him out of the water. She tried to hold her gasp when she saw the burns.

"Okay, put him here, against the hull. There's no padding. We'll just have to make do."

The surf was making the boat rock strongly, and the boy was struggling to keep himself from being tossed around.

The others were getting back into the water.

"Wait! Where are you going?"

Patrick turned his head. "Keep Kadel safe. We'll be back in a minute with our stuff."

She looked for Cyclops and saw him climbing down from the rocks. She waved, and he waved back. Whatever was going on, he was okay with it.

"Oh!" The injured boy, not much older than she was, had bumped his head against the hull.

She knelt down and put her hands to cradle his skull. "Hello, I'm Debbie."

"Kadel," he mumbled. "Burns."

"I see. The lava got you?"

He was in pain, and she didn't need the leakage through his *ineda* to know that it was horrible for him.

"Power cell. Lava broke into the factory. Cell blew. I got splashed."

She nodded, understanding a little. Scar had mentioned a horror weapon the old Cerik used, rupturing a power cell and letting all the energy escape in one instant. Supposedly, that was what the Delense had used to destroy the old City of the Face, when they made their escape attempt.

"We will get you all healed up soon enough. Do you have any practice healing?" Boys weren't given the in-depth training that girls were.

"I tried, but I just can't think straight." He was panting.

"It's okay. Just relax." She focussed on his head, cradled in her hands. There was a trick she had learned from Betty, not six months before, and just as quickly was told never to use it. Gently, she reached into an area near his brain stem and caused a slight increase in nerve signals. Quickly, he relaxed, nearly asleep.

She could feel his body, almost tied into knots by the pain, ease up.

As she pulled out of her light trance, she realized that there were men on board, pulling crates of equipment into the tub and stacking them against the other side.

Cyclops knelt down by her. "Good. I'll take over for a little. I see you have him stabilized. Where did you learn that?"

She didn't answer and he was too distracted to follow up. An older man with gray hair seemed to be directing the loading. She remembered something Robert had said. She moved to the older man's side. He was startled to see her.

"We have to balance the load," she said. "This isn't like a boat. There's no compensation. Even it out, side to side, front to back."

He frowned at her. "Who are you? Did they rescue you, too?"

"No. Festival girl. I was a recruit. I'm Chief Gardener, but we were short of people when we heard about your situation, so I volunteered. I'm no expert here, but we do have to balance the load."

He nodded, and began directing the others to move crates.

She moved back out of the way. If she stuck her foot in the wrong place, it would be too easy for all these experienced workers to ignore her as an ignorant little girl.

As the cargo moved, she noticed the crunching sound of the hull on the rocks. As the load shifted, so did the tub's position on the beach rocks. She'd be glad when they were done. They were running out of space. People would soon have to sit on their cargo.

She looked down at Kadel. Cyclops was talking to him quietly. Her attempt to put him to sleep had worn off, or Cyclops had adjusted it.

That's good. Cyclops has experience with burns. He can help.

Patrick put his leg over the side to get out. She glanced at the empty carts sitting on the shore.

"Aren't you done loading?" she asked.

The older man beside her explained, "Oh, no. We've got another five carts to bring down."

She glanced up at the hill, and had a flash of clairvoyance.

"No!" she yelled. "Patrick, get back in."

He hesitated but as she grabbed the controls and gave full power to the engines, he kicked hard and tumbled to the deck.

"Debbie?" asked Cyclops.

"What's going on?" asked the old man.

The tub, weighed down with more cargo and people than when it ground to shore in the first place, strained to move.

"Everybody, move to the back!" she screamed. More than half the people did as she said, if only by instinct.

The tub scraped, and came free. She turned it around and began racing away from the shore at full speed.

"Debbie, what are you doing? There's valuable stuff we haven't loaded yet!"

She tuned them all out, aiming at the line of tall rocks in the water.

"Lava!" she yelled. "The boat!"

Everyone was holding on tight as the tub bounced across the ocean waves.

The rocks were coming up fast. She threw the engine into reverse and coasted close.

"The boat's power cell. It's going to…"

The sky lit up, far brighter than daylight. Everyone winced at the light. Everyone except Debbie, who was guiding the tub into the sudden shadow.

Seconds later, the shockwave turned the waves into driving, stinging salt spray, and almost swamped the tub, even in their protected position. One of the nearby rocks crashed into the ocean, knocked from its ages-long perch by the blast. Again, the tub rocked dangerously, threatening to let the waves spill over the sides.

A cloud was rising, with a glowing heart of vaporized dust climbing above the hills. They watched in awe. One of the workers said, "So that's a *flick*. I've always wondered."

Cyclops spoke, loud enough that everyone could hear. "Jace, I think we're done loading. Maybe we should get out of here."

The old man nodded. "You know, I *like* this girl. I'll trade you Patrick for her."

The others chuckled and poked at the young man.

She shouted. "Hey, I've got a garden to grow. I've told the others. I'm telling you. No funny business until I'm done!" There was another round of laughter.

She turned the wheel and powered the tub out across the waters. In the distance, the edge of dawn was marking the end of night.

25

Aaron was seated with Jace and Cyclops, talking politics after the fish dinner. Robert was grumbling that even with help, it was going to be harder to keep everyone fed. There was another group that had gone with Powell to visit Sally and Edgar.

Debbie sat nearby, listening to the politics.

Aaron shook his head. "There's always some fallout between the clans when a rescue happens. You can't feel guilty about it. One of the Cerik guarding the Kakil Home was gutted for letting Cyclops walk out, even though everyone was sure that he had drowned in the ocean."

Jace looked sad. "But the current situation is dangerous. Every clan suspects every other clan of swooping in, stealing the control modules, and *flicking* the area to hide the evidence."

Cyclops nodded. "If someone shows up offering to sell the modules, all the *Names* will be interested in the details."

"Not a problem," said Aaron. "We'll need those ourselves for some time. Since the day the Delense were exterminated, the Cerik have been leaving broken machines all over the planet. We can scavenge and repair them, now that we have a boat of our own." He gestured expansively. "This facility is unknown to any Cerik clan. The Delense kept it secret all through the time of their slavery. But the technology is old. Useful, but old. You've given us the opportunity to bring it all up-to-date."

Debbie learned a lot, just listening, in spite of a regular string of men sitting down beside her, and introducing themselves. Even Kadel made an appearance, hobbling on a crutch. The pain blocks and Cyclops's extensive experience in healing burns was already having some effect.

...

It had taken twice as long on the trip back, as loaded as the tub had become. This was the first day they were all back inside the mountain, now that the submarine had returned.

Being the center of attention of every available male was nice, but she kept to her script. At least she had a number of people offer to help her with the garden work. She wasn't so sure how many of them would stick to it once they realized what was involved.

"It's getting worse by the year," Aaron was saying. "In the old days, U'tanse slaves were valuable. Not only did they fill the gap left by the Delense, but any excess could be sold to some other clan that didn't have U'tanse yet. The old Delense burrows were vacant anyway, and repair and maintenance of the Homes was minor.

"But now, there is no market for surplus U'tanse, and some *Names*, like Graddik, are actively trying to reduce Home populations."

Debbie tried not to react. That was *her* Home. Was being chosen as a Festival girl just part of the *Name's* effort to get rid of people?

Aaron looked her way. "Some, like our Debbie, were sent off to Festival, with their *Names* giving orders to bring back fewer girls than they take. I was able to recruit her with surprising ease. The Leaders are all under pressure to offload some of their girls. I'll need to do it again soon.

Aaron waved at some men across the room. "Other *Names* are taking greater risks with workers like your crew."

Jace grumbled. "So our *Name* was pleased when we were trapped with no boat?"

"Probably. For now, the Cerik are playing the role that they are benevolent, paternal guardians, taking care of their U'tanse. Being unable to risk another boat is a common excuse to reduce their slave population. I've seen it before."

Cyclops said, "The problem is that our population is still growing. How soon before they take more aggressive action?"

Jace said, "It's like the time of Baby Moses."

Aaron nodded. "Exactly."

Moses. I recognize that name. It's from the Book. I'm going to be forced to read it. There's no way around it. It's like listening to a code and I don't know the key.

26

"Aaron!" Debbie called after him, as he headed down the corridor.

He smiled and waited until she caught up with him.

"I'm glad to have a chance to see you, free from all your young men."

She snorted, "And some older ones too. But that's not a problem."

"I want to say that I'm very proud of your part of the rescue. I've heard that you saved everyone from the *flick* as the boat's power cell was destroyed."

She shrugged as she fell into step beside him. "That was just instinct. Cyclops was the brave one. That trip pushed all his fears, and he pushed back."

He nodded. "He's a particularly fine young man."

"But... I have a question for you."

"Go ahead."

"So, this place, what you do. It's all a big rescue effort, right?"

"Hmm. Something like that. I'm sorry I didn't get to have the Big Talk with you when we arrived."

"Things happened."

He nodded, "Yes, things happened. So... your question?"

She stared at the floor, frowning, as they walked.

"So, you've been rescuing people for years now. Every time a Cerik discards a worker, or someone gets injured, you sneak in and save them, pretending that they died."

"Yes," he answered quietly.

She stared up at him, with tears showing in her eyes. "Then why didn't you save my father? Why couldn't you have done something about my mother?"

They walked in silence for a few more paces, then he stopped and faced her.

"The headhunter attack on Graddik Home was sudden and brutal. I couldn't have gotten there in time, even if I had a boat of my own. Linda bar Franklin's death was a great shock to everyone, even me. But sometimes, there's nothing you can do."

Debbie's face was tight and strained, but she nodded.

"As for Karl bar Ezra—his loss was what started me on this life task— saving lives that the Cerik have thrown away. Without it, I would never have made the decisions that led me here.

"But even if I had started earlier in life, I couldn't have saved everyone. There have been many deaths that I couldn't prevent. For one thing, without a boat, I'd only been able to work on the West Coast. One man, working alone, has limits. Our new friends would have all died if you hadn't stepped in."

He hesitated, then said, "I didn't choose you by accident. I didn't scan the records of all the Homes looking for a good gardener. Some of the Festival girls will live happy lives in their new Homes and never give a thought about their position as a slave to their *Name*. I suspected, and hoped, that you in particular would take to the hardships of this new life, as a free U'tanse."

"But you have an out. Come next Festival, you can return to that life."

She shook her head. "I can't go back. Not after all I've learned. It's like the old life was an illusion."

He smiled. "There's still more to learn. A lot more to learn."

She gave a tight grin, "I know. I know."

...

It was late, and she was very tired, but she went to her garden plot and sighed at the native weeds popping up in the soil. She would have to pull each and every one of them.

She went to the shelf where she had stashed the seeds and pulled out a small pouch. The soil was still moist and soft underfoot as she walked into the middle of the plot. Gently she scattered the soil she had collected from Graddik Home across the new dirt.

"Mother, Father, this is our new home. Help me make it strong."

27

The next Full Large Moon, nearly a year later, Festival boats began to land and unload their troops of wide-eyed, frightened young girls, all arrayed in white. They entered and received their indoctrination speeches.

A few hours later, Howard was chatting with Hannibal when he noticed the airlock controls blinking. "Who is that?"

He walked closer and saw a familiar figure, pulling off her breathing mask. She smiled as she entered.

"Debbie bar Karl."

"Hello, Howard."

He looked at her outfit, a festival dress only dyed a pale blue. "Have you come back to join us?"

She beamed, "Oh, no. I'm here to trade, and to recruit! I need a healer, and a cook, and a gardener's assistant." She looked over at a cluster of puzzled girls in white, listening in. "And you should know, where I live, the boys are very cute."

Appendix

Slave Races

A variety of species were conquered by the Cerik as they scavenged Star-damaged planets. Most stayed on their home worlds. Only a few could survive the Cerik atmosphere and were valuable enough for the Cerik to make the effort to bring them home.

Species	Type	Value
U'tanse (Human)	erect bipeds	Technically talented and could design and repair tools
Dadada (BaBaBa)	radial symmetric turtles Triangles at birth, add legs as they age.	Young ones used as pets. Older ones as slow transport. Can carry heavy weights and understand spoken directions.
Uuaa (Wob)	quadruped with long multi-jointed arms and thicker hind legs for jumping	Favorite pet of the Cerik because they jump the same way. Used to quickly climb trees and harvest fruits and nuts that the Cerik can't reach. Not vocal, but they can be trained.

The Ko Calendar

Ko's moon is in a highly elliptical orbit that brings is close enough to regularly trigger quakes across the globe. The Large Moon, at closest approach, dominates the sky much more than Earth's full moon, regardless of which phase it is in. While the Cerik have noted that certain stars are in the sky following a 'yearly' pattern, it makes no difference in their lives. With no noticeable yearly weather pattern, months are the dominant measure of calendar time.

When the U'tanse arrived, Father began documenting what he could. He had a wristwatch, by which he determined that a Ko day was slightly more than 20 Earth hours. A Ko lunar month was a little over 58 Ko days.

The U'tanse set up their own calendar system, one that more closely matched the human norms. A Normal week was seven Ko Days, with the same names Father and Mother were used to. Each Normal month was five weeks. There were ten Normal months, which didn't quite match the Cerik year, but it was close enough. The month names were: January, March, April, May, July, August, September, October, November, and December.

U'tanse count birthdays and ages by the Normal year, which is only 80% as long as the Earth year. A 20 (Earth) year old would be deemed aged 25 on Ko.

	Hours	Earth Days	Ko Days
Earth Day	24	1.000	1.198
Ko Month	1162.4	48.433	58.033
Normal Month	701.05	29.210	35.000
Normal Week	140.21	5.842	7.000
Ko Year	6867.3	286.138	342.851
Normal Year	7010.5	292.104	350.000

Cerik Terms

Cerik Term	Definition
Cerik	Literally, 'Hunter', the name of a race of predators
Chitchit	A small predator from the Cerik home world that were used to root out burrowing prey. They were also used as pets.
Dak	A substitute kill. Used when an honored soldier is killed. An enemy is killed, the blood drunk, and the kill attributed to the honored soldier.
Delense	Literally, 'Builder', the name of a race of semi-aquatic tool users. The Delense were enslaved by the Cerik in prehistory, and existed in a symbiotic relationship for thousands of years before they were exterminated by the Cerik.
Dlathe	A broad shade tree, with many low-hanging branches. It was a favorite hunting perch for Cerik.
Dul	A traditional net used to hold a captured prey
'Eeh	The bloodlust, a heightened sensual awareness.
Erdan	The long wait. A semiconscious trance state when no prey were expected, but instant alertness might be required.
Fenke dan	The meal, and the following period of tupor. In good times, a Cerik would eat once a day. Digestion has its own heavy demands and causes a deep lethargy that is not easily overridden.

Ferreer	A telepathic, hive mind alien species that had inhabited several planets.
Flick	To bomb an enemy with an overloaded TP core. Invented by the Delense to attack the Ferreer, the only race the Cerik could not attack directly face to face, it was also used in the fatal rebellion against the Cerik. It has the blast effects, but not the radiation, of a small tactical nuclear bomb.
Hatsen	mid-sized predator that feeds on small prey like chitchits.
Ineda	A telepathic block. This skill can be learned by any Cerik who needs to be leader over telepaths. An ordinary Cerik who practices ineda is by definition a suspected thief.
Janji	A freshwater fish that is edible by humans. The meat is chewy. More common in the north.
Jenna	A common saltwater fish that can be edible by humans.
Kadan	The anticipated kill wait. Like erdan, but with heightened anticipation that prey would appear any second.
Katche	The 'peace'. During the Face, all clans are bound to refrain from clan-on-clan attacks, with the threat that all other clans would turn on the aggressor.
Kede	A Broken Hunter. Any Cerik who is valuable even though severely injured. Surgery is unknown among the Cerik and it is up to the clan leader whether to support anyone crippled by injuries.
Kel	A common tree that is found near streams

Klakr	The Cerik's world's version of a triceratops. Twice the size of a Cerik. Large massive head with spikes and tusks. A spiked tail. Vegetarian with easily offended sense of territory. Nearly extinct.
Ko	Literally, 'all lands' This became the name of the Cerik home planet when they discovered that other planets existed
La	Literally, 'First', also referred to as 'Named'. the title of the leader of a clan, family or guild. A First was the only individual Cerik with a name. The First names himself when elevated to rank. All other adult males are addressed by their rank, and known unambiguously by their scent. Females and cubs are known by their scent and genealogy.
Larek	Literally, 'Second', the second in command, and prime assistant to the First. Second is also heir to the First and can usurp his position with a physical challenge. In addition to the possibility of death in such a challenge, there are numerous social and clan level sanctions against a Second who endangers the clan by a challenge at the wrong time.
Lulur	Large centipede like creature with tubular body and a pair of legs per segment. Carrion eaters for the most part, Cerik disdain them and eradicate them only for sport.
Ooro	Coastal lizards that are a food delicacy, traded to interior clans
Po	Flying reptile that nest in dlathe trees
Pree'd	To register personal satisfaction. Physically there can be a purring component, a salivating component, and/or a relaxing of the subdermal plates.

Rettik	Literally 'right eye', a close assistant, with status over other assistants. Often personal soldiers or bodyguards.
Ruff	A territorial noise and posture, a threatening purr.
Sendt	Literally, 'Runner', a grazing herbivore that make up a dominant prey species for the Cerik. There are dozens of native varieties and several off-world varieties, prized for taste or for being skillful prey.
Shash	A reed-like plant that grows along stream beds.
Soso	A trade that both parties were happy with. 'Fairness'
Ssitt	Literally, 'Take the eyes'. In battle among Cerik, the ritual death stroke was to take out the eyes of an enemy and eat them. Due to the tough skin of the Cerik, the most common death stroke in duels was a blow at the weakest part of the head, at the eyes.
Tetca	Literally, 'dance'. A guild, an organized collection of Cerik workers with their own First, Second, and lower workers. A clan First will have many tetca First's under his direct command.

The Story Isn't Over
Follow both branches of this Saga

On Earth

Or Off

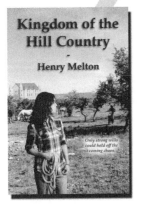

More Soon

More Soon

Small Towns, Big Ideas

Adventure comes to high school heroes from small towns as they come up against great science fiction challenges.

Emperor Dad

Roswell or Bust

Extreme Makeover

Lighter Than Air

Falling Bakward

Golden Girl

Follow That Mouse

Bearing Northeast

The Copper Room

plus

Pixie Dust

Breaking Anchor

CPSIA information can be obtained at www.ICGtesting.com
Printed in the USA
LVOW011629151212

311771LV00004B/11/P